Have Me Forever

Theirs to Keep 1

Ally Blythe

Contents

Have Me Forever

ISBN-13: 979-8-9875092-0-3

Published by Boldly Bookish Publishing
Cover design by Mitxeran
Proofread by Kate Wood Proofreading

1

Elias

"You said your dad will be gone all weekend, right, Ang?" our friend Thomas asks, leaning over his girlfriend, Violet.

Ang props an elbow on my knee, glancing at Tom. She waggles her eyebrows. "Yeah. He left last week and won't be back till Sunday. He's got some stupid conference. Something about some dead author and how the writing is symbolic for—"

Tom cuts her off, pretending to snore. "Sounds boring as hell."

She laughs as if it's the funniest thing she's ever heard. "Yeah. Glad you cut me off, that's all I can remember. He's told me at least six times but, yeah. It's boring."

It's the International Authors' Convention, and he goes every February. I want to say as much, but I bite my tongue instead. I don't need to butt in on the conversation. This is his third trip, and he always comes back so excited, ready to talk about the authors he's met, and books he thinks Ang would enjoy. Unfortunately, she hates reading, so he's stopped telling her about them. This past year, he came back and gave me a few recommendations. He tripped over his words at first, maybe worried I might react like Angel, but I was happy to have more books to read. I went to the on-campus library soon after and it had most of the recommendations Mr. Baker gave me. I've always thought it was funny how much he gushed about others because he's a published author himself. He nerds out and acts like a superfan, when thousands of fans would kill to meet him.

Ang is more of a physical person, playing softball and basketball, swimming—pretty much anything that keeps her active. It's part of the reason Mr. Baker had a heat pump installed in the pool. He wanted Ang to have the option of swimming any time of the year, even during the winter in Southern California. I haven't seen her use it this winter, she prefers to spend most of her time partying with friends, but it makes days like today nice. It's a brisk and sunny sixty degrees. Most people are floating around the pool, warm despite the cool air, and some of us are relaxing in chairs nearby.

"Guess what that means…" Tom says while pulling a bag out of his pocket. Ang claps her hands, excitement lighting her eyes as he pulls out a few rolled joints. She grabs one, twisting it between her fingers as he lights the end.

I tense as the smoke plumes around me. If my parents smell that stuff on me, I'll be in so much trouble. I may live on campus now, but they drop by unannounced often, and make me go home at least three times a week. I haven't seen them in two days, so I'm expecting them to drop by my dorm sometime this evening or early tomorrow. They have the strict, overbearing parent thing down to a science. That hasn't changed even though I'm living on campus. I don't want to imagine the punishment if they found out. I'm a sophomore in college, older than the rest of my class, but I might as well be ten. That's how they treat me.

I took a year off to visit relatives in Mexico City last year, where I helped local churches and spent a year with my father's family, who were almost as controlling. Wherever I went, my parents kept tabs on me, which made parties like this inconvenient. It's also why Ang cares more about partying now, I think. She wasn't happy when I left because our relationship was so new, even though we'd been friends since childhood. Despite the distance, we stayed together, though she got lonely a lot and partying was her way of meeting new people. It strengthened us in the long run, making me certain I'd found the one, just like *mi padre* and *Mama*.

Despite that knowledge, the idea of getting caught partying makes me nervous. My parents would kick my ass. I'd prefer to hang out with her one-on-one, but that's been hard lately because she's so busy. "Come on, guys. We're already drinking. Do we need to smoke too?"

Ang rolls her eyes and shoves my shoulder with hers. "You mean we're drinking, and you're pretending to drink?" I squeeze her hand where it's resting on my leg to get her attention.

When she looks at me, I mouth, "What the hell?" She rolls her eyes again like it's no big deal. It is to me. I've already drunk one beer because Ang told me I was being uptight, and she was right. It's already swimming through my head because I'm a lightweight. I need to have the ability to get home tonight, and if our friends notice I'm not drinking, they won't let it go until I give in. More beer, shots, anything they can find. I'm lucky my parents let me come here at all, and drinking heavily would put an end to that.

It's no secret they don't like Mr. Baker, Ang's father. After her parents' divorce, mine sided with her mother, Debbie, which was convenient because Ang ended up living with her and we could keep hanging out. Where Mrs. Baker was also strict, Mr. Baker let us be ourselves and take risks, as long as we were safe while doing it. I didn't know if it was in hopes that Ang would be more open with him, or something else entirely. He was a teen when he had her, so maybe he thought this was better than being strict. It was certainly more enjoyable than how my parents ran their house.

Ang only lives with her father now because her mother is traveling the world with her boyfriend. They thought it would be too hard to travel with a teen, and it was pointless to take her along at the time, because she was starting college. Even though it's been a few years, they rarely return home. I think Ang has only seen her a handful of times since.

Originally, Ang wanted to live on campus because she didn't know her dad back then, but he made a deal with her: he would pay for anything she needed at school, tuition included, if she lived at home with him. She thinks, even now, it's because he wants to control her and stick it to her mom. I think he wants to get to know her again, which she doesn't always make easy.

My stream of thought is cut off as someone shoves a joint into my hand. "Stop being such a pussy, Eli," Tag yells, bobbing in the water. I swear under my breath as I pinch it between my fingers, a flicker of annoyance vibrating under my skin. Also, would it hurt Tag to be less offensive? I hate when people use that term. It's overused and sexist.

Tom snorts at Tag's comment and I cringe. "You know how offensive that is, right? I don't care if you call me names, but you could at least be a bit more creative. Less sexist." A collective groan echoes around the pool, except for Vi, who doesn't join in.

My girlfriend's annoyed groan is the loudest as she pinches her face. I get it—I'm not the coolest. I don't drink, I don't do drugs, and I try my best to not offend others. I am who I am, and I'm fine with that. I pass the joint to Ang and she takes a hit, exhaling the smoke with a carefree smile on her face.

"Okay, how about this? You're a pansy. Does that work better for you?" Tom adds, helping Tag. God, I have the worst friends sometimes. No, it's no better, and he damn well knows it.

I run a hand through my hair, leaning forward, ready to respond when I see that look from Ang. The one that means I need to shut up or face her wrath. It's somewhere I don't like to be, so I keep my mouth shut.

"He'll try it," she answers for me. Then, she leans close to my ear. "Just stay here. If they ask where you were, say you had to stay at the library late studying and you'll go over tomorrow."

I shake my head. I'm pretty sure they track my phone if I don't respond to them or let them into my dorm. They have an app set up to spy on me whenever they want. "They're going to stop over tonight. I need to be back at the dorms." I pitch my voice low, making sure no one else in the group can hear me.

"Please. I'll do something for you… later. If you try this for me," she says with a suggestive smile. I hate saying no to her, bribe or not, and I want to make her happy. I know I shouldn't, but I'm human.

I grab the joint again, the tip sending up a lone tendril of smoke.

Before I take a drag, I hear a noise. "Do you guys hear that?"

"Jesus fucking Christ, take a hit, man," Tag yells from the heated pool as he snakes his arm around a girl. I think her name is Dana? Everyone chants, "Do it, do it, do it" so I take a drag before passing it back to Ang.

The noise has to be my paranoia. My parents wouldn't come here looking for me. I think. I hold it in for a few seconds, doing my best not to cough.

As I exhale, I hear a few of our friends gasp. I follow their line of sight, frozen, praying to God it's not my parents.

"Angel, I'm home." A deep, rumbling voice echoes through the crowd. Hell. Why is Mr. Baker home already? He's never returned from the conference early. An uncomfortable swirling sensation starts in my stomach causing me to squirm in my seat, which catches his eye. I have to keep reminding myself he's cool, nothing like my parents. He won't get mad that I smoked some pot. And that we're drinking.

Ang looks at him, annoyed by the interruption. "What are you doing home early?" She passes me the joint, and like an idiot, I hide it behind my back. I'm certain he catches the movement because his weighted gaze flicks to my hand, then back, his lips tilting up in a hint of a smile. I wince in response. Logically, I know he doesn't care, but all my instincts are screaming at me to hide, lie, seem as innocent as possible.

I look around, everyone frozen to the spot, uncertain how he might react. It seems like everyone's feeling the same way. No one besides me and Vi has met Mr. Baker outside of the classroom so it makes sense why they're nervous.

Vi is Ang's best friend, so she's here almost as often as me, but Ang only invites the rest of the group over when he's gone. Considering half of them only know him as their professor, a strict but fair one, I'm sure they're ready to shit their pants.

"I had to come home for a meeting with my agent. Are you having fun?"

"Dad." She shoots daggers at him, tilting her head in the universal signal to get lost.

He puts his hands up in surrender. "Alright, I'm going. Have fun, be safe. I'm going to order some pizza." He looks at the crowd. "I'll order enough for everyone."

"Great."

He steps closer to her, lowering his voice, intending the rest of the conversation only for her. I'm close enough to hear it, though. "Everyone's staying here, right? No drinking and driving."

"I know the rules, Dad." She rolls her eyes.

"Okay. Just making sure. Have fun, sweetheart." He squeezes her shoulder, and she shrugs it off, rubbing his touch away. What I wouldn't give to have my parents be this cool. "I'll let you know when the food's here."

"Yeah, sure."

He faces me again, "Eli, hope you're doing well?"

"Dad."

His eyes flick to his daughter, his jaw tensing. "Okay. I'm going." He makes his way back into the house, leaving everyone in stunned silence.

"Damn, I wish my dad was that cool," Anders calls out from the hot tub. A few mumbled agreements circle the group.

"Where have you been hiding Daddy, Ang?" Dana asks as she fans herself, Tag's arm still wrapped around her. Ang glares at her and Tag makes a disgruntled noise. Dana isn't wrong. Mr. Baker is young and handsome, objectively speaking. He had Angel as a teenager, so he's already younger than most of our parents. He could pass for twenty-six, except for when he smiles. Whenever he smiles, lines crease his eyes from years of laughter. Or so I've been told by his female students. I wouldn't notice something like that myself.

Ang snaps. "Shut your fucking mouth, Dana."

Dana says something snarky back, which seems to relax everyone but me. I get this itching, unsettled feeling under my skin, like if I don't move right now, I'm going to go insane. I can't tell if it's the weed or getting caught, but I can't sit still. "Ang, I need to walk. I have this like… I don't know how to describe it. Does weed make you paranoid?"

She doesn't respond, too caught up in a story Tom's telling. "Ang." I tug on her arm, but she bats my hand away. "Ang."

"What? Oh my God. You're being so annoying."

"I feel like I'm going out of my skin. Does weed do that?"

"No. Take another hit, it'll relax you."

"Okay." I do, then pass it back to her.

I wait for the sensation to go away. I check my phone, fifteen minutes pass, then thirty, and I still feel that sensation under my skin. "Fuck," I whisper under my breath. I need to move.

My cursing and the shifting of my legs must grab her attention. She rolls her eyes, shoving my beer into my hand. "You'll be fine. Drink this, it'll help." I'm not a doctor, but that definitely doesn't seem right. Turning to Ang to say as much, I notice she's already listening to Tom again.

I try it anyway. She knows better than I do. I take a sip, hating the taste. It's cheap and warm, making it so much worse. My stomach lurches, feeling the effects of the nasty, warm liquid. My skin feels overheated as I look around, wondering if anyone else is feeling this way. They all seem fine. Maybe water will help? Getting to my feet, I tell her where I'm going, and shrug when she doesn't respond, not wanting to wait for her acknowledgement.

I take a step forward, a wave of nausea rolling through me. *Mierda*, I might be sick. I walk to the kitchen in search of a cup. My stomach lurches again as I grab one out of the cabinet.

I flinch as something lands on my shoulder. A hand. I turn too quickly, my stomach churning angrily as my surroundings tilt. I close my eyes, trying to swallow down the bile, the hand a weight steadying me as my mind swims.

"Elias?" The hand shakes my shoulder, rocking me like I'm on a boat, back and forth. Oh no. Stop. I attempt to say that, but I don't know if I manage. If I open my mouth, I… I think I'm going to throw up.

I try to turn to the sink as my stomach cramps, the only warning I get. Bile rises, burning past my throat. I heave, expelling the contents of my stomach with angry abandon.

"Fuck," the voice mutters. Two warm points brace my shoulders, steadying me as I continue to heave.

When I empty the last of my stomach, my eyes pop open, making me feel significantly better, but then I realize who I've thrown up all over. My face heats, as I squeeze my eyes shut, trying to will everything away. It doesn't work. The acrid scent of puke wafts through the air. Powerful enough I can't ignore it. *Mierda*. I reluctantly open my eyes, and I'm met with a concerned, stormy blue gaze and high cheekbones. "Hey, are you okay?"

I shake my head. "I'm so sorry. That's so fu—Ehm, so embarrassing." I stare ahead, not meeting his eyes. Instead, I stare at his forehead, catching sight of a brown curl that falls out of place as he nods to acknowledge my words. My hand twitches, reaching out to push back the curl, but I miss as I'm manhandled into a seat.

A long sigh leaves bowed, demanding lips. The kind of mouth that's used to getting what it wants. I bolt upright at the thought. Fuck, where did that come from? What a weird thing to think. Then, that same mouth tells me it will take time to feel better. "Try to drink some water. Don't move if you can help it, okay?"

I stay silent, accepting the command.

2

Noah

Angel's boyfriend sits at the counter, vomit soaking his shirt and pants. His usually bronzed complexion is pale and clammy looking. How much has he had to drink?

I ask, but I don't get a response, only a glazed, faraway look. Okay, that tactic won't work. I place water in front of him, then look down at my shirt, and my floor, which is also covered in puke.

"Stay there. I don't want you slipping on the floor. I'm going to change and bring you something as well." I wait until he nods in acknowledgement before hustling to my room.

Stripping out of my clothes, I change quickly and grab another shirt and some basketball shorts. I bundle the dirty laundry under my arm and throw it in the wash before heading back to the kitchen, where I find Elias in the same pose I left him. It makes me chuckle despite the less than stellar circumstances. "I didn't mean literally stay in the same position."

The comment brings some color back to his cheeks, a line puckering between his brows. "Right."

"Here's a change of clothes. Leave yours in the bathroom and I'll throw them in the wash. How are you feeling now?"

"Not great. I'm still a little dizzy, and my stomach's cramping again. I, uh, don't think I'm gonna throw up again, at least."

"That's good." I grab the paper towels and kneel next to the puddle, scooping it up before tossing it in the trash.

"No, let me do that." I watch as Eli rises, unsteady on his feet, trying to get to the mess on the floor.

I scoop another pile. "Go change."

He pauses, his eyes widening, a flush creeping down his neck. "O-okay."

I toss the last pile into the trash before spraying the floor with disinfectant. I can't help but wonder why he drank and smoked so much tonight. Whenever Angel has people over, he tends to avoid that part. At least, he has in the two years I've really known him. I don't blame him, either. His parents are overbearing, and keep him on a tight leash even though he's in college. As long as I've known them, they've kept all of their children under strict watch, especially the oldest and Eli. And they look down on me because I don't do the same with Angel.

Regardless of my feelings toward his parents, I like him. He's always polite, respects my daughter, and keeps her out of trouble. Unfortunately, she's good at getting him to cave. Which is probably why I have a cross-faded twenty-year-old changing out of clothes he puked on in my bathroom. I refill his water as he walks back into the kitchen, sliding onto the stool, his feet planted firmly on the ground.

"Mr. Baker." His voice sounds raspy, deeper than normal, as he says my name. I watch him as he sways in his seat, placing his palms against the island, as if he's trying to settle a rocking boat.

"Yes?" I respond when he adds nothing. He seems more coherent now. Tipsy still, but less sick.

He shakes his head to clear it, wobbling on the stool, then gives me his full attention. "I read all the books from last year."

I tilt my head, unsure of what he's talking about. "Hmm?"

"Oh. You probably don't remember." His chin lands in the crook of his arm, which is resting on the counter, making him look dejected. "From the last conference. That list of books you told me about. It's okay if you don't remember."

Ah, the list of books I tried to get Angel to read last year. I hoped she would read one. Just one. After she told me reading was lame, I ended up giving the small list to

Elias. He must have thought I made it for him. "No, I remember. You read all of them? There were at least fifty."

He nods his head, widening his stance on the floor in an attempt to steady himself. "My favorite was the high fantasy one with the dragon, and uh, the guild. I'm trying to remember the name. I swear I read them all." That same hand he's resting his head on snakes around, covering his mouth like he didn't mean to share.

I suppress a grin at his antics, his happy frustration infectious. He's so eager, and it's endearing. It's also nice knowing he read the books I suggested, it's more than Angel's ever done. I wonder if he's ever read mine.

The doorbell rings before I get the chance to ask, so I check him again to make sure he's okay, and head up front to grab the pizza.

When I return, he's sitting exactly as I left him, though the water is gone. I grab a plate, throw a slice on it, and refill his water, placing it all in front of him. I order Elias to eat. He inhales, his face pinching into an unreadable mask. I repeat myself before he listens. I throw another slice on his plate, then make my way to the pool area, calling the rest of them inside.

Pizza disappears as the vultures descend. I watch them eat, looking content with the world, acting like a bunch of dumb teenagers. At twenty, I had a toddler to take care of. While she's been the greatest blessing, it isn't what I want for her. The sight makes me smile, knowing she's enjoying life, not having to grow up too soon.

"Dad," Angel calls out, irritation lacing the syllable. "You can leave now." She rolls her eyes, a habit she got from her mother. I love my daughter, but that move grates every time I see it. "I'm sure you have a book to write, or read, or something." She quirks a brow, clear dismissal in her tone.

I put my hands up in surrender. "Alright, I'm going."

A quiet voice cuts through the chatter. "Ang, come on. He let our friends stay and bought us dinner. If he wants to eat, let him."

I scan Elias as he argues with Angel, something he rarely does.

She pinches his arm to silence him. He flinches, but otherwise ignores the gesture. I don't want to cause a fight, and there's no reason for me to be in the kitchen with them. I should be in my office, preparing for my meeting this evening. Elias grimaces, so I squeeze his shoulder to show my thanks. My mind's already focused on my book as I turn from the group, but I swear he leans further into the touch and I wonder why.

"I get it. I'm cramping your style." She brushes me off when I try to kiss her hair. I can't say it doesn't sting, but I get it. Parents aren't cool.

"I'll take that forehead kiss, Mr. Baker," a young girl giggles. She waggles her brows, sending a crawling sensation down my spine. I know I'm younger, but that creeps me the hell out. I'm old enough to be her father.

"Dana, I already told you to shut the fuck up," my daughter hisses.

I grab a few slices and water out of the fridge. "I thought you were leaving?" she says.

Sheesh. Right to the heart. "I'm going. I'm going."

***

I get back late that evening, the meeting with my agent replaying in my mind. If I write through the night, I'll be back on schedule to publish my next book, which is good, but my writer's block has been in full swing lately. Maybe having attended the convention will be the key to getting my creativity flowing. I'd love to talk through my ideas more, maybe over a glass of wine, but my friends Tony and Beth are out of town.

One blessing is that everyone seems to be passed out in the living room, or about to nod off in front of a movie blasting through the surround sound. A relatively quiet night for Angel.

There's more beer scattered around, along with paper plates and water bottles. I do a headcount, noticing my daughter and one or two others are missing. Elias is asleep on the floor, piled among blankets and pillows with one of my current students, Violet Hartford, asleep near him.

I make my way over to check on him, seeing if he's recovered from earlier. His chest rises and falls evenly, and he's not surrounded by a puddle of puke, which is a good sign. I step over him, intending to look for Angel, when I see his face. Someone took a marker and drew all over him, a dick going down the length of his face. I shake my head at the immaturity, my jaw tensing, and grab a towel from the kitchen, along with a water bottle and his clothes. I set it all near him, hoping that will be enough to help when he wakes up.

Then, I take the stairs two at a time, in search of my daughter. I knock on her door lightly and hear a groan. Crap, I didn't mean to wake her. I just didn't expect her to be asleep already. She must have headed upstairs when Eli passed out so she could get some sleep in her own bed. The door clicks, barely inching open as she rubs her eyes. When she notices that it's me, she steps out of the door, closing it firmly behind her. "Hey, honey. I didn't mean to wake you. I just wanted to make sure you were okay since I didn't see you downstairs."

"Well, as you can see, I'm fine." I'd love to talk to whoever told me pre-teen girls were the peak of difficulty. They clearly didn't talk to nineteen-year-olds.

"Right. Good. I'm headed to bed. Sleep well." I pull her in for a hug and she pushes me away. It makes my heart ache, and I wish our relationship was different, but I know I wasn't there like I should have been. I wish I knew what I could do to fix it. "I love you." I try to tell her every chance I get.

She opens her door, slamming it in my face, leaving me waiting for a response I know I'm not going to get.

3

Eli

I was right about my parents. They went to my dorm the night I stayed at Ang's house and tracked my phone when I didn't answer. So I got to deal with that along with the faded outline of a dick on my face. Which my parents lost their ever-loving shit over. I don't know who did it, or who left me the towel, but I can at least guess on the second one, which makes me embarrassed all over again. That night was a complete mess, and I owe Mr. Baker a huge apology for throwing up on him, among other things.

I wish that was my most pressing concern. For the past two weeks, I've been at my parents' house. I'm not "grounded." Instead, they're giving me this time at home to reflect on my actions. A time for me to determine if my sins are forgivable. They also told me if it happens again, they'll pull my funding for the dorms and make me move home where they can monitor me. Honestly, I'm just thankful they didn't show up on Mr. Baker's doorstep. I love my parents, but half the time I feel like I'm suffocating. They've told me they watch us closely "so we're not tricked into temptation." I'm not so convinced that's why they act this way. But they love me, so what can I do?

Mama's searing tone interrupts my pity party. "Elias, sit down and eat before going back to campus. You can't get food like this back there." She speaks in fluent Spanish, despite growing up in Atlanta, Georgia.

My parents met when my mother went on a mission trip with her church to Mexico City at seventeen. They married a year later, after exchanging letters and getting approval from both families. To keep our culture alive for Papa, we only speak Spanish at home. It seems silly, considering we do nothing to appreciate Mama's culture, but I've never said as much. Plus, sometimes Spanish is the only way to truly express what I'm feeling at that moment.

Crap, I need to stop woolgathering. I take a seat, choking on the argument I want to make. They agreed to let me go back to campus, and I don't want to jeopardize that by arguing.

"Yes, ma'am." I pull some barbacoa, tortillas, rice, beans, and veggies onto my plate. It smells good and I am hungry. Really, I don't need to fight this. It's just food. Maybe they won't use this as another opportunity to lecture me. They ask me to say grace, and we all go around the table telling each other what we're thankful for that day. A small tradition we started many years ago.

Once done, Mom shoots Dad a knowing glance, making me freeze, my food halfway to my mouth. Of fucking course, I knew this was going to be more of the same. I have seven siblings, six still at home. The triplets, Adriana, Danielle, and Valeria, who are fourteen, and my three younger brothers, Manny, Alex, and Miguel, who are twelve, ten, and seven, respectively. They might as well be ghosts with how much attention they've gotten from my parents since I've been home. No, it seems I'm the only target.

My father clears his throat. "Now, Elias. We are allowing you to return to campus with the understanding that you took this time to reflect on your actions. Have you prayed for guidance? Do you believe He's forgiven you?"

I muffle a frustrated sigh. I've already answered this a million times. I know they love me, and this is how they think I need to be protected. I keep repeating the words, hoping they will stick. It's hard to believe it when I don't feel like I can be myself. I can't make mistakes, or talk about my worries.

I wonder if my siblings ever feel the same way. I don't know if my sisters and brothers are actually quiet, if they agree with our parents, or if it's all an act. Do they have passions and dreams outside our home? I don't know if they buck against the rules like I do. Every aspect of our life is regimented and monitored. Or they leave me alone to babysit, putting me in the role of guardian, where I'm enforcing the rules. We're not given the chance to know each other outside of a specific dynamic. "Yes, sir. I spent much of my time reflecting and praying to God. He is forgiving of mistakes and I pray he will continue to guide me down the right path."

"Do you understand why we asked you to reflect?"

"Yes, Father. I shouldn't have been at Angel's house without permission and I shouldn't have stayed the night."

"Yes. Very good. And you know we don't approve of that man. He doesn't have any morals. He's lucky he hasn't corrupted his daughter."

My mother chimes in. "That would be her mother's doing. She's such a good woman."

The judgment pricks my skin, an overwhelming sensation threatening to take hold and destroy my control. I want to say, "judge not, that ye be not judged." I clench my hands under the table, holding back any sign of my reaction. If I so much as run a hand over my face, and they decide it's a sign of disrespect, I might be stuck here longer. "I know, sir. I'll do better. Promise." As I speak, I force my jaw to relax.

My father looks to my mother, seeking confirmation that the conversation was good enough. Her lips are a tight line, but she nods her head. We drop the subject and turn back to our food, the only noise coming from the silverware clinking against plates.

***

Thankfully, dinner passes quickly, and I'm back in my dorm, unpacking my stuff while Tom sits on his bed, staring at the TV, trying to kill zombies unsuccessfully. I'll never understand his obsession with video games, especially with how bad he is at them.

"Fucking hell, motherfucker. How? How did that son of a bitch kill me?" I cringe at his outburst. The noise was so loud and full of rage. He throws the controller at the wall, leaving a small dent, then turns to face me. "So, were they really mad? Like, two weeks at home… That's pretty fucked up."

I roll my eyes, something I've picked up from Ang, which I'm trying to cut back on. It's proven to be a hard habit to break, though I don't do it nearly as often as she does. "They were definitely not happy. Really, it was my fault. I knew they were going to stop by that night or the next. I shouldn't have stayed the night. And it wasn't bad, I spent most of my time at church."

He flops back onto his bed, putting his arm behind his head. "Now that's some BS, man. I would not let my family harass me into going to church anymore. Not that we go. You gotta stick up for yourself."

I laugh, not knowing how to respond. He doesn't get it, but that isn't his fault. Most people wouldn't understand. Besides, whenever my parents stop by, I usher them back out the door as quickly as possible and make some excuse to do something far away from campus. Tom has only interacted with my parents once or twice, for less than five minutes.

"I mean, this is college, y'know? You should be able to do what you want whenever you want. That's the real philosophy there. Anyway, I'm going to meet up with Vi. You gonna invite Ang over? I'll be gone all night." He smiles, dimples popping out on each cheek. He may be oblivious to some things, but he always knows how to make me feel better after a long stretch with my parents.

I chuckle despite myself. "Nah, she said she had some project she needed to work on. I'll probably see her tomorrow or the day after."

He winces, then clutches at his heart. "That hurts. I hurt for you, my dude. Right in here, where my heart should be."

"Somehow, I think I'll survive."

***

I walk out of the business building after my last class of the day, a cool breeze ruffling my hair. It feels good after the stifling, stagnant air of the lecture hall. Talking about data tables and financial statements nearly put me to sleep—one of the biggest reasons I hate the business degree I'm getting. The breeze, however, makes me hopeful today will turn around. It's been three weeks since I've seen Ang, a whole week since I've been back on campus, so I need as much hope as I can get. I miss spending time with her alone, hearing her sassy tone as she tells me about her day, her favorite show, or what's annoying her at school. It's fun being with all our friends, but I'm ready to have her to myself.

Tuesdays seem to be her slow days, which means, if I time it right, I can catch her before she starts homework. She shouldn't be out of class yet, so I text her to see if she's free.

> Eli: Hey, hun. I miss you.
> Ang: I miss u 2, bb. U free 2day?
> Eli: Yeah. Can I see you? I miss hearing your voice.
> Ang: Yea. Meet @ my place!
> Eli: Ok, I'll be over there in ten.
> Ang: Dad gone rest of day ;)
> Eli: Really? :)
> Ang: Do me a fvr?
> Eli: Anything.
> Ang: Get in the pool.
> Ang: Naked.
> Ang: Get ready 4 me. Itll b so hot!

I stare at my screen, disbelief causing my brain to short circuit. What? I… I can't do that. God, it sounds hot, but not where one of our parents can catch us. I let her rope me into a lot of things, some of them adventurous like this, but is this too much? I call her, and she sends me to voicemail. The tone of each ring does little to calm my racing heart as I punch the number again. Damn it, Ang. Answer your phone.

I try her phone one last time. She picks up on the fifth ring, her voice sounding waspish. "What? I'm still in the middle of class."

"You can't be serious. I can't do that. What if your dad comes home?" I attempt to keep my voice quiet, not wanting the entire class to hear the details of our conversation. I'm not sure how successful it is, considering I get a few odd looks from students walking past.

"Come on, he won't even be home. It'll be so hot, babe."

I count to ten to slow my racing heart. In theory, yeah, it would be. I try to compromise. "I'll wait in your room, or somewhere on campus. Like that one time. How about that?"

"Be in the pool when I get home or go back to your room alone. Your choice." Her tone is cutting. Final.

When I don't respond, her voice turns angelic, sweet, and coaxing. "I just want to have fun with you, babe. I love you. We've done stuff like this before. It's been so long and I thought you'd like it. I'll be so excited. C'mon, baby. Do it for me?" She makes a kissing noise as if we settled the matter, then disconnects the line.

I pocket my phone before massaging the muscles in my neck. That's not what I was looking for when I asked to see Ang, but I want to be close with her again. It seems like we've been drifting, orbiting one another, but never finding the right time to connect. It's not like I don't want to sleep with her, to do something new and, yes, exciting. It's just… I want to spend time with her, not jump into bed. Or pool in this case.

What if Ang's dad comes home? He usually keeps a tight schedule, but that's proven to be fallible. Over the years, Mr. Baker has been warm and welcoming, despite what my parents have said about him, but that doesn't change the fact he's her father. He likes me, but I don't think he would appreciate me corrupting his daughter and pool. Plus, I'm in love with his books. I'm a hardcore 'Bakehead'—the name lovingly bestowed on his fandom—and I don't want to disappoint him or give him reason to doubt my integrity. I clank my keys against my palm, trying to weigh out the pros and cons as I navigate the crowded sidewalks to my car.

I'm a glutton for punishment. That's the only explanation as to why I'm in the pool ten minutes later. I haven't taken my trunks off yet because there is a lot of yard, and the fence line doesn't seem all that high. I did search the house for Mr. Baker, but he isn't home. One minor victory, I suppose.

In an effort to relax, I swim a few laps. The water flows through my fingertips, gliding along my chest and bubbling down my legs as I kick. The repetitive motions give me something to lock on to, and I continue for another ten minutes. As I pick up the pace, the splashes match the pounding of my heart.

With a new level of clarity, I think about how she loves me and wants to have fun with me. I can do this. I want to do this with her. Just like that time on campus. It's going to be so hot, having Ang against me, her wet skin gliding against mine. I'll sit on the stairs, stroking myself. She'll swim up to me and I'll settle her over my lap. Running my hands down her neck, grazing her body, until I… I stop swimming and reach into my shorts.

The image of hot, wet skin grinding against me causes my dick to twitch, so I run my hand up my length, a small gasp parting my lips. I think about the last time she wrapped her pouting mouth around me, her golden hair tickling my thighs before I wrapped it around my fist.

I squeeze my dick as all the blood in my body travels south at the idea of a hot mouth wrapped around my shaft, sucking me dry. Swimming to the shallow end, I rest on the stairs and throw my trunks onto the concrete. My hand returns to my shaft, gliding up the side, circling the head, and parting the sensitive slit. I hiss out a long breath as my body quakes at the sensation. *Mierda*, that feels good.

My hand slows as my brain tries to take the reins. It's no easy feat, as my body's wracked with searing, mind-numbing heat. All it wants to focus on is the pressure from my hand, but my mind won't settle. This awareness takes hold, though I can't put a name to it. I look around the pool, each stroke slower than the last. My finger dips into the sensitive spot under the head, causing my hips to buck above the water.

The odd sensation prickles my skin, almost like I'm being watched. I'm too far gone, my body refusing to do anything other than move me closer to an orgasm. In fact, my cock perks up at the idea, bobbing above the water.

My heavy-lidded gaze travels to the glass doors, hoping to see Ang. Hmm… Maybe she went to change into a swimsuit? I turn my attention to the second floor, hoping to catch sight of her in her bedroom window, but the curtains are shut. I stroke myself again, my eyelids fluttering, fighting to stay open, when something catches the corner of my eye from the second floor. I can't focus on it. My lust is riding me hard, distracting me from what my rational brain is trying to tell me. I make myself stop, long enough to inspect the second floor, but I don't see anything.

I look down at myself, the head bobbing above the water, a bead of pre-come leaking from the tip. Using it to rub a circle around my head, I then slide down, using the other hand to cup my balls, tugging on them lightly. I think about blond hair running through my fingers, a hot mouth swallowing me whole, a rough scratching sensation rubbing against my inner thigh.

Long, lean fingers grabbing my hips as I run my fingers through… brown hair. A tousled, just got out of bed look. My cock jerks angrily, ready for release. In the fantasy, I look down, expecting to see blue eyes peering up at me, so light they look almost like ice, but I'm met with a stormy dark blue gaze.

My breathing quickens as my hand pumps faster. Fuck. I'm so close to coming and I know I need to stop for some reason. I squeeze the base of my cock, trying not to come, to wait for Ang to get here. My hips thrust faster, higher, ensuring my cock continues to bob out of the water, completely ignoring the rational side of my brain. Each breath grows heavy as my orgasm threatens.

Vibrations wrack my body, my balls pulling tight as I bite my lip to muffle the sound of my release. Ropes of come shoot between my fingers, landing on my stomach as I stroke up, slowly, wringing out every drop. I tilt my face up as small shudders rock through my body and this time I see the curtain flutter, though I can't see inside. Until I hear the glass doors open, I don't stop staring. As my body falls back into the water, I clean myself off.

"Babe." Ang cries out, panicked, as I refuse to open my eyes. I run my hand behind my neck, my blood pumping thick and oily through my veins.

The sun is blocked off as footsteps race closer. "Babe, my dad's home. You need to get dressed, now." And there's the nail in the coffin. The last miniscule hope that I was wrong about who was upstairs. I pop my eyes open, meeting the icy blue eyes of my girlfriend, as she launches my swim trunks at my face.

I end up leaving, not wanting to run into Mr. Baker, and going without seeing Ang once again. Which might be for the best. The idea of seeing him, if he was in that window… God, I'd die of embarrassment.

He wasn't though, and that's the story I'm sticking to. I'm still in knots about what I did. I cling to one thought as I make my way home; according to Ang, fantasizing isn't cheating. That's what she always says when she shares her own fantasies. Sometimes it's me, other times it's some celebrity, one time it was a guy who was a barista at a coffee shop we frequented. Or that one time, on campus where she convinced me to touch her in an empty classroom, and another student stood outside the door. She whispered to me, telling me to let her watch, and I agreed. She always said, no big deal if I don't act on it, right? I'd agreed at the time.

Now, this feeling rolling around my gut, choking the breath from me… It doesn't seem harmless. Even though I don't know if he was actually at the window. The air conditioning could have kicked on, making the curtain move, and I didn't see it until I already came. Plus, lots of people have brown hair and blue eyes. I was so caught up in the moment my mind must have played tricks on me. It was a girl. With brown hair and blue eyes.

As a rule, I don't share my fantasies with Ang. She never asks to hear them, and I never volunteer. I don't want to appear weird or needy in the bedroom. I never told her that the same barista showed up in my dreams after she shared her fantasy, all three of us there, and he wasn't touching her.

4

Eli

I'm not proud of it. It's imperative I put that on record, even if only in my mind. I've been actively avoiding the Baker household for over a month now. Ang told me he's been there more than usual, and she hates spending time with him, so it took little convincing to go on dates elsewhere.

Once with Tom and Vi, and once to a party on campus. So, is it actually avoiding Mr. Baker if Ang doesn't want to be at home either?

Besides, we only have five weeks of the spring semester left, which means I've been buried in projects, papers, and exams. If I'm not doing schoolwork, I want to spend time with Ang, not her dad. Not even if I looked forward to the days we would catch up as I waited for Ang to get back from one thing or another. Like that time two months ago, well before the event that never happened. I sat in the living room, waiting for Angel to get ready, as per usual. Mr. Baker walked in, clearly staring at the TV. When he saw me, he said the customary hello, but kept walking toward his room.

"Don't leave on my account." I picked up the remote and tossed it to him as he stood on the other side of the couch.

He caught it, but hesitated for a minute, glancing at the TV again. Taking a seat at the other end of the couch, he ran a hand through his hair. "You're not going to want to watch what I'm putting on."

I furrowed my brows. "Why not?"

"Well, I thought I was home alone." He twisted away from me, his thumb rubbing against the power button. Okay. That sounded… unusual. My mind short circuited, attempting to find a response. He whispered, "I have a secret obsession with Avatar: The Last Airbender…"

And I had a dirty, disturbed mind. "Oh, I love that show. Toph is my favorite."

"Really? Angel always makes fun of me for watching it. Says I'm too old."

I snort. That did sound like something she would say. "Well, I don't mind. It's for all ages. Besides, you're not old."

He smiled warmly. "I don't know about that, but thanks. I'm guessing you watch it because of Miguel?"

My eyebrows popped up, stunned he remembered something so innocuous. "Yeah, actually. Good memory."

He settled himself against the couch, shifting a few times. He put one arm up, using it as a headrest, his bicep bulging as his shirt rode up, revealing a strip of skin. "You look surprised."

I startled and cleared my throat as my eyes flicked back to his face. I swallowed a few times to wet my dry mouth. "Well, I didn't realize you remembered any of my siblings' names."

"Of course I do. You said you think your mom has him follow you around to spy on you, so you've spent a lot of time figuring out the best ways to distract him. Watching TV works. Building Legos does not. Ice cream definitely works." He said it matter-of-factly, like he was checking off a list. I supposed he was, in a way. A list of distractions from personal family drama.

My mouth gaped as I tried to remember when I told him that. I knew Ang wouldn't have told him because I didn't talk to her about that stuff. The one time I did, she told me I was being too sensitive, and at least I had a mom who cared.

"Uh, yeah. That's right."

He opened the streaming service and moved around in the episode guide until he found what he was looking for. He clicked on it before tossing the remote to the side. It was the episode where Toph was introduced in the show.

Why am I thinking about Mr. Baker? Again. What I should focus on is my surprise for Ang.

Her last class lets out soon, and I want to make us dinner, even at the risk of running into him. Thinking about seeing him still has me on edge. I shiver, and squarely attribute it to the negative reaction side, because that's where it belongs. *The surprise. Focus on the surprise.* On our second date, I made her a homemade carbonara with garlic bread and salad, and I got groceries to make it for her tonight. I also got a few candles and a bottle of wine, purchased by one of our upperclassmen friends, Danny. I feel like I've neglected our relationship, and I never want her to think she isn't important to me.

I drive to the house and park in the driveway, noting Mr. Baker's car is gone, which is a good sign. Ang deserves to be comfortable tonight, and she always gets prickly when I do stuff like this at her place and he's home.

I grab the food from the back seat and let myself in with the spare key hidden in a potted plant on the porch. Once I place everything on the counter, I open the cabinet where Mr. Baker keeps his cutting boards. I grab it, a faint crying noise cutting through the quiet. I pause, listening for it again, but shrug and turn back to the task at hand. Must have been something outside.

I pick my favorite blade, which happens to be Mr. Baker's favorite knife, gifted to him by his best friend Tony. I grab the prosciutto, but decide I'd like some music playing while I cook.

At the front of the house, I sort through his stack of vinyl, hearing the weird noise again, only this time, it's louder. I go to the window and peek out, looking for an animal, or even a kid, but I don't see anything. Maybe someone left a TV on upstairs? I jog up the steps, and sure enough, the noise gets louder as I land at the top.

"Fuck," Ang calls out, her voice throaty, wild sounding. A deep groan follows her cry. Bile rises as my stomach churns, warning me not to go into her room. My feet don't get the signal, guiding me forward, though I already know what I'll see. I push the door open, watching Ang on her hands and knees, head bowed back as Tom drives into her from behind. "Tom. Fuck." She sounds breathless, turned on. More into it than she's ever sounded with me. He slaps her ass and adjusts his grip around her hair. And I can't turn away.

He catches me first, a twisted grin curling his lips as he continues to pound into her. Mocking me. Where I should feel rage, there's only emptiness.

Her eyes flutter open, locking on mine, her mouth widening into a horrified O. "Eli. Shit." She pulls from Tom's grasp, attempting to scramble off the bed.

My name snaps me out of the trance, pulling me out of the room and down the stairs. She calls out to me, yelling she's sorry, that we've been drifting apart for a while, but I can't hear any of it. I race to the kitchen, grab my keys, and hightail it to the front door, jumping out of the way when it swings open. In walks Mr. Baker, apologizing when he knocks into me, unaware of the shitshow unfolding before him.

Ang races down the stairs wearing a robe, her hair mussed from where Tom had his fingers in it, stuttering to a halt at her father's appearance. His face pinches, looking between us, probably assuming we hooked up. He clears his throat awkwardly. "Eli. Good to see you. Angel told me about your parents grounding you all of last month. She said she was worried you'd have to move home and she wouldn't see you as much." I look at her, his words like jagged needles aimed at my heart. Was she worried… or excited at the prospect of getting to screw Tom without the risk of getting caught?

I stand there, speechless, feeling like the biggest idiot. He's not done. He turns to Angel, saying, "Anyway, I should, uh, probably let you two get back to…" He winces, obviously uncomfortable.

"Dad, shut the fuck up," Ang cries out.

He gives Angel a look, before turning back to me. "I'm interrupting something. I'll take my leave."

"No, Mr. Baker, I'm leaving." If I can get my legs to work. *¡A la verga!* I'm frozen to the spot, darting my gaze from Angel to Mr. Baker.

Tears pour down her cheeks and my body jerks like it wants to go to her. She might be right. We have drifted apart, and her tears still get to me, but they also make my stomach heave. How did we get here?

She attempts to reason with me again. "Babe, please don't go. Not like this. Let's talk."

I look at her father, his expression growing more concerned. I force myself to turn away. He's not the one I need to focus on right now. I shouldn't care what he thinks about all of this. It's not like that fucking day at the pool meant anything to him, if he even saw something. I'm nothing to him, just like I'm nothing to Angel.

Tom strolls to the top of the stairs, looking smug, and it hits me all over again. *Me chingué.* I am so incredibly, irrevocably screwed. Where am I supposed to go? I can't live in the same room as him and I refuse to go home.

"Eli, buddy," he calls out, before spotting Mr. Baker at the bottom of the stairs. His entire demeanor changes as his gaze darts to Angel, then me, wondering if I've ratted him out. I can't help the laugh that breaks out—stuttering, cold, robotic. It was bad enough seeing it myself, but now Mr. Baker's witness to my absolute humiliation. Fucking perfect.

I see the pity written on his face as I storm to the door ignoring Ang's pleas and Tom's sputtering. My hand's on the knob when I hear Mr. Baker call my name. I pause at the gritty sound, but I refuse to turn. What could he possibly have to say to me?

***

I'm wallowing. I know it, I see it, I smell it. As I sniff my shirt, I wince. If wallowing was a scent, this would be it. Tom's been AWOL as I've nursed my wounds, thank God. I turned my phone off after Angel's tenth call, and Tom's sorry-not-sorry text. That got a laugh out of me. How was I so blind? All the small touches when they were together, how she hung on his every word, not making time to see me—it all made sense. I was the dumb fuck who hadn't realized it.

The one saving grace in all of this is that Tom hasn't come back to the dorm once. It makes me wonder where he could be. His side of the room is still messy, clothes everywhere, but his gaming system is gone. He's somewhere he felt comfortable enough to stay long term if he took it with him.

It hits me then. He's at Violet's, in her off-campus apartment. He wouldn't, right? After getting caught, he wouldn't go back to acting like everything was normal? I don't want to think about it, how twisted that would be. How uncaring he would have to be to play Violet like that. Don't have to think about it too hard, though. I have to tell her.

I turn my phone back on and call after call streams in from Angel. Apologetic at first, but angry at the end. I laugh at the last one, where she's blaming me, telling me how angry her father is. Like I'm the one who caused all this. Fuck that. Fuck her.

And one from Tom, threatening to beat the shit out of me if I tell Violet, which gives me my answer. Lucky for me, he taped her work schedule at the bookstore's coffee shop to his desk. I don't want him answering her phone, or being anywhere near her when I tell her the news, so catching her at work is the best bet. Despite what my ex-best friend and ex-girlfriend think, Vi has the right to know. I check the time, and she's going to end her shift in twenty minutes. I race to the showers, not wanting to smell like a rotting heap of garbage.

I make it to the shop with five minutes to spare, and I glance through the window, looking for Tom or Ang. Thankfully, I don't see either. It's been over a week, so they probably think if I was going to tell her, I already would have.

"Hey, Vi," I call out to her as she comes around the corner. She has a bright smile, the almost-hidden freckles on her nose scrunching under the open expression.

It slips off her face as she takes me in, replaced by concern. "Hey, you okay? You don't look so good." I shift uncomfortably, trying to comb through the unruly black mass that is my hair. It never looks nice on a good day, so I can't imagine what it must look like now. Apparently a shower isn't enough to fix ten days' worth of vegetating.

"Um. No, not really. Do you have a second to talk somewhere a little more private?" She assesses me, her look more concerned by the second. She must realize something's up because she nods her head and pulls me through the employee-only entrance.

She turns to face me, placing a palm against my forehead, my brows furrowing at the motion. "Tom told me you were pretty sick. You should probably be resting, Eli." She pulls her hand away, then feels her own forehead. "At least you don't have a fever."

That pulls a smile from me. The first one in days. "Violet, I'm not sick. I, uh, I don't know how to say this.

I'm not good with softening blows, so I think it'd be best to just come out and say it."

A line forms on her forehead, and she waves her hand, motioning for me to continue. "Okayyy."

I clasp my hands together, then pull out my phone with their texts and calls, shoving it at her as I blurt everything out. "Tom and Angel are sleeping together. The other night, I went over there, and they were in bed together. I… I thought you had the right to know. I'd want to know if I were in your shoes." She scrolls through the messages, blood draining from her face. She stumbles back a few steps, so I guide her to the nearest seat. "I'm sorry. I shouldn't have told you, right?"

She shakes her head once, twice. Then, like a dam breaking, tears burst forth, running black from her mascara. "No, no, you don't need to apologize, Eli. God… when did you find out? He… We… This morning we…" A hiccup rocks her body as more tears pour down her face. I pull her into a hug.

We sit there for a while, until she runs out of tears. When she catches her breath, we notice a buzzing sound. "It… it's m-m-my ph-phone." The tears pick up again, turning her voice raw and unsteady. I snatch her purse up, pulling out the phone, and sure enough, it's Tom.

I turn the phone toward her. "You want me to answer it?" She nods her head yes, then clutches my hand. "Tom."

"You little fucker. I'm going to kill you. I told you I'd kick your ass if you told her." He continues to scream down the line as I pull the phone away from my ear. It makes Vi cry harder, so I release her hand and pull her into my side, wishing I could take away her pain.

"You need to be out of her house before she gets home. If you're not, we're calling the cops." I don't know if they'll actually do anything, but it sounds serious enough. I hang up before he can respond, then turn the phone to do-not-disturb. She watches me, eyes wide, in awe. "Sorry, I should have let you make that decision…"

For a moment, she seems unsure, her gaze darting around the small space. Eventually, she straightens her shoulders and tips her head up high. "No, that's what I want. Fuck him. Uh, th-thank you. Will you come back with me? If he's not gone… um, I don't want to see him."

I'm glad she asked, because I don't want her going back alone with Tom making those threats. "Of course. I'll be right by your side." I slip my hand from her shoulder, grabbing a tissue from the box to hand to her. She thanks me, wiping her cheeks. It's a far cry from her normally flawless makeup, but it cleans the streaks. "I'll drive. We can come back for your car later."

She nods.

We pull up outside of her apartment building and I walk her to the door, entering before her. A key sits on her countertop along with a note. I ignore it, knowing the note is none of my business, even if it is from the *pendejo*.

I check every room to make sure he's gone, then give her the all clear. "Thanks, Eli. For everything." She hugs me again, small, infrequent sobs still stuttering through her.

I rub my neck after she lets go. "You don't need to thank me, Vi. I did nothing worthy of a thank you. I mean, I made you cry." To show I'm joking, I twist my face up, but it falls flat.

She looks around her apartment, looking a bit lost. "Hey. I mean this in the most platonic way possible, but… do you want to stay the night?"

I sigh. I want that. It's been miserable all on my own. Alone in the dorm with my thoughts, it isn't great, but the alternative is going home, which is worse. Plus, I've figured out my parents' pattern. They'll track my phone tonight to make sure I'm on campus, ready for all the tests I told them I had coming up to avoid going home. "I can stay for a while, but I can't stay the night. I'm sorry. It's my parents. They track my phone."

"Oh, no. I get it. No worries. Maybe I can convince my sister to come and stay with me." She shifts on her feet, dropping her gaze. "Can I call you? We're still friends, right?" The words shatter me. I can hear the pain and uncertainty lacing her words, and I know once I leave here all of those emotions will threaten to overwhelm me again. It's like staring in a mirror. When everything crashes, you don't know what's up or down, or who to trust, including yourself.

I pull her into a tight hug, my cheek resting on the top of her head. "We will always be friends. You call or text whenever you need me, okay? We'll get through this together."

She takes a long, shuddering breath, then pulls away. A small, wobbly smile crosses her face. "Yeah. You too, Eli."

5

Noah

I hear Angel slamming the kitchen cabinets from all the way down the hall. The house is icy, and it's been that way since Eli ran out, devastation clear in his hazel eyes. I want to see him, to apologize, but I don't know if he would appreciate that. To him, I'm only the father of the girl who broke his heart. He wouldn't care to hear from me. Plus, after what happened, everything I saw, even if it was a matter of seconds, I should be thankful I won't see him again.

I sigh, listening to pots and pans clanging as the cabinets ricochet. I have no fucking clue how to deal with that. One stupid remark, that's all it took to make our house a war zone. She's an adult, she can be with who she wants, but she should have ended things with Eli first. Something similar may have fallen out of my mouth as Tom hovered at the top of the stairs that day. She didn't like that, so she left with him.

I hate being angry at her, but I can't help the simmering disappointment when I think about what she's done. I don't know what to say, so I've stayed silent, hoping I'll find the right words. All I can see is Angel going further and further down the same path her mother carved out in her twenties, and it scares me beyond belief.

The little asswipe she slept with doesn't help matters either. He reminds me of the guys I used to fight back in high school. The ones who Debbie would flirt with to rile me up. When I saw him strut down those stairs, happy, arrogant, it didn't sit well.

A particularly loud slam makes me jerk in my seat. "Dad…" Angel yells.

I walk to the kitchen, expecting to see some pots or pans, or food—some artifice to show she wasn't slamming the doors just to get my attention.

"Angel, take it easy on the hinges, please." She huffs, crossing her arms, and I know I've already fucked up. Wrong thing to say. I try again. "Can I help you with something?"

She bites her lip and bats her lashes, angling for something. "I have to go to work soon. After I get off, Tom is coming over. He's going to stay for a while."

That kid is a dick, but I can't just say no. This is her house too. "Why?"

She rolls her eyes. "He was staying with Vi, but Eli had to fuck things up for them, and now he's got nowhere to stay."

"Seriously?" She can't actually believe that, can she?

She vibrates where she stands, her back going ramrod straight. "Are you seriously taking his side? You're my father." She emphasizes the word my, making me flinch.

"I'm not taking sides. Come on, you know Eli isn't the one at fault here."

"You don't even know what it was like, Dad. You have no idea how suffocating he was. He never wanted to do anything fun."

"It's not going to happen. He can't stay here."

She storms off, and I hear the click of the front door swinging open. She shouts one last time, "Fuck you. This is my house too, and he's staying here."

I inhale and exhale a few times. I open my mouth, needing to say something, but stop. This conversation isn't productive, and won't lead anywhere, and I don't want to say something I'll regret later.

"Oh," she calls out loudly, "might I also remind you, by keeping Tom out of the house, you're consigning your poor, precious Eli to living with him. I wonder how that will go." The door slams behind her, not giving me the chance to say anything. I drop my head into my hands, resting them against the counter. That was a clusterfuck. What am I supposed to do? The kid's trouble, acts the same way in class, but Angel's an adult. She has the right to make her own decisions, but this is also my house, and I'm not comfortable having him here.

Digging the palms of my hands into my eyes, I replay the whole exchange, looking for the right answer. I know I could have handled that better, but I think I made the right call. Tom is a user, and I will not give him unfettered access to my daughter.

The doorbell chimes minutes later, as my thoughts swirl. I pray it's not Tom because I haven't calmed down enough to have that conversation. I glance through the peephole and see unruly black curls, a hard jaw, and stubble.

What is Eli doing here? Should I pretend I'm not in the house? My car's in the driveway, so he knows I'm home. I can ignore it. That's what I should do. My hand turns the knob before the rest of my brain is on board. He straightens, locking eyes with me, and the image of his sorrow lingers in his hazel eyes. I feel the need to banish that look. I analyze every feature, searching for the happy person from a few weeks ago, when I notice a light bruise stretching the length of his cheekbone. It's nearly black, but partially hidden by the scruff.

"What the fuck happened to you?" I pull him inside, not thinking straight. Under the hall light, it looks darker—swollen and angry looking. I trace my fingers over it without thought, currents of electricity stinging my fingers. Static shock. That's what the electric feeling is.

"It's not important." He clears his throat, pulling his face away from my grasp. I drop my hand and it lands on his bicep, not ready to let him go. Still feeling the urge to protect him. He doesn't pull away from me either, a low, simmering something roiling through my stomach at the realization. "I'm sorry to drop in like this, Mr. Baker. I, uh, I probably shouldn't have. I knew Angel would be at work, and I had a few things I needed to get from here. I'm not ready to see her yet."

Of course he's here to pick up his stuff. Why else would he be here? Certainly not so I can act like a caveman, staring at and touching his bruises. I might have gone postal for a moment, my younger years of brawling, fighting for stupid reasons, rearing their ugly head. Thank you for that one, Debbie.

"Yeah, that's not a problem. Go on up and I'll grab some ice for that." I take a reluctant step back, releasing his arms. He absentmindedly brushes the bruise, his fingers tracing the same path mine traveled. He looks at me again, turbulent emotion causing him to tense, before he nods and races up the stairs.

I need to get control of myself. What the hell am I doing touching him, grabbing him? It's not appropriate. I put ice in a bag and wrap a towel around it and after a few minutes he joins me in the kitchen. He's holding a few items, looking uncertain, awkward. He rubs the back of his neck, something I've noticed he does when he's nervous. When I don't speak, he fills the silence. "I"—he clears his throat—"I'm okay, Mr. Baker. I should go."

"No." Well, I've lost my filter today. If Angel knew he was here and I didn't rush him off, she would be livid. As is, if she notices his missing things, she's going to go nuclear. "Please, sit. I actually wanted to apologize."

He hesitates, eyeing me, but doesn't argue. Perching on a stool, he places his things on the island. I get a sense of déjà vu—Elias sitting there, as I take care of him. I circle the counter, eating up the distance between us to place the ice on his cheek. His lashes lower, hiding his thoughts from me. "And, please, call me Noah. We've known each other long enough, and you're not…" Shit, probably not a good idea to remind him he isn't my daughter's boyfriend anymore.

He inhales sharply and I can't tell if it's my words or the fact I'm still holding ice against his cheek. "It's okay. You can say it. She isn't my girlfriend anymore." He grabs the pack, his hand over mine, as if he's trying to comfort me. I don't let go and he tightens his grip.

"I'm sorry," I whisper, analyzing every inhale of breath, every twitch of skin as I watch his face. This tugging sensation starts, telling me to get closer to him, protect him.

"You don't need to apologize. You didn't do this… Noah." His words sound ragged as they tumble from his mouth. I turn my gaze to those lips as a shiver runs down my spine. I lean closer, tipping his chin up with our clasped hands so he has to look at me. It feels different, his skin, covered in a light dusting of hair.

I can't remember the last time I stood this close to someone and felt this comfortable intimacy. "Still, I want to apologize."

He swallows, and I track the motion. Somehow, without my notice, his other hand found its way around my bicep, clinging to the arm caressing his jaw. Wait, when did I start that?

Squeezing my arm, he mumbles something under his breath.

"What?"

His voice stays quiet, intimate. "I said, is that all you want?"

"What's that supposed to mean?" My mouth goes dry, my heart picking up speed.

The hesitation from moments ago is gone. He lets go of my arm, placing his palm against my chest before closing my shirt in his fist. "You saw me that day."

Every part of me goes taut, trying to deny his words. "I don't know what you're talking about."

"In the pool." He looks up at me then, his hazel eyes dark, pupils blown.

I shake my head, but fail to deny it with words. "For a second. I swear I walked away when I saw…"

"I was thinking about you. I knew it was wrong, but you can't help what you fantasize about. Right?"

Fucking hell. I know I couldn't. My hand clenches around his jaw, controlled by a mind of its own.

He lunges off the stool, his lips clashing against mine, short circuiting my brain. I… Do I like this? I don't know why I fucking ask. Of course I do, just as much as I did when I caught him naked, outside, in my pool. And that makes me… I don't know what. Nothing good.

He pulls away when I don't move, color draining from his face, interpreting my hesitation as repulsion. Without thought, I pull him back to me, leaning into the kiss, running my tongue along his lower lip, teasing a small gasp from him. I use the opening to mold my tongue against his, coaxing it to follow mine. I drag my fingers against his jaw, leaving an abrasive, tickling sensation behind. It shouldn't feel this good, but it's never felt so right, so perfect.

His chest molds against mine, long fingers tangling through my hair, tugging at the ends. I moan, which only seems to embolden him. Every hard, toned inch of his body melting against me, his hard length grinding against my own. My hips thrust forward, a grunt falling from his mouth. I move my hand to his lower back, trying to get him closer, and I feel his cock twitch in response.

I'm losing my mind to the sensations rioting through me, but… I should stop. Right? There's a reason this isn't okay, and I've never been attracted to a man. I'm thirty-fucking-five, I feel like I would have noticed something like that before. I fall back, chest heaving, wondering what the fuck I just did.

He jolts back, his large, firm body heaving like mine. His erection strains to break free, twitching under my gaze. My body heats as he adjusts himself, making me picture what he would look like without clothes. His hand rubbing the sensitive head and… I can't. Fucking. Take. My. Eyes. Off. It. Apparently, thirty-five years means fuck all, because I'm so hard I don't want to stop.

6

Eli

His heated gaze pins me to the spot, my chest heaving, wondering what the fuck I just did. Grabbing my hips, he hoists me onto the counter, his rough hands shoving my knees apart, his body slotting between my legs. His mouth finds mine, his tongue sweeping in a passionate, consuming caress. He overwhelms every sense, commanding my body. I moan under his demanding touch.

"So fucking good," I mumble against his mouth as his hands run along my chest, down my stomach, and to my thighs.

A grunt is his only response as he grabs my jaw, angling my head so he has better access, licking a trail down to my collarbone before nipping it.

He does something wicked with his tongue and I lose all rational thought. My sole focus is on more pleasure. I rake my nails down his back, then grab him through his jeans. He's so hard the heat pulses through his clothes. "Fuck." He grinds against my palm, his voice like gravel.

My cock responds to the sound, needing more—that quiet, animalistic sound. I'm not kidding myself, he's my ex-girlfriend's father, and has never given any indication he's into men, so this won't go further than right now. We've given in to this tension, this pure insanity, but that's it. It feels right, and I'm going to take everything I can while we're in this moment. Every touch, every breath feels amazing, and I want more.

He nips at my neck, then licks away the sting, drawing me away from my negative thoughts. Instead, I focus on the path he's licking and sucking. "Fuck, Noah. So fucking hot."

He hums against my skin, pleased. The vibration leaves a warm, molten feeling in my bones. I run my fingers through his hair, tilting my head back to give him more access.

A loud pounding comes from the front hall, and my hands stop, freezing at the sound. We take a second to process what's going on. "Fuck." His chest heaves, hands tightening on my neck. "Fuck." His voice sounds panicked, but he doesn't release me. I tug at his hand, making him take a step back so I can slide off the counter. "Stay here," he whispers as he readjusts himself.

He hurries out of the kitchen, leaving me to worry alone. I fucked up. I squeeze my eyes shut, wincing as the pain from my cheek and stomach returns. What was I thinking, coming here? I knew it wasn't a great idea, but knowing Angel still had the album my grandfather gave me, or the notes and stories I wrote for her didn't sit right.

I may have come here with pure intentions, but those flew from my mind when Noah put his hand on my cheek, when he caressed my jaw, at the look he gave me. I thought I read the same fire in his eyes that I felt in myself. Grabbing the items, I walk toward the hallway and listen, choosing to ignore everything that's shouting at me to freak out. I crossed the line, but I'll have plenty of time to over-analyze later.

Noah's deep voice echoes down the hall, the gravel of lust absent, replaced by annoyance. "What are you doing here?"

"Ang said I could stay here, sir." *Pendejo*. Angel wants that dickhead to move in here? All those tears she shed, the calls she sent, they meant absolutely nothing to her. She only wanted to save face. I can't say I didn't expect that, but it stings. And I'm a fucking hypocrite. God, what did I get myself into?

"I'll tell you what I told my daughter. You are not welcome here and you certainly won't be living here." I glance around the corner, risking being seen, to see the happy, smug smile wiped from Tom's face. It's the least he deserves after following through with his threat. I rub my face again, a ripple of pain striking at the memory.

He turns, as if to walk away, clearly stunned. It's weird, I've never seen him at a loss for words. It doesn't last long.

He takes a few steps, stops, then turns back to Noah, his face contorting in rage. "What is Eli doing here?" *Mierda*, he must have seen my car parked on the street. He shouts my name.

"Stop shouting. Eli isn't here." The lie falls smoothly from Noah's lips. The same lips I kissed only moments before, which still seems unreal. I don't know what I was thinking when I launched myself out of my chair, practically mauling his body. He's just so kind, and he seemed so genuine in his concern for me.

His hand was warm, brushing against my jaw, holding ice against my cheek. Every move made me ache for him, and so I'd jumped, taking the risk, not expecting he'd return the kiss.

Tom looks behind Noah's shoulder, and I fall back, hoping he didn't notice me. I know he's not going to buy the lie, but catching me hiding will probably make things worse.

Spur-of-the-moment, I decide I should go up the back staircase and come down the front like I'm getting stuff from her room. I came here to do that, so it's a believable reason. If he sees me leave with my things, there's no reason he should be suspicious.

"I know he's here," he grinds out between his teeth. "Is he waiting for Angel, trying to beg her to take him back? He's so fucking pathetic."

"Watch your mouth. If you have nothing else…" I lose track of the conversation as I race up the stairs with my things. Once at the top, I descend the front stairs, stopping a few from the bottom. I see Tom's stance shift the second he sees me. His stupid, smug grin falling back into place.

"I thought you said Eli wasn't here." Then he looks at me again and his eyes widen. "What the fuck? Are those hickeys? Did you hook up with Ang, you son of a bitch? It wasn't enough to get me kicked out of Vi's place… but now." He stops, tension radiating through his body, causing him to vibrate on the spot. "No, no. Ang wouldn't do that to me, which means you were cheating on her too, you fucking asshole. Why'd you rat me out when you were doing the same fucking thing?" I resist the urge to cover my neck and look guilty. I didn't cheat on her, even if I've made quite a few questionable choices recently.

If looks could kill, Noah would have surely managed it the way he's glaring at Tom. "I told you to leave my house." He tries to slam the door in Tom's face, but Tom catches it, taking a menacing step forward, sights set on me. Noah catches his arm, yanking him back. "Get out before I call the cops for trespassing." Noah looks my way with meaning. "Or assault."

Noah lifts his brows, staring down someone who I thought was a close friend, threatening him for me. All I see now, as I watch Tom, lost to his rage, is a complete stranger. Someone who betrayed me, punched me, and hates me. I want to ask him what I did, because it has to be more than telling Violet, but I don't know if the answer will make it any better.

He hesitates another second, then turns, grabbing the door and slamming it on his way out. I collapse, the adrenaline coursing through me giving out, leaving me half sprawled across the stairs. "Fuck," I shout, wincing at the outburst.

I lower my voice and start again. "Sorry. I didn't realize that would make it worse. I thought if Tom saw me, he'd leave, satisfied he was right."

Noah comes into my line of sight and I stare up at him—his short brown hair, messy from my fingers, his eyes full of compassion and worry. Worry for me. All those thoughts and feelings I did my best to bury jump to the surface as he takes my hand and pulls me up. All I see now is a handsome man who let me kiss him, who seems to care if I'm okay or not. The same man I want to kiss again. I can't though, which makes this whole situation worse.

Then there's the fact that I'm pretty sure he's only into women. He was married to a woman and Ang has said she's seen him with one or two women since then. And I'm supposed to be straight. I'm totally straight. I replay the exchange, wondering if I took advantage. He's a nice man, and all he wanted to do was comfort me. Fuck, the hesitation, it was plain as day. I should have stopped after I mentioned the pool. I kept pushing, and I ended up kissing him. What the fuck is wrong with me? My mind keeps oscillating between hurt, confusion, anger, arousal, and back. And I have to say, I don't love the mixture.

"None of that was your fault. He's the asshole. It wouldn't have mattered if you came out here or not. He was looking for a fight after I told him to leave."

"Yeah, why did you do that?" Shit. I need to learn how to filter my thoughts better. I don't know if I want to hear the answer. In equal parts, I fear it and crave it. Did he do it for me, or was he just being protective of Angel? That I'm even asking should clue me in on how truly fucked I am, but my stupid, bruised heart doesn't care for logic. It wants to hear that he did it for me because we shared one kiss that he might not have wanted.

"It was the right thing to do." My heart beats harder. "He assaulted you, and I will not give him the chance to do that to Angel in a fit of rage." My heart sinks. Right. The right thing to do for his daughter. I shouldn't be upset by that. Obviously, I don't want her hurt either. But I want it to be, in part, because of me. And that's problematic.

"Right."

He switches the conversation. "We should talk about this."

I'd rather not. "No."

"Eli."

"It never happened."

"It did."

It did. And it felt fucking perfect, despite every reason it shouldn't. If Angel finds out, she's going to think I made a move out of revenge. That wasn't it. The pool was one of the hottest things I've ever done in my life until now.

What I shared with Noah was wrong. Hot, but wrong. Yet it was something more. Honest, at a time where everything in my life feels like a lie.

Even knowing it wasn't some ploy to get back at her, it leaves me wondering if I did something more unforgivable than what she did to me. I may not have kissed him until we were already over, but I've always felt close to him, and there was that day in the pool.

I rub the back of my neck, looking away from Noah. I can't think about those things right now, not while I'm still in front of him. Not when it looks like he wants to say more. I think it's time for me to leave before I do anything else extremely dumb, like try to kiss him again, when he is clearly freaking out.

"Well, I got the things I came for. I, uh, should probably go?" I don't mean for it to come out like a question. I'm not sure if he'll drop the subject or if he'll force me to talk about it.

When he says nothing, I sigh, moving toward the door and opening it, already thinking about the best ways to avoid him altogether. It shouldn't be that hard, since there's no reason for me to be at this house, and I've never once run into him on campus. I spend most of my time in the business building, which is two miles from the English building, if not more.

"Eli."

"Bye." I shut the door and race to my car, not looking back at the house once. I arrive back on campus having reached a decision. About Tom. I'm still not thinking about Noah. I won't go home to my parents and I'm not running away from my dorm. Either he needs to find somewhere else to stay, or deal with it, because switching rooms isn't an option for me. It will give my parents enough ammunition to pull their financial support. One saving grace is the fact that I have a full ride for tuition, but that doesn't include housing expenses. Which means they can keep me under their thumb.

I make my way to the room, listening outside the door before cracking it open. He isn't there, thankfully. He's left his mark though.

He took everything that's mine and threw it around the room. He ripped open boxes of food, smearing it all over my shirts. My bookshelf is tipped over. The one picture I have of me and my grandpa while I sit on his lap, his record player resting behind us, smashed. I race to it, pulling it from the shards, heart pounding as I pray it's otherwise unscathed. I analyze every inch, relief coursing through me, as I determine it's in one piece and barely rumpled.

With that realization, my body goes numb, unable to process the destruction of all my property. What the fuck is wrong with him? How could anyone do this to someone they once called a friend? I don't have answers, and I know I won't get any from him. I look down at the picture again, finding a folder to slide it into, then go in search of my Resident Assistant. Tom is such a piece of shit. I may not be leaving our room, but after what he did, he will be.

7

Eli

I wait for Vi outside of her classroom. She asked to grab lunch with me today, and I know I can't keep hiding out. Neither of us have socialized in weeks and she's determined it's time to break out of the pattern. I can't disagree, especially because I want to make sure she's okay. We text almost every day, but I need to see her in person. I know I'm still struggling, even though this past month has shown me Ang and I were already drifting apart. Cheating was only a small part of it all. I'm more worried about continued retaliation from Tom.

Being out in the open on campus makes me antsy, worried I'll run into him. The RA moved him to a different room, but it's still on the same floor. He said without proof, that's the best the university can do.

The door to Vi's English class opens, reminding me of the other reason I feel anxious. I don't want to accidentally run into a six-foot-something, hot-as-sin professor whose body I became intimately familiar with earlier this week. It's like now that I've done it, the floodgates are open, and I can't stop remembering every second of the encounter.

Now, did I spend that first night and next day hoping to hear from him, and also dreading I might? Yes. True. Did I also look up the university policy book to make sure there wasn't an explicit rule that would get Noah in trouble? I did. That's something I did. Not because I was hoping it would happen again. Not at all. Only to make sure what we did wasn't a violation that could get him fired. It's... very strongly frowned upon. It's really ambiguous at best, so he should be fine. Thank fuck.

After the initial disappointment, when I realized he wasn't going to reach out, I decided it was for the best. Nothing good would have come from speaking with him again. I can't like men, and I especially can't like Noah. So I'm standing outside the door, hiding in the last hoodie I own... hood up. It's almost seventy out, so I probably look absolutely bonkers, but *ni modo*. It is what it is.

I wait another five minutes before she walks out, the classroom next door pouring out as well, causing a large amount of congestion. Her normally sunny smile is more reserved, but otherwise, she looks okay.

"Hey, Vi." I wrap her in a hug, resting my cheek on the top of her head. She folds her arms around me, squeezing tight.

Her nose pinches as her face rubs against my hoodie. "Why are you wearing a sweatshirt?" She pulls her head back but doesn't let me go. Probably sensing I need the hug as much as she does.

"I was cold," I say, lamely.

She tilts her head, unamused, clearly not believing me. Yeah, I wouldn't either. She flips the hood down, staring at my neck. First shock, then confusion. "No. Eli, tell me you didn't!"

I look at her, confused. "What?"

"Please tell me you didn't hook up with Angel." Oh, oh. Shit. I almost forgot about the bite marks on my neck. I cover them, my face boiling. They've faded significantly, but they're still there.

I shake my head. "No, not Angel. I swear."

A single sculpted, fiery red brow rises so high it almost disappears behind her bangs.

Her look says everything, so I reassure her. "I promise. No going back. Only forward."

"Well then. Someone's been busy. Who is she?" She pokes me, waiting for a response.

"No one."

She huffs. "C'mon, tell me."

"I don't kiss and tell."

She pulls my hand away, inspecting it again. "I mean, good for you. They don't deserve a second of our time, right?"

I change tactics, pulling her into my side, propelling her forward through the crowd. "It's no one. You're right though, they don't deserve another second of our time. Now it's you and me against the world."

She snorts, bumping me with her shoulder. "Yeah, I suppose it is."

The crowd thins enough to reach the other classroom, and I glance in, making direct eye contact with none other than Professor Noah Baker. Shit. He startles, sloshing a bit of coffee over his mug, but recovers quickly. His eyes fall to my mouth, boring into me, an unreadable expression on his face.

Violet must notice the hitch in my step because she stops, glances up at me, and catches my line of sight.

"Shit," she whispers, close to my ear. "I didn't think about his classroom being so close. I'm sure you don't want to see him either." She doesn't even know how true—and false—her words are.

He walks out of the classroom, stopping in front of us, blocking our exit. I drop my arm from Vi's shoulders, breaking the silence first. "Professor." I hope if I lead by example, he'll say a quick hello and leave us alone. He assesses me, his eyes flitting from one spot on my face to the next before subtly glancing at my neck.

Vi echoes me. "Professor Baker." She nods her head, but I can tell she's uncomfortable. His daughter also ruined her relationship, so I imagine she's not thrilled to be around him.

"Mr. Ruiz, Ms. Hartford." He acknowledges our greeting and I try to steer her around him. I'm not quick enough. "Can I speak with you for a moment, Mr. Ruiz?"

Vi peeks at me, trying to gauge my reaction. "Actually, professor, we have to be on our way." She tugs at my hand, and this time he lets us pass, though I feel the weight of his stare on me.

"Eli, please."

I look at Vi, then ask her to meet me outside. I have to know what he wants to say. He leads us down the hall as Vi makes her way out, and we arrive at his office. He shuts the door, and I stand there, waiting.

When he doesn't speak, I take in his school office. It has all the usual—books upon books, stacked anywhere he can find room. Everything else is tidy, each item in its place. He watches me, his hip propped against his desk, arms crossed.

"This kind of screams you. A sort of organized chaos." I don't mean to speak first. It just slips out, but I can see it catches him by surprise.

"Yeah, I suppose that's true."

"Why'd you ask to see me, Noah?" I set my backpack down and turn to face him. I mirror his position, too close for comfort. It's like I can't help myself. He's magnetic, and something about him pulls me in.

"What we did… It can't happen again."

"Because you're straight."

It's not a question, but he answers it anyway. "No. Because you're my daughter's ex-boyfriend. I'm fifteen years older than you. I'm a professor at your university and it's inappropriate. Take your pick. There are plenty of reasons."

"So you're not straight?"

He clenches his jaw. "That's not relevant to the conversation. It's not… your business."

"That's bullshit. You know that's an excuse. I want you."

He takes a step back. "Then there's the university."

"They don't have a policy against it. I looked it up."

His brow quirks before he rubs the crease between his eyes. "They may not have a rule, but it's still not okay, Eli."

I run my hand along my neck, suddenly overheated, and I can't tell if it's anger or being in his presence, but I need to cool down. I yank my sweatshirt over my head, and toss it onto a chair near his desk, the movement bringing us within inches of each other.

He swallows as he looks at me, much closer than is appropriate. I didn't do it on purpose, but I'm glad we ended up here. "Fine. It won't happen again. Just tell me I need to leave. That you don't want this."

He pinches the bridge of his nose, eyes shut, the motion causing him to brush against my chest. When they pop open, his pupils are dilated, and he stares at my mouth. "This isn't going to happen again." His hand twitches, reaching for me. "You should leave."

I grab his hand, placing it on my chest over my shirt. "Should is not the same as telling, professor." His hand tightens against the material.

"Eli." His voice sounds tortured, and it makes me bold enough to close the distance between us.

"Yes?"

He grabs me with his other hand, and I can't tell if it's to pull me closer, or push me away. "Fuck." He crashes against me, taking my mouth in a deep sweep of tongue and teeth. It's everything I've been wanting for days, since that first kiss.

I run my hands up his back and curl them through his hair, pulling tight, hoping to get him as close as possible. I break away to turn his head, wanting to run kisses along his neck, but someone knocks at the door. He jumps back, racing behind his desk as lust and fear shine through those dark, beautiful eyes. The door swings open, a fellow professor in the English department stopping just inside the door.

"Oh, sorry, Noah. Didn't realize you were talking with a student. I can come back later."

He clears his throat. "No. No, I'm free. Please, come in."

The dismissal is clear, final. I gather my belongings and race from the room. What the fuck did I do? Again.

I make my way out of the building and find Vi, pretending that absolutely nothing happened. I grab her bag and sling it over my shoulder. It's something my parents ingrained in me, a habit I've tried to break because Angel complained about how misogynistic it was of me to assume she couldn't carry her own bag. Vi chuckles but doesn't say anything, continuing to walk in silence.

"Welcome back. What did he want?"

"Thanks. To apologize for Angel. Ready to eat?"

"Yeah. That's kind of weird of him."

I don't respond. What can I say? Certainly not the truth.

We walk, silent for a few moments. "You know, I can't believe he had the nerve to come up to us. I know it's not his fault. He isn't Angel. But he had to know we didn't want to see him. That you wouldn't be comfortable talking to him. Even if he apologized for her. I swear, that family, they are the worst. Well, the worst after Tom. No offense, he's still number one on my shit list." Her lips quirk, and it looks more like her usual smile.

"Let's not think about them for a while. Let's just enjoy our lunch. It's such a nice day. Want to eat outside?"

She pinches her brows, thinking about my question. "Mmm, yep. Sounds like a plan."

"How'd your study group go for finals next week?"

***

I'm lying in bed late in the afternoon, a show playing in the background, relaxing after my last final. Thankfully, I've convinced my parents that I need to stay on campus

71

for summer school, so I'll only have to go home for a week before I'm able to come back.

They have actually assigned me to the same dorm, so I won't have to move my stuff. I've packed a small bag, ready to leave in the morning.

This will be the last night of privacy I have for an entire week, and I intend to enjoy every second. I'm going to order a pizza, watch TV, and zone out.

Only one topic is off limits for the night. Of course, the more I tell myself it's off limits, the harder it is not to think about him. The way he felt against me, his mouth on mine, teeth grazing against my neck. Or later, in his office, his body pressed against mine. I groan, my fist clenching on the sheet. I am not supposed to think about Noah Baker. My dick doesn't get the memo. It stands at attention, liking where my thoughts are going. Naturally, my hand slides under the fabric of my shorts.

I squeeze, and my eyes fall shut, a short breath stuttering from my mouth. It's the last chance I'll get to do anything for a week… One time won't hurt, even if I'm thinking about him.

I pull my pants and boxers down, grasping the base before sliding up. I use the pre-come beading at the tip, drag it back down, and picture his strong, nimble hand. Reaching into my side table, I retrieve the lube and squirt some into my palm. I slick it down my length, shuddering at the contact. Then I grab my shirt at the back of the neck, pulling it over my head, tossing it to the ground.

I imagine Noah's mouth back on my collarbone, but it travels lower and lower, over my chest, then my abdomen. His tongue teases me after each biting kiss, dragging a line back to my throat. He palms my cock, stroking it in a lazy, unhurried motion, teasing me, in no hurry to push me over the edge. A hand glides lower, slipping between my cheeks, pushing against the sensitive ring of nerves.

My phone vibrates, making me jump, my hand retreating to clutch the sheets. My heart hammers as I debate checking it. I don't want to look, but I don't want my parents showing up at my dorm unannounced either. Cracking one eye open, I flip it around in my hand. Unknown number. I open my phone, curious.

> Unknown: Eli, it's Noah. We need to talk. Call me
> when you get a chance.

My heart stutters, a fluttering sensation coursing through my whole body. How the hell did he get my number? I know he's about to crush the fantasy, everything about us together.

> Eli: If you want to talk about what we did, and
> how it was a mistake, I don't want to hear it.

I want him to know what I'm doing, who I'm thinking about while he texts me. It's fucking dumb. Reckless. He had a point earlier… I just don't care.

> Noah: That's just it. It was a mistake. We're going
> to see each other around campus, and I can't
> keep going without saying something. I need to
> apologize. I'm older, I shouldn't have let it
> happen. I know better.

I slide my hand down the length of my dick, his words only goading me further. I'm picturing him with his stern voice, telling me how to stroke. How fast. How hard. Of course, I'm not going to tell him what I'm doing. I want to, but I've already pushed him twice, and he's telling me why it shouldn't have happened.

Using the hand not covered in lube, I add his contact to my list, then drop my phone on my chest and focus on my rock-hard dick. It's much easier than focusing on all the complicated shit. I twist around the head and slowly pump down before the need to respond gets to me.

> Eli: There's no way that's how you actually feel.
> Not when it's happened twice. The thing is, I knew
> what I wanted then...

I click on the camera icon next to the messages, and select the video option, turning it to face me, showing only my chest. I stare down the camera, though he can't see me, my voice needy, "And I know what I want now." My hand speeds up, the audio picking up the wet slap of my fist. My hips thrust, abs contracting. Apparently, with Noah, I have no common sense. Not one fucking bit. I send the video.

And panic sets in. Shit. Shit. What the fuck did I do? I pull my pants back up, typing out another text.

> Eli: Don't open that v...

Incoming from Noah, my phone flashes. I end the call. Holy hell. I don't know what's gotten into me, but whatever it is, it needs to vacate, stat. My phone rings a second time, and I end the call again.

> Noah: Answer the phone.

"Hello." My voice is hesitant, like I have to fight to get the one word out.

His voice comes out deep, gravelly. "Eli."

"Yes?"

"I'm trying to do the right thing."

"Why is it the right thing? I want this. You want this."

"I shouldn't."

"No one has to know."

He swears again, and I think he's going to hang up. "Do you wish it was my hand, Eli?" I shudder, my dick growing painfully hard.

"Yes," I squeak out, unable to lie.

There's a pause at the other end. I wait for him to continue. I hope he continues. "You know what I would do if I was with you right now?"

"I really, really hope it has something to do with your hands and my body that doesn't involve the two going in opposite directions."

He laughs, and the sound is heady, sensual. "I'd finish what we started. This time you would be down on your knees, touching your cock as I fuck that sexy, smartass mouth."

I whimper, unable to hide my reaction to his filthy words. "Yes, I want that."

"Are you still touching yourself?" I yank my pants back down, grabbing myself, knowing he wants the answer to be yes.

"Mhm." I'm so close, I already feel myself teetering on the edge. One more dirty word and I'm afraid this is going to be over way too soon.

I want to ask if he's touching himself too, but I'm not brave enough. I lost it all in the first go. "Do you know what that video did to me, Eli?" Damn, the way he says my name sounds like sex. "Answer me."

"What?" I can't seem to string together more than one word at a time.

"It made me want to touch every inch of your body. Leave marks on your perfect skin, dirty you up a bit. You got me so fucking hard I can't think unless it's about touching you." His words cause images to flash in my mind—he's sprawled out on a bed, fisting his cock, head tipped back, cheeks flushed. Then, his body over mine, kissing and sucking down my chest, turning it to putty.

I cry out as hot jets of come land on my stomach. I ride out my orgasm, not wanting to let go of this feeling. I stroke my cock lightly as it continues to twitch post-orgasm, not softening at all. Already needing more.

"I don't think I told you to come. What do you have to say for yourself, Eli?"

All I can do is let out a breathy moan, lighting up at his words. One positive of being young, I suppose. I stroke again, making sure he hears the wet pull of my slick hand. "I'm ready for you. Again."

"Fuck," he growls. I hear each wet stroke he takes, matching my own, pushing me to the edge again. Too fast.

He's not even touching me and I'm so ready. I've never felt this desperate.

I squeeze, trying to hold it off for him. "Please, I need to come." Apparently I'm not above pleading.

"Good. I like you begging for me. Come, Eli."

I cry out, panting, as my chest tightens. That was embarrassingly quick. Both times. Noah must like it, though, because he grunts moments later, his orgasm riding him. The low, guttural sound is exactly what I needed to hear. It makes me feel powerful, desired.

The feeling is fleeting, as reality crashes in once more. Yet again, I pushed him into something I'm not certain he wanted to do. And I have to still make the assumption he's straight, right? People jack off near each other all the time. Yes? Tom probably did one time when he thought I was sleeping. I don't know. Maybe I'm thinking too much about this. I don't know what I am, but until he says otherwise, I need to assume he's straight. He was married, has a daughter, and has only ever dated women to my knowledge.

"Eli," he calls my name, and it sounds like it's not the first time. "I can hear the gears turning in your head. Stop. I shouldn't have called. We shouldn't have done that, but you're right. We're both adults, and we both wanted it."

That's just it. I don't know if he did. "No. I started it. I pushed it. Again. It's just… there's something about you. The way I feel when I'm around you. That doesn't matter though. I mean, for one thing, you're straight. Then there's that whole thing where you told me to stop."

8

Noah

I was trying to be good, but I lost all sense after opening that video. His hard muscles flexing for the camera, telling me how much he wanted me. The sound of his slick hand fisting himself to thoughts of me. And now he's freaking out. I don't blame him. There are more reasons than I can count why this is inappropriate. Yet we keep finding ourselves here.

We're both adults, maybe if we give in to this attraction, remove the illicit temptation, it will go away. That's exactly what this is—lust, want, need—because it can't be anything more.

I don't want to examine the small part of me that screams it's more. After my ex-wife, I only sought companions for the release. That's what they wanted from me. I haven't been with anyone who I know, who makes me feel… everything. Who I want to protect. It throws me for a loop that it's all for Eli. A man. My daughter's ex-boyfriend.

"… for one thing, you're straight. Then there's that whole thing where you told me to stop."

I laugh, I can't help myself. My pants are still around my thighs, my button-up pushed up to my pecs. Come streaks across my stomach, only barely missing the shirt.

I texted him while in my office trying to write, not expecting what came next, secretly thankful it had. I lean over the desk to grab a tissue and clean myself off. It makes me feel like I'm fifteen again, trying to find every opportunity to get myself off. Horny all the fucking time. My mind isn't fully on board, but my body knows what it wants right now, even if the location is suboptimal.

However, my feelings and thoughts aren't as important as Eli freaking out right now. I need to say something that will ease his conscience. He didn't do anything I didn't want from him. "If I didn't want to fuck you, then I wouldn't have called, Eli." Is that crude? Yes. However, I enjoy turning him on with dirty talk. Sue me.

His response is a slightly crazed sounding chuckle followed by an audible swallow. "It's not just me?"

"No, it's not just you, Eli."

"This is crazy, right?" I hear him exhale through the phone.

"Yes." It's fucking insane, but whatever it is, I don't know if we can end things here. He may be looking for a rebound, and I don't know what I want out of this, but it seems unstoppable. If it's only once, and no one knows, would it be that bad? It can't be long term, but he can get me out of his system, and I can work on pushing this—this rightness out of my mind.

I throw the tissue into the trash next to me and pull my pants up, zipping and buckling them. "I want to see you again. However you'll take me. Whenever you used to come over, we always talked. I miss that." Shit, most of that wasn't supposed to come out.

"You miss talking to me?" He sounds surprised by my admission.

I wish he was in front of me so I could see his expressions. His face is an open book, always willing to tell me what he's thinking. "Yeah, Eli. You've always been a highlight of my day… for a lot longer than I should probably admit. Even if all of this, what we're doing, is new to me."

If he was here, his tan cheeks would be slightly pink, his gaze lowered because he knows I can read him. The thought makes me smile.

"I'm going to have the house to myself for the next month. Would you want to come over? We probably shouldn't do this, but I'm inclined to think this is going to keep happening. It's better if we control the situation. I'll be less likely to jump you the next time I see you." Fuck, am I seriously doing this? I know better, but I can't find it within myself to stop.

"Yes," Eli cuts in before I can embarrass myself further. "I want that. Boundaries. We need them. This is just sex and no one can know."

"Agreed."

"We stop if the other one says stop."

"Absolutely. Sex, until the other wants to stop."

The line goes silent for a moment, and I wonder if he's already regretting his decision. He has just as much to lose.

"This seems like it's going to backfire," he says. He's right.

"We will stop before that happens." God, if Angel finds out about this, she's going to hate me forever. I shove that thought down, only for another to pop up. What if the university finds out? Fuck. I'm so close to tenure.

"Okay." His voice is quiet but sure.

"Okay."

"Does next Wednesday work? I'll be back on campus by then and I'll have some free time after my class gets done at two."

"That works." I pause, debating my next words. "Eli, if you come over and change your mind, that's okay. We don't have to do anything. You don't owe me anything. What I'm trying to say is, this is all in your hands."

"And if I want something else in my hand, too?" he says cheekily, my dick perking up, making me grimace as it rubs against my pants. I groan. He is going to be the death of me.

He chuckles at my apparent misery, so I decide he needs to be punished. "The next time you get me horny and you don't finish what you started, there will be consequences. Understood?"

A strangled moan falls from his lips, followed by one stuttering word. "U-Understood."

"I don't know if my cock can take much more of your filthy mouth."

He responds, sounding indignant, "My filthy mouth? What about yours?"

It makes me harder and I squeeze myself trying to calm down. "I need to get off this phone before we start this process all over again. I've got to get back to my writing." I also promised I'd pay for all of Angel's clothes while she shops for vacation outfits as long as I could tag along to spend some time with her. She's renting a condo with a few girlfriends for the next month, which she's extremely excited about. I wish she would stay so I can spend more time with her, but I can't say it isn't convenient. It gives me the time to make a very dumb decision with someone who is very wrong for me but makes me feel different. Special.

"Alright, alright. I'll see you Wednesday. Happy writing."

"See you then." I end the call as I hear the garage door open, announcing Angel's arrival. I expect to feel guilty about what I did, and that I have plans to do it again. Instead, a buzz skates over my skin, ready for it to be next Wednesday.

"Dad," Angel calls out. I pull my shirt down and use the black screen from my laptop to check my reflection. Then, I peek at my watch realizing she's twenty minutes late. The door opens, and I've never been more thankful my daughter cannot make an appointment on time to save her life. "What are you doing in here? I thought we were going shopping. I need plenty of time to find the perfect outfits."

"I'm ready, sweetheart. Let's go. Maybe we can grab an early dinner on the way too?"

I grab my wallet and keys off the desk and slip my phone into my back pocket.

"Only if you're paying," she sings, making it sound like a joke. As if I don't already pay for everything, happily. I try to wrap my arm around her as we walk, give her a side hug, but she shrugs out of my hold. "Dad, stop. You know I don't like being touched." She flicks her hair with a hand before opening the passenger door and sliding into her seat.

9

Eli

The week with my family was torture, especially knowing I would see Noah soon. I didn't get a moment of privacy, and thinking about him took up most of my time. It made for a lot of uncomfortable nights. And days. Especially when Manny was trailing me at my mother's request.

Every night, dinner was the same. Asking me about my business classes, if I was still on time to graduate since I had to take so many "pointless" electives, like art classes and English. Those words stung, especially because they knew it's what I love, even as they brushed it off as a hobby.

They didn't ask about Angel, which was the one saving grace. They did spend all weekend ignoring the triplets and my brothers. Instead, the focus was on me. It was driving me crazy. Honestly, sometimes I think they put more pressure on me because they don't have contact with my oldest sister, Carmen. We don't even talk about her anymore. She left us after college and never looked back. She's twenty-six now. That's all I know about her. I hate it.

As promised, I'm back on campus in time to go to a party with Vi, which is a distraction from my morose thoughts.

"Heyo," she shouts as she jumps into my car. "You ready to par-tay?" She looks a lot happier than she did even a week ago after I picked her up from her English class, and I'm glad to see it.

"Oh, I'm ready for something, I just don't know if it's a party." She frowns at my words, and I can't help but chuckle at her face. She looks like a dejected puppy. "Okay. Stop with the look. Yes, I am excited to party with you."

She knocks her shoulder against mine. "Aw, shucks. You know how to make a girl blush." She scrunches her nose, then boops my own.

I swat her finger away. "Hey. No distracting the driver. And ha-ha, your flirting skills need work."

She smiles, sticking her tongue out at me, all while grabbing her phone from her pocket. "Yeah, you're a real ray of sunshine. You know I have a secret undying love for you. How much worse does my flirting have to get?"

I roll my eyes at her theatrics. She doesn't give me the chance to answer. Instead, she says, "Nah, I have my sights set on someone special. Remember that guy from the intro psych class we had to take last year? He sat two rows over and one seat ahead of you."

I try to recall the classroom, and I vaguely remember some guy with long blonde hair and a surfer-bro vibe. "One: rude, I am totally special. Two: yes?"

She tries to boop my nose again as I dodge her finger, keeping both hands on the wheel. *Woman, I am driving, remove your finger from my face.*

She eventually gets the message and stops, laughing her ass off. "Well, his name is Ambrose, and he is my target for tonight. It's his party. I ran into him the other day and he invited me. So that might be hopeful?" Her brows draw together, troubled, all the easy laughter gone. I want to say something but the look is gone as fast as it came and I can tell she's not ready.

I tug a strand of her hair. "Hey, you know it's okay if you need more time. It's also okay to talk to someone new. No judgment from me. Yeah?"

"Yeah. Thanks, Eli. I know you wouldn't judge me. We should have been closer friends a long time ago. Probably could have saved ourselves a lot of trouble dealing with the other assholes."

I nod my head in agreement, thankful for her as well. Despite the shitty circumstances, growing closer to her has been great.

I pull up to the curb, taking in about twenty to thirty cars, each one nicer than the next. It takes me a moment to find a spot near the sprawling mansion. The lawn and bushes are perfectly manicured, highlighting the deep red and brown brick of the house. I sit there, wanting to have fun and dreading it in equal measures. What if everyone heard about the breakup? I don't know if I want to spend all night answering questions.

"Hey, Eli. You ready?" Vi pokes her head back into the car and I startle, not realizing she got out. I was too busy staring at the house thinking about all the ways this could go wrong, which sounds about right for me.

I clear my throat. "Yeah. Coming." I trail behind her as she keeps up a stream of quiet chatter. I'm thankful for it, though I don't think I'm holding up my end of the conversation well. We step through the door and I'm instantly assaulted by the loud, pounding music coming from somewhere, probably the basement. I look toward the back of the house and spot a kitchen lined with twelve different hard liquors, and an honest-to-God keg sitting in a bucket of ice. I thought those were more of a prop in movies. Apparently we weren't going to the right parties.

I'm taking in my surroundings when I hear a familiar voice shouting over the bass. "Eli, brother. What's up, haven't seen you in a while?" The voice pauses, then calls out, "Vi?" Tag comes barreling into me, doing some elaborate man-hug where you can't actually fully touch before giving the usual back slap. "What are you two doing here together? Are Tommy boy and Ang joining us soon?"

Huh, it's strange our friends don't know. The university is small, and it's not uncommon for the student body to know everything about everyone.

He doesn't seem inclined to wait for an answer to his question. "Ah, hell. Who cares? I'm just so happy to see you guys. Let's get you a drink and then we can head downstairs. I brought Donna, I'm sure she'll be excited to see you. The last time we were all together was at Ang's pool party that afternoon. That was a whole lot of fun, minus you being a major buzz kill as per usual, Eli." He pauses to snort-laugh, "You know I'm just joking, buddy." I can't help but glance at Vi, who looks amused by the constant stream of words.

"I thought you were at the pool party with Dana, Tag?"

We enter the kitchen and he pumps a beer into a red Solo cup. "Oh yeah, I was, but that wasn't anything serious. I don't know if you guys heard, but Donna and I made it official, she's for sure my girlfriend now." He pauses, I think for dramatic effect, or maybe he's waiting for a reaction from us.

"Congrats?" Vi says.

"Yeah, yeah. Thanks. Now, I know what you're thinking. I don't seem like the kind of guy to settle down. And, you're right. Don't worry, Donna knows that. All of us should go on a date together sometime. Or maybe we can all hang out at Ang's again. I'm sure her father will be gone again soon, he always is. For a dude who teaches at the school, he sure disappears quite a lot, which is weird.

Good for all of us, right?" He hands the red cup to me and pours another.

He takes a breath, and I'm sure he's about to start again when Vi cuts in. "Hey, Tag. I actually wanted to take a couple shots before going to dance, and Eli was going to take one with me. You go ahead and bring that beer to Donna, I'm sure she would appreciate it."

"Oh yeah." He does an actual finger gun at her. "You're right. She would like that. Okay, I'll see you guys down there. Save a dance for me, Vi. I'm sure Donna wouldn't mind, and, well, Tommy boy isn't here." He winks before walking away.

Once he walks away I blurt, "Was he always this… over the top? Like this whole time and I'm only now noticing?"

She winces as we walk toward the hard liquor. "I'm going to have to go with… I'm afraid so. But don't worry, I felt the same. Also, you don't actually have to take a shot with me, I just needed an excuse to send him away. I do want one before I go down and see Ambrose."

"We should probably find one that isn't open?" That probably sounded super uncool or like I think she doesn't already know that. Who says those kinds of things to other people?

Instead of looking offended, she smiles softly. "Hey. You don't need to be embarrassed about looking out for me. I appreciate it. You can be my mother hen anytime." She pats me on the head and I roll my eyes. Opening a cabinet, she finds forty other bottles hidden inside. "Help me look for a sealed one?"

I don't understand how she's able to read my embarrassment so well. Has anyone ever paid that much attention? Maybe Noah. That is not a can of worms I should think about right now. I focus on the task at hand, grabbing one toward the back that's sealed in wax. "Will this do?"

"Yup." She searches through a couple of cabinets and finds an insulated cup, pouring about a third of the bottle into it. "That way I can have more if I want. I'll just carry this around with me."

I look at her incredulously. "Are you going to drink that straight?" I shudder at the thought, my stomach lurching in remembrance of the last time I drank. She's got a much stronger stomach than me.

Her answer is to take a large chug out of it as she winces. She licks her lips, her eyes screwed shut tightly. "That whole 'it goes down smoother the older it is' seems kinda like bullshit to me." She holds the cup out to me, quirking a brow in question.

Shaking my head no, I say, "Drinking isn't my thing." She shrugs her shoulders, then slaps the lid on before grabbing my arm, ready to party.

10

Eli

We head down to the basement, the music getting louder and louder with every step. All I can see are bodies grinding against one another in time with the music. In the corner, a couple is making out against the wall. On the other side of the bodies, I can just barely make out a group of people sitting in a circle. Vi yells over the crowd, "Ambrose is in the circle, let's go over there." I nod and start pushing through the crowd.

It takes a couple of minutes, but we finally make it over, and it's significantly quieter on this side because the speakers are facing the other direction. I can just make out voices talking in the circle. Ambrose turns around as we approach, and he smiles over at Vi. He must have cut his hair recently, because this time, it only falls to his shoulders.

"Hey." He stands and makes his way over to her. "I'm so glad you could make it." He looks at me next. "Um… Eli, right? We had psych together last year?"

"Yeah. Good memory. Ambrose, right?"

"Thanks. You can call me Cade. Only my parents call me that. Ambrose Caden Albrecht the third. And yes, I know it sounds super pretentious." He laughs at himself good-naturedly. "Why don't you two come join us? Vi, you can sit next to me." She giggles, but takes him up on his offer. Apparently this wingman stuff isn't hard at all. Didn't even have to do a single thing.

"Eli," a girl with red hair and dark black eyeliner calls out to me. "Come and sit next to me." I don't think I recognize her, but it's close enough to Vi I don't mind. "Hey, Eli. How are you doing?" She pushes close to me, her arm wrapping around my bicep. It makes me uncomfortable, so I try shifting away from her, but she only moves closer.

Thankfully, I don't have to come up with an answer. "Back to the game," a guy named BJ shouts to the group. "Vi, Eli, we were playing fuck, marry, kill—professor edition. We have a laptop pulled up to the faculty page in case you don't know who the professor is. Vi, you wanna go first?" Who thought it was a good idea to use professors? I shudder, thinking of my business professors. They are not my cup of tea. There is one professor that I'm thinking about, and I hope no one calls on me.

She laughs, subtly moving closer to Cade as she takes another drink. "Sure. Give me your worst."

They list off three male professors and end up looking up two because Vi doesn't know them. Each man is old with gray hair and tiny beady eyes. They have a terrible reputation among their students, and their pictures say it all. The third is an older guy, but friendly to everyone, who taught a few of her freshman year English courses. She lists her answers as Cade slides his hand onto Vi's knee. She gives him a wide, flirtatious smile. I turn away as the girl next to me pushes closer. Close enough I can see down her shirt. My skin breaks out in a sweat as I attempt to extricate myself. Her hands feel like tentacles suctioning against my skin. She won't let go, so I turn my attention away and do my best to ignore the sensation.

A few more people go around, and by the time someone gets back to me, Tag stumbles over, a bad feeling opening in the pit of my stomach. They explain the rules to him quickly and he smiles. "Whose turn is it?"

Everyone chants out my name in response. "Ohhh, I have a good one." He pauses like he did upstairs, leaning over to someone I don't know and stage whispers, "Donna just told me Ang dumped Eli." A few people snicker and I feel my cheeks heat. Moments later, I realize the embarrassment is the least of my worries. He raises his voice to full volume. "Eli, your group of three are Senorita Alvarez, Professor Dottie, and Professor Baker." Everyone oohs and ahhs at the options as I freeze. Logically I know no one knows about me and Noah, but that doesn't stop my mind from interpreting every glance as one of suspicion.

I sit there uncomfortably as if someone is going to rescue me. The redhead reprimands Tag. "That's not how the game is played, stupid. You can only give female professors to Eli, he's straight." I could kiss her. Thank you for saving my ass.

"Well, it's not like he'd have a hard choice. Ang dumped his sorry ass, so what's a better way to get revenge then to kill off her pops?" He laughs like it's the funniest thing in the world while Donna tries to pull him away from the group. She manages to budge him and my heart stops as I spot Tom and Angel. Tom glares at Vi, who's wound her way around the crowd to stop by my side. Angel glares directly at me as if this whole situation is my fault. Shit. Does she know? How could she?

When I don't respond she storms over to Tag. "Shut the fuck up. You're such a dipshit." I sigh, hoping since her priority is yelling at Tag, that we won't have to talk. I want nothing to do with her, especially after everything I've done. She can't know. He certainly wouldn't have told her, but I'm paranoid enough to believe she might see it in my eyes. I'm ready to leave, and I'm pretty sure Vi feels the same way.

Tom and Angel close in, sights locked on us. Apparently it was wishful thinking that they were going to leave us alone. "What the fuck are you two doing here?"

Tom shrieks loud enough that some people stop dancing to stare.

Neither of us respond, too stunned by their anger. Tom decides now is a good time to add, "Oh, I get it now. You were moving in on Vi, you piece of shit. That's who the hickeys were from. How long has this been going on behind our backs? And you were trying to play the fucking hero, Eli." He seems crazed, his eyes wild, chest heaving. I inch myself in front of Vi, afraid of what Tom might do. He looks at her. "You're such a fucking slut. You kicked me out of the apartment so you could be with Eli, didn't you? How long were you two cheating? Fucking pieces of shit."

He clenches his fist, taking a step toward Vi, so I step in front of her, blocking his path. I'm not a fighter. If he punches me, this is going to fucking hurt. "Back the fuck off, Tom."

As if she's knocked out of a daze, Angel finally processes Tom's words. Her eyes water as she looks at the two of us. Her voice is quiet, accusatory. "You slept with Violet? What the fuck, Eli?"

She turns to Tom, not waiting for a response. My chest tightens. Even though I didn't cheat on her, what I've done with her father isn't much better. It's actually a lot fucking worse.

"Were you going to tell me, Tom?" She shifts, crossing her arms over her body, a single tear rolling down her cheek.

Tom doesn't acknowledge Angel, so she moves to walk away, squeezing between us. In the same moment, Tom lunges, fists up and flailing, unable to stop as he realizes he's about to hit Angel. I grab her, shoving her back before Tom can land a blow. I'm not quick enough to guard myself and I feel his fists rain down on the side of my face, my ribs, my stomach, as I see Vi pull a flailing Angel back further.

The next blow lands on my temple, and I fall to the ground, hard. I throw my hands up to protect my face as he kicks. I feel each point of contact as I scramble to find my footing. Another kick lands just under my ribcage, knocking the wind from my lungs. I can hear the girls screaming behind me and I worry Violet might try to intervene. I try to pull myself up again, knowing I need to get back on my fucking feet. If I don't, who knows what he might do. I get one foot under me, a hand next, but that's a mistake.

My guard is open, leaving enough space for his foot to connect with my face. It doesn't land. Someone wrenches on his shoulder and I use my free hand to grab his ankle and yank it hard. It's enough to knock him off balance. It gives someone enough room to grab us, one pulling me off the ground, the others holding him back.

Three people pull Tom back but I don't have time to see who. Vi has tears streaming down her cheeks as I stumble forward, trying to get to her with little success. "You okay?" I croak out as she rushes to my side, helping to prop me up.

I look at Angel, checking to make sure Tom didn't get her. "You okay, Angel?" I watch as she looks at Tom, fear in her eyes. She turns her gaze on me, shaken, but rushes to Tom's side, ignoring me.

She grabs at his neck, pulling his face into view. "Are you hurt?" He sports a small cut on his brow from where he landed on my elbow as he fell down, but he doesn't respond. He just keeps glaring at me. She tries again, "Come on, let's go back to my place. We'll finish getting ready for our trip."

He jerks against the hands holding him back. "Get the fuck off me. All of you." When they let him go, he pushes past Angel, storming up the stairs.

Vi and I look at each other, a silent message passing between us. I say, "Don't leave with him. We'll get you a ride home, Ang."

Her face goes blank as she watches us. It's unsettling. She walks off without a word and I intend to go after her, but when I take a step out of Vi's arms, I stumble to the side. Cade catches me then puts my arm over his shoulders before turning to Vi. "Let's get him seated. There's a room through there."

We walk to the room at a sedate pace, every step causing a dull throb in my ribs. I plop onto a bed, flinching when it jars me. Cade says, "I'll go get some paper towels and some antiseptic for the cuts."

Vi nods as she kneels next to me.

"I'm going to lie down." I slide down as slowly as possible, avoiding any sudden movements. The light burns my eyes, so I close them, letting out a small sigh.

I blink them back open when I hear a sniffle and see Vi, her face streaked black. "This is all my fault."

"Hey, no, it's not your fault. The only one at fault is Tom." That only seems to make her cry harder, so I push myself back to sitting and grab her hand. "Why do you think it's your fault?"

"I'm the one who dated him. He's pissed I dumped him. Jealous that I might be with someone else." She lets out a bitter laugh before rubbing her eyes. "The reasons are endless."

I lean forward; the motion causes my head to swim. I swipe my arm over my face, trying to push the sensation back to focus on the conversation. "Even if you never dated him, he still would have slept with Angel. He'd still hate me for whatever reason. Tonight would have ended the same way. You know that, right?"

She sniffles. "You're probably right."

"Good." The light in the room feels like it's scooping out my eyeballs, so I close them again.

"We should call your parents to come and get you, Eli."

"No. Absolutely not. I'm fine. No way can my parents find out."

"Eli, come on. You're not fine. They're your parents, they would want to know. I know they're strict, but…"

"No."

"Eli."

"No."

"Fine, but someone needs to make sure you're okay. You might have broken bones, or a concussion. You need someone who can watch for the signs and get you to the hospital if needed. I'm drunk enough that I shouldn't drive, and I don't know what signs to look for to make sure you're okay."

She's right. I know she is. I absolutely refuse to call my parents.

"I… I have someone I can call." I grab my phone out of my pocket, but Vi yanks it out of my hand.

"I'll call."

"It's okay, I can make the call." I hold out my hand, but she doesn't seem to budge.

I stare at her and she stares back at me for a few moments as blood trickles down my brow, along the side of my face, until it splashes on the collar of my shirt, both of us refusing to back down.

"Hey, I found the supplies." Cade looks at the two of us in our standoff. "What's going on?"

"I'm ensuring Eli has someone to watch after him tonight instead of him lying to me and saying he does when he really doesn't. He's going to let me call a friend of his."

I respond, refusing to break first, "I can't leave you alone either, you're drunk. It's not that bad. I'll be fine."

"I can get her home, man." That solves one problem.

I say, "Thanks, Cade."

I can't help but smirk as Vi glares over at Cade. She clearly doesn't want to leave me alone. "I appreciate the offer. I'll be ready to go as soon as I make the call for Eli. Thanks for your help, Cade." He nods, sensing the dismissal. Placing the first aid kit on the bed, he raps his knuckles against the door once and exits the room.

She pulls some paper towel off and wets it with the antiseptic. "Is there any particular reason you don't want me knowing who you're going to call?"

I wince at the sting as she places the antiseptic against the cut over my brow. While she's distracted, I try to grab my phone, but she swats my hand away from where it's sitting on the bed. "I can make a frickin' call by myself. I'll call someone."

"I don't believe you. Just tell me who to call, Eli." She tosses the paper towel to the side and grabs another one.

"A friend."

"The girl you don't want to tell me about? She can't be that bad. It's not like it could be your best friend's girlfriend." She tries for humor, but it falls flat and she gives an awkward grimace.

"No. Not the person I won't tell you about, as you like to put it."

She rests an elbow on my knee, careful not to jar me. "Then I don't see why I can't call for you."

"You wouldn't understand."

"Try me." She raises her brow and unlocks my phone.

My face involuntarily scrunches. "How did you know my passcode?"

She rolls her eyes. "Don't change the subject. Who should I call?"

I heave a sigh. She's not going to let this one drop. Who can I call? I want to call Noah, but I can't do that if she insists on being the one to call. And I will not contemplate why he's the first person to pop into my mind. I certainly can't call my parents. That's when it hits me. I could call Carmen. I doubt she would answer, but it's someone that I can give her. In fact, that's perfect, because I know she won't answer. The perfect distraction until I have a second alone to call someone else or sneak away and drive myself home. "Carmen. Call Carmen, please."

Nodding her head, she scrolls through my contacts before punching the number into her own phone. The phone rings while she holds the paper towel against my forehead. She puts it on speaker and tosses it on the bed. This was a dumb idea. I wheeze. I shouldn't have done this. She should hang up the phone. "She's not going to answer." I try to grab it, to hang up before Carmen has the chance to send the call to voicemail.

She dodges me again, sliding it out of the way. A chill breaks out over my skin as I try to slow my breathing. It rings for what feels like an eternity. I match each breath to the tone. Shouldn't it go to voicemail by now? "Hello, this is Carmen." I focus on one spot in the room as I do my best to ignore the panic rising in me.

Mierda. I didn't think she'd actually answer. "Hi, Carmen. This is Violet, Eli's friend."

"Eli? Elias Ruiz?"

Vi looks at me oddly and mouths, "Does she not remember who you are?" Hell, does she think this is the girl I hooked up with? That's horrendously disgusting. I shudder. "Um… yes. Elias Ruiz. Maybe we shouldn't have called."

The line is silent for a second. "No. No, I… Um, what's wrong? Is he okay?"

Vi continues to eye me. I can only imagine how weird this conversation seems to her. "Well, um, actually…" She trails off, looking at my cuts.

I catch her eye, pinching her hand in mine. I mouth, "Tell her I'm fine."

Her eyes narrow. "Not really. He should be okay. I don't know the signs of a concussion, and I'm kind of drunk, and we need a ride from this party, though. I didn't want to leave him alone even though it's what he said he wanted." I squeeze her hand again, widening my eyes at her. *Stop.*

"Concussion? What happened? Where are you?" Vi rattles off the address and there is another moment of silence before she comes back on the line. "I'm about thirty minutes away, can he wait that long? Does he need to go to the hospital?"

Her gaze turns back to me, assessing. "I don't think so. He seems coherent and can answer all my questions even though he's been stubborn as fuck. Keeps eying me like he's going to kick my ass, so he'll probably be okay."

Carmen laughs. "Yeah, that sounds like him. I'll be there soon. I'll text this number when I'm outside."

11

Vi and Cade get me up the stairs and out to the porch with emphatic swearing given every step feels like another punch to the gut. As we sit and wait, I take stock of my injuries. Despite the punches, kicks, and hits to the face, I can still see fine, which means I hopefully have minimal swelling around the eyes. One small miracle, I suppose.

While his punches were weak, his kicks had some power behind them. I know I have several minor cuts, and one large cut on my face above the brow, but I haven't looked at it, so I can only go on what I feel throbbing. Honestly, the worst damage seems to be to my ribcage, where he got most of his kicks in. I can breathe and move, so I think they're just bruised. All in all, I got lucky.

Knowing that I'm okay, though extremely sore, I tune in to the conversation with Violet. She keeps insisting that she's going to go back with me. "No, Vi. I'll be okay. Go home and get some sleep. All I'm going to do is crash. Let Cade drive you home."

I think her adrenaline has waned because she's shaking, though her tears slow. Pulling her into my side, I do my best to hide a flinch as the throbbing pain intensifies. "I'm going to be okay. Even if I look hideous, I don't think I'm that bad. Though I might have already looked like that before Tom kicked my ass. Besides, Carmen will take care of me."

She sniffles but snorts half-heartedly. "You promise?" I squeeze her hand and nod my head. "Swear to me… if she leaves, you'll tell me. I'll be right over. I don't know her, so I don't know if I can trust her. She didn't seem happy to hear from you."

"She might not have been happy to hear from me, but she will take care of me. If it makes you feel better, I'll call you in the morning to let you know I'm okay."

"Hey, Eli." She stares out at the lawn as she's perched along my side.

"Yeah."

Tears roll down her cheeks as she gathers her words. "I'm so sorry I made you come tonight. This was all my fault."

"Look at me." She shakes her head. "Please look at me." She sniffles, then looks at Carmen as she walks up the stairs, and finally at me again. "This wasn't your fault. Tom started this. Don't waste a second of guilt on them. They don't deserve more of our thoughts or time."

My gaze catches on my sister as her lips tip up on one side. Worrying about Vi this whole time kept me from freaking out about seeing my sister for the first time in five years. Everything floods to the surface as we stare at each other. Each emotion is like a storm, threatening to leave chaos in its wake. She clears her throat. "Elias. *¿Qué te pasado?*"

"Nothing happened. Can we go?" I didn't mean for my words to sound accusatory or aggressive, but it looks like that's what I'm going with tonight.

I look back at Vi. "I'll call you tomorrow. Thanks for giving her a ride home, Cade." He nods his head at me as I struggle to my feet. My sister reaches forward, catching me under the elbow as we stumble to the car under my clumsy weight.

Once enclosed in the space, she says, "I'm guessing you don't want to go home to our parents, so where would you like me to take you? Should you go to the hospital?"

"I don't need the hospital, I'm just sore. I have a dorm room at the college. Drop me off there. Sorry you had to come all this way to get me. I'm sure you had better things to do." Again, accusatory. I need to get this shit under control. I don't want her to think she's getting under my skin.

"It's not a problem, Elias. I'm glad you called."

"I go by Eli now."

She clears her throat. "Right. Eli."

The car is silent, tension bouncing around the space as she winds through the streets. "One more right turn and the parking lot for my dorm is on the left." She nods, following the directions, then pulls into an empty spot.

"Wait in the car, I'll come around and help you." I don't listen to her. A grunt of pain stumbles past my lips as I push the door open and jostle my rib cage. I know I'm acting like a rebellious teenager. I recognize that and I don't care. Launching half my body out of the car, I make it a step or two before falling back into the seat with a loud thud, jarring every aching bone in my body. "Yeah, that's why I told you to stay in the car, *cabrón*."

Mierda, that fucking hurt. I glare at her as she comes around to the door. She may be helping me, but she doesn't get to act like everything is okay between us. That's not fair. She can't just call me a dumbass like she knows me. Not after she abandoned all our brothers and sisters. But I can't get out of the car myself right now, so I'll have to fucking deal with it.

Once I'm settled on her shoulder, we waddle to the backseat, where she grabs a small bag. It's then I notice intricate black lines criss-crossing her arms, leaves and flowers spreading from what seem to be twisting vines. All I can think as we make our way up the stairs is that our parents would flip their shit to know that their daughter has tattoos. I also wonder what the black ink would look like on my slightly darker skin, if I was ever brave enough to get one.

I open the door myself, the throbbing pain more of an ache now. She places me on the bed, then tugs one shoe after the other off my feet like I'm an invalid. As she leans closer, her hair falls forward and I notice how the underside is dyed purple and blue, contrasting drastically with the rest of her black hair. I don't know how I didn't notice it earlier, because it's bright.

"Our parents would kill you if they could see you now." She flinches at the sentiment, and I have a moment where I feel a little regret, but I don't have long to stew in that feeling.

She responds, "Get some sleep, *hermano*. I'll see you in the morning."

***

I become conscious too soon, my stomach, ribs, and face throbbing. I groan as I lift my head, trying not to move the rest of my body. When I sit up, I realize the room is empty. Figures that Carmen left me as soon as I fell asleep. I shouldn't have called her in the first place. I pat my pockets, looking for my phone before noticing it's plugged into the charger on my desk. My body protests as I hop off the bed and make my way over to it. I need to call Vi and let her know I'm okay.

The door opens again to reveal Carmen. I look at her dumbly. "I thought you left."

"Nope. I went to get you some ice packs so that the swelling won't get worse. Here." She comes across the room and places one in my hand. She stands there awkwardly, looking at anything but me.

I look at it, then at her, as if the ice pack is going to bite me. It would make sense, considering it's provided by a sister who abandoned her family. "Thanks."

"No problem."

I shift again, wondering if I should say anything else.

I don't. Returning to my bed, the ice pack pressed against my forehead. I shoot off a quick text to Vi. There's also a message from my mom, but I don't have the mental capacity to deal with that right now.

Carmen says, "Look…"

I say, "So…"

We both awkwardly chuckle. "You first," I respond.

She nods her head twice. "I-I'm glad you called me."

"I didn't think you'd answer after you dropped off the face of the Earth. You know our brothers and sisters needed you, right? And you left them. Like it was nothing."

Her face pinches before she lets out a bitter laugh. She runs a hand down her face then gathers her hair into a messy bun. Almost like it's an unconscious, nervous habit. "I'm not surprised that's what they told you."

"Would you rather have them say nothing at all? No explanation why our older sister left us without a word. Who wouldn't return our phone calls or messages?" She crosses her arms and my eyes catch on the tattoos again. "Was being rebellious that important to you? Getting a bunch of tattoos and changing your hair color was more important than being there for Adriana or Miguel, or any of the other four?" I wanted an explanation. How could she leave them? I didn't want to be there a lot, I got that part, but I'd never abandon my siblings.

"Keep going," she whispers.

"Our parents aren't great… but our siblings needed you and you weren't there. Who does that?" I throw down the ice pack, my breathing labored as I force myself to take deep, even breaths. I look at Carmen, really look at her for the first time in years. She's clasping her arms around her, not in defense, but in comfort. Her eyes are glassy, not with rage, but with a deep, distant sorrow. It catches me off guard, my mind unable to process what's in front of me.

She clears her throat. "I know you needed me, and I wasn't there. You have no idea how sorry I am. I should have been there even if I didn't think you'd need me. As for our siblings, I knew they had you. You were always better than me."

I don't know what to say to the last comment, so I choose to ignore it. "I don't need anyone. Least of all you."

She smiles sadly. "I hope that isn't true, Elias."

"Why didn't you call?"

Her body sways. "I couldn't." I'm about to call bullshit when she continues. "Look, I don't want to offend you by saying I don't think you're ready to hear my side of the story. You're an adult, and you're old enough to make your own decisions, but you need to decide if you're ready. I can imagine, vividly, what Mom and Dad told you. I can also guarantee it's not the whole truth." She waits a second, giving me time to let her words soak in. None of it makes sense. She left us, they said she couldn't stand being at home with everyone anymore. They told us not to call her, that she wouldn't answer. And she didn't. Not once out of all the times I tried.

She's not done. "Whatever you decide, if you want to hear my side of things, I'll tell you. For what it's worth, and I'm sure it doesn't sound believable, you can call me. After this many years, I thought leaving you alone would be the best thing to do. Maybe I was wrong? I love you. I didn't…" Tears shine in her eyes as her words trail off. She shakes her head twice before falling completely silent.

I copy the motion, not believing one thing she's said. She cut us out. That was her choice, and she's only backtracking now trying to make herself sound better. It's only empty words.

"I can tell you're not ready. Mama and Papa love you and you trust them. That's fine. If you ever want to hear it, or you ever need someone to talk to, you have my number. I'd love to hear from you again." Before turning to me, she walks to her bag and packs the couple of items she took out from last night. She gives me a small smile as she opens the door to leave. "You are more than just the family, *hermanito*. You are an individual, completely separate from the rest of them. I meant it when I said I love you. All of you. I won't pressure you into hearing my side, though."

Not expecting a response, she walks out the door. After staring at it for a few minutes, I put the ice pack on my face and fall back onto the bed. I should not have called her. I'm already dealing with enough bullshit. As I slap another ice pack on my ribs, I groan. I don't know how I'm going to make it to class tomorrow.

The rest of the day, I'm in various levels of consciousness. I only wake to throw the packs of ice in the garbage. The last melted about an hour ago, and that's when I finally looked at myself in the mirror. The bruise around the cut is thankfully a dark brown instead of nasty black. Another one rests on my cheekbone, slightly darker than the one on my forehead. My ribs are angry shades of purple and blue all along the left side. All things considered, it could have been worse. Mostly, my body feels like hot garbage. Not ideal, but not the end of the world. I should be well enough to make my next class.

I text Vi, asking if there is any magic makeup voodoo she can do to cover the bruises on my face. While I don't have any experience with makeup myself, I know she's pretty skillful. She responds that, yes, she can do something, but she doesn't think it will completely cover everything.

> Vi: Plus, makeup can't cover up that big cut you have on your face. You sure you don't want to take it easy for the next few days?
>
> Eli: I need to try something. Come over before my class tomorrow? Pleasssseeeee. <3
>
> Vi: Fine. Fine. You don't have to beg.

12

I sit in my seat, as straight-backed as possible. That seems to be the most comfortable position for my poor, still very bruised ribs. This class seems to go on forever, especially because I'm only half paying attention. I should have listened and stayed home.

After this, Vi asked me to stop by the other side of campus so that she could see the makeup, make sure it's still holding up. There is still some color peeking out through the foundation, but it's light enough that most people won't notice. Everyone's so busy with their own lives. I did run into someone from the party, though. They gave me a disdainful look before scurrying away to class. The rumor that I cheated on Angel seems to have spread. Though I don't love that fact, I know the people who matter most will know it's not true. Although, I'm sure no one would have believed she was the type to cheat either, so who knows.

Regardless, I'm meeting Vi, but this time it's at a coffee shop away from the English building and not the same place where she works. I'll be less likely to run into Noah there. I texted him last night saying Wednesday wouldn't work for me anymore and that we would have to try again next week. He was worried because he thought I called to tell him I regretted what happened between us. It took some reassuring, once he actually let me speak, but he calmed down when I told him I had a family obligation. He knows how intense they are, so he didn't question it. I'm hoping a week will be enough for the bruises to fade.

Now that I know he's as eager to see me as I am to see him, it feels like cruel and unusual punishment not getting to see every part of him. Yet another reason to be pissed off at Tom—cock-blocking *pendejo*. But I don't want Noah to see me like this, so I'll just have to deal with it.

It wasn't too hard to convince Vi I didn't want to run into Noah again either, not after the last time, when he wanted to speak with me, which is why I find myself on my way to this coffee shop. I try not to drive on nice days like this, but given how bad my ribcage is, I gave in. It takes about ten minutes to find a parking spot, and my phone starts to ring as I enter the building.

I ignore it, assuming it's my mom or dad. I see Vi approaching me rapidly, her phone against her ear. "Red alert," she whisper-yells. "I thought this place would be safe. Unfortunately, he's in the back booth with a few of the other professors."

"What?" I turn in the direction she points and catch Noah's eye. They light in excitement until he surveys the rest of my face. His gaze zeros in on the bruise and his eyes turn a stormy, dark color that looks almost black. *Chinga.* I break eye contact, and usher her into the line. "Well, he's seen me, so it's too late now. We'll just have to grab a quick coffee and hope he doesn't approach us. I hope Angel didn't tell him some lie about how I tried to beat the crap out of Tom or something."

Violet gives me a weird look. I backtrack. "You know, 'cause she also said I cheated on her. I don't want him to get any idea that I wronged his daughter. My face already has enough bruises," I end, lamely.

She leans into me. "I don't think a professor would beat you up, even if you 'wronged his daughter' as you said. Also, you sound like you're from *'The Tudors'* when you say stuff like that."

I snort, and the movement makes me cringe. "Ouch, no making me laugh. It hurts."

She scrunches her nose in sympathy. "Sorry."

We order our drinks and snag a table where Noah can't see me. Vi takes a moment to look over my face. "I think it's definitely working. Unless someone knows you well, they might just think it's weird lighting hitting your face. There is one spot right by your cut that's kind of peeking through. Take this and do what I showed you this morning. You'll need the lighting in the bathroom."

My eyes involuntarily dart to the section of the shop where I last saw Noah. He wouldn't follow me into the bathroom, right? "Oh, I don't know. I don't think I'll be able to do it myself."

"It's either do it by yourself, or have me do your makeup here at the table out in the open where anyone can see. You really want that added rumor going around with everything else?"

I snatch it out of her hand. "Alright, I get the picture. Thanks for those very kind, super motivating words."

She gives me a wicked little smirk. "Oh, you are so welcome."

I make my way through the shop, going behind a few tables to avoid Noah's direct line of sight. Maybe if he can't see me, I can get in there and sneak back out without a confrontation. A few students glance at me as I walk past, and one or two turn to their friends to whisper. I thought this was supposed to be a mid-sized school. How is it that everyone knows my business? I shake my head, trying to ignore it.

I walk through the door and make sure the two stalls are empty before approaching the mirror. I take out the stick thing Vi gave me and warm it between my hands like she told me to do. It makes it "glide on nicer for a more even finish," or so I'm told. I bring it to my face when the door creaks open and quickly slams shut, the lock clicking in place. I don't need the mirror to tell me who it is barging into the bathroom, but I lock eyes with him anyway.

He's across the small space in a flash, grabbing my shoulder with one hand to turn me, while lightly gripping my chin with the other. I cringe, trying to hide the pain from him jostling me. His eyes flick from the cut to my cheek, and back. He frowns, his hand lifting to wipe at my cheek as I say, "No," trying to stop him from seeing the full effect.

His eyes darken as the makeup brushes away, but his hand remains light on my face. His body radiating tension, his jaw tightening, I can tell it's taking every ounce of his control to remain calm.

He grits out through his teeth, "Please tell me this isn't from who I think it's from."

I lightly tug out of his grip, and he releases me. Even though I want to step closer, I take a step back. "I'm okay."

"Is this why you rescheduled on me? You didn't want me to see this?" He takes a step closer.

I take a step back, bumping into the sink. He steps forward again, seeing I have nowhere else to go, his body flush against mine. I shiver from the contact, which makes me flinch, my ribs groaning at the movement. And he notices. He grabs the hem of my shirt and pulls it up before I can protest. He hisses out a breath before growling, "I am going to kill him."

He drops the material and spins around, moving toward the door as if he's going to hunt Tom down right now. I rush after him, grabbing his arm.

"Please don't. That will make things so much worse for all of us."

"You can't expect me to sit by while he's hurting you."

"I was just trying to help Vi and Angel. It's fine."

"What?"

"The fight, he was trying to go after Vi, and Ang got in his way. I pushed them behind me, but my guard was down. It won't happen again."

"He tried to hit my daughter?"

"Not intentionally. But, she, uh, she left with him. She said they were going to pack for a trip?"

He turns murderous, picking up his phone to dial her number. His body shakes, trying to contain the anger rocking his body. "She told me that was with girlfriends." Fucking hell. I can't believe I didn't think to tell him before.

I let go of his arm. "Sorry. I should have thought about that. Um, I'll go so you can call her. Hopefully she hasn't left yet. I'm so sorry. I should have known. Should have told you sooner."

"Stay. I'm not done speaking with you, either." His piercing gaze ensures I don't move from the spot.

It's so wrong, I know it's not the time, but excitement courses through my veins at the sound of his voice. He calls her number again, running the pad of his thumb across my bottom lip, accurately interpreting the heat in my eyes.

The phone continues to ring as he moves his hand to my jaw, his body inching closer and closer. He puts pressure on my throat as I swallow, and my dick starts to grow under the possessive gesture.

It goes to voicemail, so he hangs up and tries one last time. While he's waiting for his daughter to pick up, he leans in, whispering in my ear, "I'm guessing you think I'm mad at you?" He waits until I confirm, then continues. "I'm not. I'm worried for my daughter's safety. I'm worried about you. They are completely separate things. For now, I need to be a father." The phone goes to voicemail again.

He gestures between us as he lets me go. "This conversation isn't over. I'll call you later." He shocks me by placing a light kiss over the bruise on my cheek before walking away.

I lean back against the sink as he unlocks the door, giving me one last look on his way out. I let out shallow pants, feeling winded as I try to recover from the extreme emotions coursing through me. My cheek tingles as I run my fingers along it, trying to hold on to the feeling of his lips on me for a little while longer. If I'd had any worries about him still being attracted to me in person, I don't have to worry anymore. That was quite possibly the second hottest... mmm, maybe the third hottest moment I've ever experienced.

After what feels like hours of reeling my emotions in, I turn back to the mirror and quickly apply the makeup. I look at my phone when I'm done applying it and notice it's been fifteen minutes. Crap, there's no way Vi isn't going to be suspicious. Although this shit takes a while, hopefully I can pass it off as being incompetent with the stick thing.

Capping the lid, I race out of the room, and over to our table where I find her flirting with Cade. I've never been happier to see the guy either, if it means she was distracted and didn't notice how long it took, or that Noah probably left the shop looking like he had murder on the brain. I wait until there is a lull in the conversation. She glances up at me, and she looks happy, and I absolutely love that for her.

"Hey, I have to get to the library. I reserved a room for studying. I'll see you later." She stands up and gives me a hug, subtly grabbing the makeup out of my pocket. Did we need to be so covert? No, probably not. It does make me feel better knowing we're less likely to get gossiped about again. "See you later, Cade."

"See ya later, Eli. Glad to see you're feeling better."

I nod my head, then grab my backpack and head to the library. I don't have a room reserved, but I do need to study. Maybe it will help me get my mind off a certain hot English professor who might have a bossy streak that I find way too intriguing.

***

It's been three days and I still haven't heard from Noah after our run-in in the bathroom. I'm thinking he reconsidered this whole deal. He said he wasn't done talking to me, but it sure feels like it with this radio silence and I'm going a bit stir crazy in my room.

I asked Vi to hang out, but she was busy. I've had a few friends from our old group reach out via text, some messages good, others bad. It's a lot easier to ignore it all when I don't have to see anyone, but my mind does a pretty good job of replaying all the comments. From Tag's, "*Good job banging the two hottest chicks in the group*," to some girl named Emma's "*I heard what she did to you. I'm here if you ever need to talk. Or anything ;)*," I think it's that redhead from the party. Either way, it's been a nightmare.

I've watched endless amounts of TV hoping it will drown out all the thoughts running through my mind. Normally I'd read a book, but I'm too on edge for that. The only positive thing is that I am barely sore anymore, the bruises on my face have faded to yellow, and I've avoided my family and thinking about Carmen this whole time. Go me! I'm winning at life. I've also caught up on a lot of sleep and it has been glorious.

Someone raps on the door, and I let out a long sigh. My thoughts have manifested my family. I thought I'd managed to keep them at bay, but apparently that's a lost cause. I glance at myself in the mirror, making sure I look somewhat presentable, before grabbing the food off the desk next to me and tossing it in the trash can. I'm about to say hello to my mom, the words at the tip of my tongue, when I pull the door open and come face-to-face with Noah. "Mm-Noah. What are you doing here?"

I glance down the hallway, thankful that it's deserted. It's summer, so it's not usually busy, but this is kind of risky.

"I'm here to finish our conversation."

I step back and he walks through the door. Have I stepped into the twilight zone? Am I dreaming? Why is Noah Baker in my dorm room? "Oh." Wow, I sound so articulate.

He smirks at me before observing the rest of the room. "This room does not scream Eli to me."

"Um…" I glance at my surroundings. He wants to talk about my room?

A chuckle rumbles through his chest. "Sit down, please."

I look at my desk chair, then my bed, and the floor. "The chair will do for now." I glance at him, and the smirk has turned into a full, extremely attractive smile. It's truly not fair how my body begs to obey his words.

13

Noah

I survey his room, and I know it's making him nervous, but I can't help exploring his space. He's become more outgoing with me the more we've spoken, but there's still so much I don't know about him. Not that this arrangement is about getting to know one another. I thought his room might tell me more about him, but the longer I think about it, the more ridiculous that seems. His parents have spent his whole life shaping how they want him to be. I doubt he'd have anything super personal at home or in this room, which isn't his own.

The one item in his room that looks well-loved is his desk, and it's not because it's the same furniture students use every year, it's the papers strewn about, pens and pencils scattered, and books stacked everywhere. He also has a little bookshelf off to the side of the desk filled with books. For someone who lives close to home, it's odd to see enough to make a small library. I'm expecting to see mostly school books, but I don't expect to see all the books that are published from my two series that are currently out. Nine books in total.

They are on a shelf of their own, a few fan-art knick-knacks hidden among them. A warmth spreads in my chest as I look at the shelf. Each spine is cracked and well worn. The tops of the pages have several smudges along the edge, right where someone would hold a book. It's a small thing, but it shows someone was running their finger over the pages again and again—some wild emotion overtaking them as they read through different scenes. These books look cherished, beloved. Eli walks up behind me, and I can hear a long breath leave him. "Those, um, yeah… Those…"

"… are my books. I didn't know you were a fan. You want me to sign them?" I say it to tease him, but his eyes light up at the question.

He clasps his hands in front of him. "Would I be absolutely awful if I said yes?"

I laugh at his excitement. No matter how bad a mood I'm in, he always cheers me up with his kind and caring demeanor. And now his adorable, nerdy side.

"No. I think it's cute." He blushes, and I can't help but admire how it looks on his high cheekbones. This wasn't part of the plan when I came here to talk, but I'm liking the direction this is going.

I can't get too sidetracked though. I came here to talk about what happened, and how he thinks I'm mad because he didn't tell me about Angel being in the middle of the fight. Or that the trip was with Tom. Those were concerns, but now that I've dealt with it, with no less than five hours a day of screaming on Angel's part, I'm ready to have that talk.

Choosing the newer series, the one I haven't finished yet, he picks them up with care. He carries all four carefully, like they're made of glass. He has a container sitting on his desk, and I shuffle the pens around until I find a purple fine-point sharpie. I hold the book up out of his view and write a message. I put small notes in each book, swatting his hand away each time he tries to grab one so he can read it. "No. These are only to be viewed the next time you actually read them. Understand?" What he doesn't know, and won't until he reads them, is that the notes are a story in and of themselves. My story, or a part of it.

He swallows, and I track the motion, instantly intrigued. How is he so damn distracting? I shouldn't feel any of this, but I do. And it takes all of my willpower not to command him again, the hazy lust in his eyes giving away how much he likes it. I clear my throat and drag my gaze up to meet his own.

"Understood," he responds. Honestly, he might be the death of me.

I clear my throat. Glance at his mouth. Clear my throat again. "We need to address what happened the other day."

He winces as he picks up the books and returns them to the shelf. "We don't. It's okay, I get it. I would have been mad if I was in your shoes." As he continues, I lift a brow. "I promise I still tried to make sure Angel was okay when it all went down. I also get why you'd be upset that I didn't think to tell you she was planning a trip with him."

I stalk closer as each word comes out of his mouth. He looks nervous, but under that, I can tell he's excited, so I draw nearer still. I crowd his body against the desk, noting once again that I don't have to bend down to talk to him face-to-face. He's as big as me, and the thought sends a thrill through my blood. Despite our similar heights, I tower over him as he bends back, curving around the desk. I cut him off by running my finger over his jaw, ending on his bottom lip. "I need you to listen to me. Can you do that?"

He nods his head, swallowing as I release his lip to graze his jaw with my hand, tilting his face closer to mine.

Standing there for a minute, I take in what exactly I'm doing, and it shocks me how right this all feels. Like he should be in my arms, taking my orders. He's still leaning against the desk, but I reluctantly release my grip on the surface. I've never been attracted to a man before. Granted, I haven't truly lusted after anyone after my messy divorce. I've slept with a few people, but I haven't needed them like I need Eli. I could lose my daughter, my job. He could lose his family and his scholarship. Even if the school and Angel weren't issues, fifteen years is... not ideal.

Everyone would look at us and automatically assume I'm taking advantage. But I'm here now, and the millions of problems we face seem to fade.

Despite it all, when I'm around him, when I think about him, I don't know. I run my hand over his palm, unable to stop myself. "Eli, I'm sorry I left like that the other day. Angel was about to leave for that trip and I had to get there before she could." He nods his head. "You took that as my not caring about you." He opens his mouth, his head already shaking to deny it. "No. Don't deny it, I know you were upset." He crosses his arms over his chest, but I can't tell if he's being stubborn or doing it to protect himself.

"I do care, Eli. About you. More than I should considering our positions. We could go around and around talking about why it's wrong, that I shouldn't, and believe me, I am and have. At the end of the day, I do care. Whatever this is with us"—I gesture to him and back to me—"it's not nothing, but I'm still a father. That means she will always come first."

I clench my fist, looking away, before whispering, "When I saw those bruises on you, still seeing them on you now, it makes me want to go insane. I want you to hear me when I say that I'm going to do my best to protect you too. You deserve better than what you've gotten."

He swallows, head bobbing in acknowledgement. "Shouldn't we stay away from each other?"

I laugh half-heartedly. "That would be the smart thing to do."

He's shaking his head before the last syllable. "I don't want to be smart. I want to do really dumb, terrible, hot things. To you. You to me. Anything."

"I can relate." My hands tighten their hold on him. I fucking want anything Eli's willing to give me, too.

14

I can't help but stare at Noah as he promises to protect me. The words squeeze around my heart like a vise that won't let go. In response, I tell him the truth. I am so tired of doing the smart thing, the right thing, toeing the line and never making waves. Where has it gotten me? Nowhere good, but maybe it could be better…

Noah's close to me, but not close enough. I want him hovering over me, whispering dirty things in my ear, just as desperate for me as I am for him. "I want to kiss you so much." It comes out as a whisper, as I look away from him.

He knocks my chin up with his hand, his brow quirked. "Is that all you want to do to me?"

My body heats, molten desire coursing through my blood. His words weren't even suggestive, but they have me so turned on I can hardly breathe. I need to learn how to control myself when it comes to this man. However, that day is not today.

He smiles wickedly, knowing exactly how he affects me. Wrapping his hand in my hair at the nape of my neck, he yanks me in for a deep, passionate kiss. My mind goes silent, enjoying each brush of his lips, the flash of his tongue teasing me, inviting me to let him in.

I groan and that's all the invitation he needs to delve deeper, tangling with my tongue. Each flick of his tongue is that of an expert, driving me higher, drugging me with his touch. He tugs my hair, readjusting the angle, and I let out another deep moan. His other hand runs from my neck to my shoulder, then caresses the slope of my back. In the next breath, his hand delves under the hem of my shirt, gliding a path along my abs. He walks me back, shoving me against a wall so that our bodies are touching head to foot. "God, Eli, you feel so good against me," he whispers as he breaks the kiss.

I let out an extremely undignified whine at the admission. His cock grinds against my thigh, hard and hot. Not quite where I want it. My hand lands on his ass, encouraging him to continue, hoping he will shift and give my dick some relief. Instead, he lifts me, pivoting just enough to throw me on top of the desk, widening my legs so he can step between them. I'm not a small guy, and the fact that he can throw me around like I weigh nothing has me hot and bothered. I reach for his pants. "You're so fucking sexy, but I need to see your cock. Now."

He chuckles, brushing kisses down my throat. For a minute I think about the hickeys he left last time, and how I should probably tell him not to do it again, but I can't find it within myself to stop it. I want his mark on me, to pretend that I'm his, if only for this moment. He grants my unspoken wish as he bites down, sucking at the juncture between my neck and collarbone. "*Mierda*."

"Hmmm. You like that? Good. Take this off, now," he demands, tugging at my shirt. I grab it from the back, pulling it over my head. He stops to stare at the bruises, fire in his eyes, before bending down and placing light kisses on every dark patch of purple skin. My hands trail through his hair, letting him, sensing his need to make it better.

I'm fucking impatient. "I want you naked."

He glances up at me, the sexy tilt of his lips indicating I will not be getting what I want. "I thought I was supposed to be the bossy one."

I have no words, so I tug on his hair, silently begging for something. Anything. After another pull, he crashes his mouth against mine, letting my hands explore.

Finally, finally, he lets me pull his shirt over his head. I'm mesmerized by the smooth muscles covered in a light smattering of brown hair starting at his chest, slowly fading away before picking up as a narrow happy trail.

God, I want to lick every inch of his body. I grab at the button on his jeans, flicking it open, waiting for him to stop me. Praying he doesn't. I unzip his jeans and they slide low, showing off the deep, chiseled V of his Adonis belt.

The urge to run my tongue along the line of his hip until I meet the seam of his pants is almost impossible to fight. My priority is getting my hand under his briefs to run the length of his cock, so I ignore the impulse. I stroke, stopping at the head, rubbing the pre-come around his slit.

"Eli, don't stop." With that encouragement, I tug a little harder. He reaches for my shorts, stripping me bare before rutting into my hand, each thrust fiercer than the last. "Get on the bed."

He steps away, and it takes me a moment to act because I'm so busy taking in his body—from the mussed hair to the burn on his face from where I've been kissing him. Though more subtle, I've left my own marks on him and something like satisfaction rips through me.

"Don't make me ask again, Eli."

Snapping out of the daze, I dash to the bed, reclining against the pillow with one arm behind my head.

"Stroke yourself." This time, I don't have to be told twice. I take myself in hand and glide along my length. He stands back, watching each movement I make, completely enthralled.

I call out, hoping to tempt him, tease him beyond reason, "This is what I was doing when you called me. I wanted it to be your hand so badly, Noah." I shut my eyes, lightly squeezing my balls, feeling too close to tipping over the edge for comfort.

"Eyes on me."

They flick open in time to see Noah remove his jeans and his underwear. His dick is hard and long, twitching under my gaze as he strides to the bed. It's so fucking big, a vein running along the bottom, a perfect path for my tongue. He stops just out of reach, taking himself in hand, moving in sync with my own. I speak again. "Do you know what else I was doing over the phone that I wish you'd done instead?" I sound breathy, desperate for his touch.

"What?" he bites out, sounding almost as gone as me.

Instead of telling him, I spread my legs wider, gliding my fingers over my cockhead, collecting some of the pre-come, before dragging my fingers over my balls, and down to the sensitive skin of my hole.

My hips buck at the sensation as I tease my hole. I push lightly, the muscles clenching deliciously as my finger teases it. I barely make it to the first knuckle of my middle finger before I have to abandon the plan or risk embarrassing myself.

It has the intended effect. Noah's pupils dilate, frozen to the spot, his hand stuttering its rhythm. Frustrating man that he is, he doesn't move closer. "Please," I cry out, needing something. I don't care what it is, I just know I need him to do something.

He quirks a brow.

"Noah, fucking please. I need you to touch me."

He must love seeing me beg because he climbs onto the bed, sliding up my body, trailing kisses from my chest to my mouth. Knocking my hand away, he takes both of us in his large palm. "Where's the lube?"

I hiss a breath as I feel his hard length rub against mine. *¡A la verga!* I need more. "Nightstand drawer."

Placing another kiss over my mouth, he reaches into the drawer, slicking his hand and cock. Then, our bodies are sliding together, the perfect amount of wet, heated friction. I dig my nails into his back, arching into his touch before grabbing his ass, getting leverage to move him faster. "Oh, God. Noah." He spreads my legs wider, holding one leg up and to the side, using the space to grind down, his hand creeping closer to my puckered skin. "Noah, I'm going to come if you keep doing that."

I don't know if my words are a plea or warning. I try to snake a hand down between us to stop it, to prolong the moment, but he grabs it and pins my arm to the bed. Moving the other hand from his ass, I try again, hoping to find some relief from the perfect torment. Like the first, he grabs it, pinning both hands in his large grasp. Once I can't move, he returns his hand to our cocks. "Come for me, Eli, I want to see every part of your pretty skin covered."

He leans down, sucking on the sensitive part behind my ear and that's all it takes. I explode, strands of come shooting through his grip, up my chest, and on his stomach. Before I have a chance to catch my breath, he sits back, his beautiful, hard cock bobbing angrily in front of him. I'm about to ask why he stopped, if he wants to use my mouth to finish, when I realize his heated gaze is taking me in. Tracking over my body, each spot where I came. He's watching me like I'm a fucking masterpiece.

The worry creeps in as I come down from the high. I wriggle under him, worried that he's freaking out, thinking he wasn't actually ready for this. It's one thing to have thoughts, something entirely different when the evidence is literally all over you. His hand lands on my stomach, just above my cock, which is still impossibly hard. "Fuck, Eli. You look so beautiful covered in my marks and your come." He drags his hand through the sticky liquid, spreading it over my skin before he brings his thumb to his mouth, sucking it off. "You taste even better than you look."

I, of course, flush at the compliment. It's so hot, but he can't mean that, can he?

He drags a finger down one cheek. "And there's that pretty blush I like so much."

I'm fucking ready to go again. This time, I want to give him pleasure. He should be in my mouth and on my tongue. I glance down at his erection, only a little apprehensive at the size. "Noah, I want to taste you. I need to taste you. Please." I'm begging, and I don't have one ounce of shame about it. He leans forward, giving me a hard kiss, and I taste myself on his tongue.

"You want my cock in your mouth?" The whisper sounds like gravel, one of the few signs of how turned-on Noah is. He's still too in control. I want to see him snap, taken over by lust, just like I am.

I nod my head in response.

"Then take what you want." He releases my hands and I flip him below me, knowing that we are this way only because he allowed it. I'm not weak by any means, but strength and power radiate from him. He's in charge and he knows it. Somehow, it makes the moment that much better. This beautiful, intelligent, experienced man wants me and whatever I have to offer. It's a heady sensation.

I run my hand over one pec, watching the way his muscles twitch at the contact. I drag my hand lower, following the path with my mouth. He lets out a soft moan, fisting the covers. I lick the spot where his leg meets his hip, getting ever closer to my goal. I enjoy every shift of his body, every thrust of his hips as he spirals higher. He grabs my hair, tugging up until we make eye contact, his voice one breathy rasp after another. "Stop. Teasing. Me. Put me between those fucking lips."

Not giving him a chance to change his mind, I swallow it eagerly. His cock hits the back of my throat, and I choke.

I back off, cough, and try again, albeit more reserved this time. A bead of pre-come leaks from the tip and I drag my tongue across the slit. Then, I slide my mouth down, experimentally, taking things slower. I hollow out my cheeks, sucking hard. He likes that. I do it again. And again.

His hips flex, but he's holding back, not wanting to hurt me. I swear in that moment that I'm going to make him lose his mind. Even if my throat is fucked raw. I bob up and down, faster, using my hand on the part I can't swallow.

"Fuck, Eli." His hand tightens in my hair again. "Holy fucking shit."

I take that as a good sign, keeping the pace. His cock grows impossibly harder so I take his balls in hand, tugging on them. He bows off the bed, forcing his cock past my gag reflex. This time, it feels fucking amazing and I hum, loving the power it gives me. I'm causing every twitch, every moan, every swear. I pop off him. "Noah, fuck my mouth."

He looks down at me, uncertainty bubbling up alongside the look of lust. I don't give him time to argue. Instead, I grab his hips, pulling him so far down my throat that a tear leaks out.

"Fucking hell, Eli." He thrusts, tentative at first, but each thrust reaches the back of my throat.

I scratch my nails down his legs and he stops holding back, fucking into my mouth hard and fast. My cheeks burn, tears streaming down my face as he does what I've been imagining for months. I'm out of my mind with desire and I thrust into the sheets, searching for relief.

"Eli, fuck. I'm going to…" He tries to pull me off his shaft, but I dig my hands into his ass, sucking him down hard. Like hell he's going to take his come from me. The hot, salty liquid shoots down my throat and I swallow it as best I can, some of it leaking from between my lips and dribbling down my chin. He gives a few shallow thrusts as his dick pulses. Then, he pulls me off and watches me, his eyes full of some emotion I can't name, the expression soft but sexy.

He tugs me in for a kiss, but I push back, the remnants of his orgasm still running down my chin. I can't imagine he wants to taste that.

He must see the indecision in my expression. "I don't care about a little come. Kiss me."

This time our lips connect, his tongue delving into my mouth for a long, languid kiss. He pulls back, wiping my face and sliding his thumb into my mouth, feeding me what I missed. I suck it, wanting every drop of him, and I shiver at how dirty it feels. How is anything else ever going to feel the same? He fucking changed my world with a few orgasms, but it's not like we can be together.

With that thought, reality comes crashing in. Right now, I'm lying in his arms, draped over his body, sweaty, while he peppers kisses on me, acting like this could be a forever thing. My body is not getting the message that this will have to end and that scares me. This is sex. Great fucking sex, but we can't do the other shit. We can't cuddle, or give sweet kisses.

I pull away to distance myself from the entire ordeal, already refusing to believe that I'm more invested in this than I thought I would be. The deal was sex, get it out of our system, and move on with our lives. Not cuddle, kiss, and act like an actual couple.

Noah sits up when I pull away, his brows furrowed. "Everything okay?"

What can I say to him? I can't tell him I'm feeling all of that. He agreed to sex, no strings attached. Totally apart from the potential of catching feelings. I set the fucking rules, for Christ's sake. I clear my throat, searching for something to say. "Yeah. I just… don't cuddle. Especially not with, uh, a fuck buddy." God, I sound like a total prick. It seems to do the trick, though.

He hops off the bed, my saliva still wetting his dick. "Uh, right. Best not to. Well, thanks for…" He trails off, gesturing between the two of us before bending over and grabbing his clothes. He covers every glorious inch of his body and my mind screams "fucking idiot."

I stand in the middle of the room, feeling lost, wishing he would have called me on the bullshit. Told me to lie with him and fuck the rest of it. He glances over his shoulder, not fully turning, as if I'm already an afterthought. "See you around, Eli."

"Maybe. Thanks for the fuck," I blurt out.

Hurt flashes, causing lines to crease on his face before he smooths out his expression into a completely blank slate. Self-sabotage at its finest, folks. No matter what the arrangement was, it wasn't something cheap, but that comment was.

The door opens and closes without a word from Noah. I flop back onto the bed, knowing that I won't hear from him anytime soon, and wondering why that seems to fucking gut me.

15

Eli

I startle awake because of a loud pounding at my door. Fuck me, I was not ready to get up. I spent an hour wallowing in self-pity last night before crashing hard, all the endorphins from the sex long worn off. I didn't even pull the sheet over me, so now I'm lying on my bed, buck-ass naked, covered in dry come, cold as hell. "One second," I yell.

"*Soy yo, mijo*," my father calls through the door. Fuck, fuck, fuck. I scramble off the bed and grab a hoodie off the back of my chair and a pair of shorts out of my dresser. I look in the mirror, trying to smooth my hair down as I splash some water onto a towel and try to clean my chest. The bruise on my face is still dark enough to be noticeable, but I don't have the time to hide it.

What the hell is he doing here? I told them I would be home on Sunday. I should still have two more days.

"*Mijo*." My dad raises his voice, annoyance evident.

This is as clean as I'm going to get. I hope I don't smell like sex. Dear God, please don't smell like sex. I pull the door open and my father, mom, and all my siblings stand outside my door. *Como chingas*. They've never all come to campus. I swing the door open asking, "What are you all doing here?"

My mom leans closer to me, turning my face to the side. "What happened to your face?" She signs the cross before inspecting it more closely.

"Yeah, and that." My sister points at the hickey just popping out from the neckline of my hoodie. Damn it, I should have told him not to do that again. At least they aren't all over my neck this time. "What happened there?" My other sisters snicker behind her.

I glare at them. Are they trying to get me killed? "I don't know what you're talking about, let me go look." My mom releases me, and I head back over to the mirror as if I didn't just look at myself. "Oh, it must be some rash. I changed my detergent, maybe I'm having an adverse reaction to the sheets."

My sisters roll their eyes. Adriana places both hands on her hips, looking at me. Dani looks at my parents hoping they will call me out on my bullshit. Valeria adds, "Oh, yeah. That doesn't look great. Maybe put some lotion on it and take some Benadryl, I heard it helps." Pretending to be helpful probably because she assumes the hickeys are from Angel.

"Ah, thanks, Valeria. I will. What are you all doing here?"

Thankfully, the distraction works. "You've been so busy lately we thought we'd do a family lunch at your cafeteria. We know you said you couldn't leave campus because you've been studying so much, so we thought we'd bring the family to you. Even if the food is not as good as my cooking." My mom smiles like this is the best idea ever.

My whole family in my cafeteria, where the school is gossiping about me, and the potential for another juicy story? I smile, pretending like that's the best idea ever. "No one's cooking is as good as yours, Mama. Can I meet you all downstairs? I just woke up and I need to use the restroom."

Mama looks like she's going to argue, probably wanting to search my room under the guise of looking around, but my father grabs her hand. "We'll be downstairs." Thank you. One thing is going my way.

I brush my teeth and run through the quickest shower I've ever had. Then I find a shirt that hides most of the marks decorating my upper chest. I pick up the makeup Vi lent me, but worry my sisters will tease me endlessly. I set it down and grab my wallet, keys, and phone.

Feeling marginally better, I make my way downstairs where my brothers are running around acting like little terrors. My family keeps up a steady conversation as I lead them to the cafeteria, my sisters commenting on how cool the school seems, my brothers talking about how boring it is, and my parents asking me a million questions about the campus as if they don't visit it almost every other day to spy on me. Asking how much I'm enjoying my major, which classes are my favorite, and what I've studied lately. As if they don't know all the answers.

My brothers are the first to bound into the cafeteria, and I swipe my card with the lunch attendant. The guy asks, "All nine of you dining today?" I nod my head yes as he gives my brothers a dark look, but doesn't say anything else.

We all shuffle to a table, trying to herd the boys into seats. I thought telling my brothers to come with them the next time my parents visited would be enough to deter them. They don't love being out in public where the boys are more rowdy. I suppose I should be thankful they didn't stop at the dorm last night. Yet another reason as to why it was necessary to fuck things up and almost guarantee Noah won't talk to me again. If I keep telling myself that, maybe I'll believe it.

Mama and Dani stay at the table with the boys while I lead my father and Valeria to the drink station. Adriana and I jump into the food line and I see a familiar face.

"Eli," Vi calls out, excitedly.

"Hey, Vi. What are you doing here?"

She blushes, then glances at my sister. "I was visiting a friend on campus."

The blush makes me wonder what exactly she got up to with this friend. I thought she was going after Cade, but maybe that already fizzled out. Vi's eyes flick to my sister again, who I almost forgot was there. I eye Adriana as a Cheshire cat grin crosses her face. "Vi, this is my sister, Adriana."

An 'oh shit' look crosses Vi's face and I can't help the small chuckle that falls past my lips. Yeah, Vi, I feel the same. Today is an 'oh shit' kind of day. "I was visiting my friend to study."

"What kind of friend?" my sister questions.

"A study buddy."

Adriana pops a hip. "A boy study buddy?"

I turn to reprimand her. "That's not any of your business."

Vi says, "Nope. A girl study buddy."

"Hmm, not as fun."

I shoot daggers at my sister as Vi laughs, and it makes me wonder if I was right. Was it a hookup? Is Vi pretending it's a girl, or was she with a girl?

Unfortunately, I'm not given the chance to think about it further because Adriana opens her mouth again, so I smack a hand over it. She bats it away after licking it as I wince and rub her saliva on my shorts. I'm shocked at her next words. "Join us for lunch, Vi. Unless you've already eaten?" I look at my sister, wondering what angle she's working.

Vi looks at me and I widen my eyes, shaking my head no behind my sister's back. She responds, "Oh, I don't want to intrude."

My father walks up, catching the last of our conversation. "Is this one of your friends, *mijo*?"

"*Si, Papa*. She was just leaving."

"Nonsense, have her join us. Is she friends with Angel?" Vi flinches and Adriana notices as well, looking between the two of us.

"Uh, *si, Papa*. Best friends. She hasn't seen much of Ang either. She's been so busy with the internship."

"I don't want to intrude, Mr. Ruiz," Vi adds.

He doesn't take no for an answer. We're all seated at the table, my brothers shooting furtive glances at Violet, Valeria and Mama glaring at her, Dani in her own world. My mother leads us through a prayer blessing the food and all those on campus today then locks her attention back on Violet.

I sit back, doing my best to hold in my groan.

"So, Violet, Emanuel Senior says you are friends with Angel. Do you think it's appropriate to be friends with my Elias?"

"Mama," I cry out, but she silences me with a look.

Vi looks startled, but doesn't glance my way. "Mrs. Ruiz, I don't think I understand what you mean."

My mother's eyes narrow before leaning forward, assessing Violet. My dad's eyes pinch, his face drawn, as if he's telling her to stop, but she goes on. "When I was younger, it was disrespectful to be so close with boys who

146

had girlfriends. People asked many questions because they knew the girls had no shame."

"*¡Mama, es suficiente! ¿Por qué estás siendo grosera?*" I can't believe how rude she's being. Vi doesn't deserve this.

"*¡Ciera tu boca!* I didn't raise you to speak to your mother like that," my dad reprimands, though he lets out a long-suffering sigh. He tries to hide it, but it's there. I don't have time to question the reaction because he repeats himself, making sure I don't argue again.

I stare at him, dumbfounded. Does he seriously think that Mom is being any more respectful? "Violet is my friend. You can't speak to her like that. Besides, Angel and I broke up."

That seems to get everyone's attention. The only set of eyes that are remotely sympathetic are Violet's. I bury my face in my hands, not ready to deal with this conversation. They have always been too invested in my relationship with her, always wanting her over, never asking too many questions. It's almost like they wanted me to break their rules, to a certain extent, where she was concerned.

Mama turns her gaze back to Violet. "I need to talk to my son in private. Leave."

Violet looks at me one last time, uncertain. I can tell she doesn't want to leave me here alone. I shake my head, telling her she should leave while she can.

When she's gone, Dani squeals, "I'm so proud of you. She was the worst."

Adriana, more quietly, says, "I knew it."

Valeria looks like she's about to cry and Mama looks livid. She switches back to Spanish so that others around us won't eavesdrop. "When did you break up?"

It'll only make it worse to tell her the truth, so I lie through my teeth and hope she can't tell. "Only a few days ago. I'm sorry I didn't tell you sooner, it's just been hard."

"Why did you break up?"

Well, I can't very well tell her the truth about what happened either. This feels like a minefield and one misstep will cause a bomb to detonate. "She broke up with me because she didn't feel like she had enough time anymore. You know she's getting ready to go to law school."

My father responds this time. "All the more reason to fight for her. She's probably waiting for you to show how much you want to be with her."

Mama nods at his words. "That's what I would want, Elias."

"That's not how it is. She doesn't want to talk to me."

My mother's lips tighten before she leans forward, pinning me with her stare. "Well, that's probably because you're spending time with her best friend. Can you imagine how that must look to her? You're being thoughtless, Elias. I'm going to call her and set up dinner this weekend."

"Mama, no. Please don't. She won't want to come."

"It's settled."

I want to ask why they care so much. Why are they fighting for me to stay with her? It can't be because they want me to be happy. If that were the case, they would listen to what I'm saying. Shouldn't they be on my side? For all they know, I could be heartbroken at the fact she left me. "Do I have a say in this? She upset me and I don't know if I want to be around her right now."

"Upset?" my father scoffs. "Be a man and win her back. She's good for you."

My mother grabs my face, pinching each side while giving me a look that says she knows best. "Don't be silly, son. This will make you happy. She can't say no to my charming boy. Stay away from anyone else standing in your way and things will turn out fine."

I sink further into my seat, pushing my food away as they continue to plan, ignoring me and my siblings. Adriana tries to get my attention, but I'm tuned out. There's nothing anyone could say at this point to make this better.

16

I need to call Vi and apologize for my family. She must think the worst of me. I don't even know what to think of my parents right now. I pull up my most recent contacts, clicking on her number, then flop facedown on the mattress, groaning. It still smells like Noah's soap. Fuck me. Why couldn't I have spent the morning lying in bed, remembering everything that happened last night, instead of thinking about a planned dinner with my ex-girlfriend?

"Eli, I'm surprised to hear from you." My sister Carmen's voice comes through the line. I smash my face into the bed further. Of course. Fuck today and its Murphy's Law ass.

I pull back my phone to glare at it, as if it's somehow the phone's fault.

"Eli? Did you butt dial me?"

Chinga. "No. Wrong number. I have to go."

"Please don't." I can hear the desperation in her voice. It almost sounds like she cares, like she wants to talk to me, and it makes me pause. My family has already royally fucked up my day and mood, what's one more family drama to add to the mix?

"Fine. What's up?"

She clears her throat. "Well, I'm at my friend's house for a pool party. Summer break started for my district. I'm a teacher. I don't know if you remember…" she states, her words coming out in a jumbled mess.

"I remember. Mama and Papa wanted you to get a doctorate so you could become a professor of mathematics."

"I teach art at a high school now."

What am I supposed to say? "Um, cool?"

"Yeah, I love it. It makes me happy. But that's not why you called."

"I didn't mean to call. I don't make it a habit of calling people who abandon their younger siblings."

Silence presses in from the line. I can't tell if she's regretting taking this call. If I was her, I would be. She lets out a long sigh. "I'm going to ignore all of that for now. I don't believe in coincidences, *hermano*. Is something bothering you?"

I will not tell her about the shitshow that was breakfast this morning. Not one word of it will cross my lips. I swear. I sit up, ready to get off the phone. What comes out is,

"You wouldn't understand." Crap, that wasn't what I meant to say.

"Maybe. We won't know unless you tell me."

God, I need someone to talk to. Maybe Carmen would understand. She grew up in our family. She may have run away, cut us out, but she'd understand how pushy they can be.

I tell her about this morning, how the whole family ambushed me about Angel and how I caught her cheating. The lie I told our parents to get them off my back and how it spiraled to the dinner arrangement from hell. She sat on the other side, letting me get everything off my chest, only chiming in with a few non-committal noises.

I almost blurted out what I'd done with Noah, but I didn't know how she'd react to that. After all, she knows what it's like at home. There were so many reasons we didn't do something like that or talk about things like that. And even if, somewhere in my mind, I thought it was okay, there was still a part of me that wanted to hesitate. I decide to tell a partial truth instead.

"The worst part is they wouldn't listen to a word I said. I don't understand why they care so much." My chest heaves like I've run miles instead of word vomiting through the phone. I didn't realize until I finished speaking, but my whole body's trembling, so consumed by everything swirling inside of me.

"Our parents are extremely pushy, aren't they?"

Her response takes me by surprise. Out of everything that she could have said, that's not what I would pick.

"Yes. Most of the time I feel like it's for a good reason. I told them I didn't want to see her. I know they don't know the real reason, but isn't my reason good enough? I don't understand why they won't listen to me. Why are they so invested in us together?"

"I can venture a guess."

"That they liked Angel?"

Carmen laughs, and the noise eases the tension between my shoulders. "No, not because they like her."

"Then why?"

"Two potential reasons. One, it's easier to control you when they can take away the things you like."

No, I wouldn't believe that. They cared about me and loved me. This obsession over my being with Angel wasn't about their control. Maybe they were acting like this because they wanted what was best for me. After all, they didn't know how much Angel hurt me. Maybe if I told them the truth… But that would bring up other questions I didn't want to answer. Hell.

"Or two, they don't want you to think like me. They refuse to believe they have two children in the family that think the way I think, and they are pushing you so far down a certain path to ensure it doesn't happen."

I pull the phone away from my ear, frowning at it like Carmen can see me. Seriously vague and unhelpful. "What are you talking about?"

"The reason why I wasn't allowed to talk to you or the siblings after college. Why our parents blocked my number from our landline and cut me out completely five years ago."

"You're not making any sense, Carmen. What does my problem have to do with why you stopped talking to us? You sound paranoid. Our parents aren't manipulative like that."

"Don't you hear yourself? They aren't manipulative like that, which means even you recognize they are sometimes. I told you before that I wasn't sure you were ready to hear my side of things. Do you want to know?"

First my parents treat me like I'm a toddler, and now it feels like Carmen's doing the same. I run a palm down my face. Do I want to hear this? I didn't think I'd ever want to talk to her again, but here I am, spilling all of my drama in her lap. She may talk like Mom and Dad, treat me like a child, but she's offering the chance to hear more of the story. She's offering me the chance to be more than that naïve kid. I think it's time I hear her out and stop pulling the anger I have on behalf of my siblings around me like a blanket. "Fine. Tell me."

"Oh. Okay." She sounds floored. "Um, I don't know where to start. I, uh, didn't think you'd let me explain." She lets out an awkward chuckle.

"From the beginning. That's usually a good place."

"Okay, *cabrón*. So helpful."

"I can hang up if that's easier?" This time, I can't help the teasing that laces through my voice. I don't want to tease her, or form any sort of connection, but I can feel myself softening toward her. I can't let that happen, I'm only giving her the chance to explain, not a place in my life.

"Like I said. Smartass. Okay, okay. It was my senior year of college. It was about two weeks from graduation. I don't know if you remember, but I was going to move into an apartment with my roommate, Jess. I was preparing to sign up for my grad school classes and I had a job lined up as a sub for math at our elementary school. It was the compromise we agreed upon. I choose an apartment close to home, come home for family dinner every few nights, and I don't have to move home."

I don't remember any of this. I was around fifteen. Why don't I remember any of this? "You were going to stay close to home?" My voice comes out sounding uncertain, and I hate the vulnerability it shows.

"Yes. As long as I got to live with Jess and spend time with all of you, our sisters and brothers, I thought I would be happy enough."

"Okay."

"Then, one night Mom and Dad stopped by, much like they did to you this morning. I'd never warned Jess about our parents. I should have, but I always got them out of the dorm as fast as possible so that they wouldn't interact." That sounds familiar. A pit of unease swirls low in my stomach.

"Well, it was a Friday night, and Jess was going out with a few people. She wanted me to come, but I knew I needed to study for finals. Math was… not great for me.

Everyone was over to pregame when our parents knocked. I still don't know why to this day, but they insisted on coming in. Maybe they heard everyone talking. Anyway, Jess came out of her room, happy to meet them."

"Okay. That's annoying, but none of that sounds bad so far." Even if I do the same thing.

"Then her girlfriend came out and Jess introduced her to Mom and Dad."

A cold sweat breaks out on my skin, the pit forming into something stone-like, weighing me down. "I don't think I want to hear the rest of this."

"Mom and Dad physically dragged me from the room, yelling loud enough to draw everyone's attention on the floor. They asked if I knew what depraved behavior my roommate was a part of. They tried to make me swear that I would have nothing to do with her because she was going to Hell. Well, Mom did. Dad stood there and let it all happen. Then they demanded I move out of the dorm and come home immediately."

"Carmen, stop." I raise my voice. I can't help it. This is not something I want to hear.

"Okay. Sorry. Eli, they cut me out. They wanted nothing to do with me after that night. They blocked my number and wouldn't let me talk to any of you. You might not believe me, but for the first year, I tried to call every night, but all I got was an error message."

A numb sensation overtakes my limbs, and it sounds like I'm hearing Carmen from underwater. "You weren't there for them."

"I know."

"You chose your friend over us."

"I didn't see it that way. I can understand why you feel like that, though. I'm sorry."

"Are you gay?" I hear myself ask without processing the words.

"No. It didn't matter to them. I told our parents I would always stand by her. That their views were small minded and love is love. They didn't like that answer."

"And that was enough for them to abandon you? You weren't even gay, you just loved people who were?"

"Yes."

Vibrations wrack my body as I struggle to breathe. A crushing weight presses down on my chest and I don't know what to do. All I know is that I believe her. A small part of me always knew about them. I was so afraid of what the answer might be… afraid of what I might be. There is also a smaller part of me that hopes it could be different for me. I am their kid. They will always love me, right?

Well, this is my answer. My sister was only a friend of someone gay, and they abandoned her for it. It makes me numb. I can't feel my body, can't regulate my breathing. "I… I believe y-you." My words come out garbled, the tremors getting worse.

"Eli, are you okay?"

"M'okay."

"I shouldn't have told you. I'm sorry. I thought—Well, I read this wrong. Do you agree with them? I'm sorry if you're mad."

A pitiful laugh escapes, but it sounds more like a wheeze. "N-not mad. You're r-right."

I can't make syllables form, and that seems to make whatever this is so much worse. My heart hurts, a shooting pain going along my arm. A light sheen of sweat beads on my skin. What's happening to me? My mind clicks along at a glacial pace, unable to hold on to any thought for long. I can't get enough oxygen. Am I going to pass out?

"Eli, you're scaring me. Please answer me."

I try to tell Carmen I'm going to pass out but the words won't come. Dizziness sweeps over me, my breathing getting heavier, more labored. "Ne-ed t-to go." Each word comes out as a stutter as I drop the phone, trying to hang it up. I scramble around looking for it, but my head swims and my fingers won't move properly. I'm going to pass out, I'm sure of it.

17

I don't pass out, but I lose track of time, caught up in the sensations rioting through my body. Though I kind of wish I would pass out. I can't get my body under control. I can't inhale for longer than half a breath before I'm wheezing, I watch my hands shake, looking more like wiggly blobs than anything else.

Hands grab at me, pulling my face up so that I'm looking at them. "Eli," they call out. "Breathe. I need you to breathe. You're having a panic attack." How would they know what's happening to me? That can't be right, I feel like I'm dying.

"We're going to breathe, follow my lead. In." The person takes a large inhale. They hold, grounding me, giving me something to focus on so I can do the same. I lock all of my attention on that one breath.

"Exhale." They show me what to do. I do it.

They repeat the words until I comply. Each breath brings oxygen into my lungs and I feel every part of my body sigh in relief. My muscles twitch and my fingers clench, tingling as my blood flow resumes. "Okay, Eli. Now I need you to count to fifty for me."

I don't question the voice, though it seems like a silly instruction. I've known how to count for years. "One..."

"Good."

"Two..."

As I continue to count, my mind processes the outside world again. Vi stands in front of me, her eyes glassy, her face pinched.

I've reached thirty-five when another knock sounds at my door. Vi assesses me before walking to the door. She pops it open about an inch. I see her sigh in relief before fully opening the door.

"Thirty-nine." My voice sounds steadier.

Carmen enters the room, evaluating me just like Vi. She has her arms down at her sides, but her hands are clenched and she worries her lip. I can't hear anything they say because of the rushing in my ears, but it gradually decreases as I calm down.

"Forty." I can't place the feeling that runs through me at seeing her here, but it's warm.

She takes a hesitant step toward me as Violet trots back to my side. Vi finishes the last ten numbers with me.

"How are you feeling?" she asks.

I roll my shoulders, doing my best to rid the tension from my body. "Better. Thanks, Vi." She pulls me into her side, refusing to let go.

I look at Carmen as if she has an answer. Her hand twitches before falling back down. Does she want to reach out to me? Do I want her to?

Instead of answering Vi's question, I ask one of my own. "How'd you know to come here? And how did you get in?"

"Your sister called me. She was worried about you. Was it because of lunch?" She looks up at me, her eyes full of guilt. "What your parents said, I know you don't believe it… but still."

I shake my head, thankful for the reminder. So much has happened since then that I almost forgot. "No, not that. I was planning on calling you to make sure you were okay. I'm sorry about my family. They shouldn't have said any of that to you."

"I'm not worried about me, dummy. Are you okay?"

"Um, excuse me. I'm the invalid. Shouldn't you be nicer to me?" That gets the reaction I want. She pushes me, an amused smile tilting her lips, the concern wiped from her face.

Her attention turns to my sister. "If he's already back to being a smartass, he'll be just fine."

That gets a chuckle out of Carmen. Then I realize, Vi called her my sister. "Am I going to get in trouble for not telling you Carmen is my sister?"

"Obviously." She smiles cheekily.

"Shit. I expected as much."

"I'll leave you two alone. It looks like you might have a few more things to talk about." I almost call her back, tell her not to leave me alone, but that's only pushing back the inevitable.

"Yeah, alright. I'll see you later, Vi. Thanks for helping."

She squeezes my hand. "Of course."

The door closes quietly behind her, and I turn to face my sister. She still looks unsure and is hesitant to start. I start for her. "I'd rather not talk about it."

"Eli, come on."

I cross my arms. "There's nothing to say. I'm fine."

"I'm sorry I called your friend. I didn't know how fast I'd be able to get here and I didn't want you to be alone."

She thinks I'm mad that she told Violet? I guess five years of distance makes it hard to read someone. "I'm not mad. I just don't want to talk about it. Really, I'm fine."

She puts a hand on her hip. "*¡Eres tan terco!*" I'm being stubborn? How about her! "You're clearly not fine."

I stay silent, but uncross my arms, hoping to look amicable. If she thinks I have nothing to hide, maybe she will be more likely to let it be.

"Is it Mom and Dad? Are you worried they'll cut you off now that you know the truth?"

"No."

"Okay, then what happened? I can't help if I don't understand what's going on."

"Maybe I don't want your help."

She tilts her head back and forth. "I know that's true, but whatever it was, you want to talk about it."

Crap. I can't tell her the truth. I can't lose my family. Saying the words out loud, putting them into the universe, it's too real. Whatever happened between me and Noah… it's over now and it was a mistake. I can't, I won't, I don't like men. It was an experiment, and it never needs to happen again. My family is more important. They will always be there. If they don't know, then I can't lose them.

"Okay, you're right. That's what I was worried about, why I was freaking out over the phone. I don't want them to be mad at me if they know I talked to you. I'm already on thin ice from lying to them."

Carmen watches me as I sit as still as possible. The intensity of the stare is uncomfortable. It's as if she wants me to crack, to catch me in a lie. "Well, I'm clearly not going to talk to them. They don't have to know."

"I think it would be best if we don't talk. At least for a while."

Her eyes turn glassy. It hurts me to see, but even if it was our parents who made her leave, she still left. Something that big doesn't just go away after one phone call. She wants me to trust her? With something this big? I don't think so. There is enough to deal with in my own life. I can't—*can't*—worry about more right now.

"You don't mean that. Whatever's going on, I want to be here for you. I know I haven't been the big sister you need, but please don't do this. I'll be better."

"Nothing's going on. I want you to leave."

"No."

"Yes."

"Stop giving me a bullshit excuse, Eli. I get it, you're mad at me. I left when you needed me and I'm sorry." She raises her voice. "I'm here now. I'm trying."

"Leave."

"You're queer." It isn't a question. I reel back like someone has slapped me. It can't be obvious, can it? Is that what my sister meant about my parents pushing Angel so hard? They can't possibly have known. I didn't know. Not fully. Not until, well… Noah.

"You're trying to fight it for them."

That loosens my lips. "I'm not gay."

"Okay."

"I'm not… queer." I won't let myself be. Not if it means losing my family.

She nods her head. "Okay. I was wrong. I shouldn't have assumed, I'm sorry."

"You need to leave. I don't want you here."

Finally, finally she gives up, and walks out the door.

18

Noah

Angel's been avoiding me because I forced her to stay home from the trip with Tom. Normally I would seek her out, ask her to spend time with me, but I've been avoiding her ever since Eli kicked me out of his dorm the other night. I just can't tell if I'm avoiding her because I feel guilty about what I did or the fact that I want to continue what we started, even though he wants nothing to do with me. It's not a great place to be in. I haven't heard a single word from him, and I feel it acutely. Whatever this is, I think it's already over and it fills me with longing and regret.

I've tried to escape in my writing, to block all thoughts of that night, but I haven't even had that luxury. Everything I write seems so trivial, so boring, that I couldn't possibly use it. I'm thankful I spent the last two weeks ahead of the deadline, otherwise I'd have my publisher breathing down my neck again.

Tossing my blue-screen glasses onto the desk, I make my way out of the office. Maybe a snack will help get my mind right. I look around the house, wondering if Angel's even home as I go in search of something to eat. If there aren't any slamming doors in an effort to show how mad she is, then she must be out with a friend or something. I get why she's angry. I was a controlling ass, especially during the conversation, but I will not let her get into a dangerous situation. The guy has assaulted Eli twice. Like hell am I going to let that happen to Angel. I just can't tell if she genuinely likes this guy or if she's doing it to get under my skin. And if it is to get a reaction from me, what does she hope to gain from it? Should I say something or let her figure it out for herself?

I open the fridge and rifle around, looking for something quick and easy. Ah, hummus. Perfect. I grab the dip, a glass of water, and a bag of pretzel chips from the pantry then slide into a chair at the island. The only sound is my crunching, and it's not quite peaceful.

"Daaaaaadddd," Angel yells from across the house. There it is. That's more like it.

"I'm in the kitchen, Angel."

Footsteps stomp down the stairs and through the hall before I catch sight of my daughter, tears streaming down her face. I'm around the counter in an instant, pulling her in for a hug. "What's wrong, sweetheart?" I stroke my hand down her hair, and she allows it. I swear under my breath. This has to be bad.

She lets out a loud sob. "My friend Dana went on that trip with Tom and a few others. They all went to a club last night. They were dancing and having fun." A hiccup interrupts her story.

"Oh-kay," I say evenly, not knowing how to react yet.

"Well, Dana saw Tom making out with some bitch out on the dancefloor. H-h-he cheated on me." She buries her face in my chest and my heart aches for her. God, I want to punch that little shit. I don't want her anywhere near him, but obviously she didn't stop dating him, and I don't want her to hurt. Thank fuck she didn't go on that trip.

"I'm so sorry, honey. That was super shitty of him."

"I know. Dana got a picture and I'm so much prettier than she is. I don't understand." She pulls her head back, looking up at me as her lower lip quivers. "Why wouldn't he want to be with me?"

I sigh, wiping the tears off her cheeks. "It had nothing to do with you, sweetheart. I promise. You are smart, beautiful, fun. Anyone would want to be with you. I know it hurts, but don't give up on all of them. You just haven't found the right one yet. Not everyone can be as cool as your dad." I crack a joke, hoping it will give her the distraction she needs. What I really want to say is, good fucking riddance. But I don't want to lose this moment, and I know if I go too far she's going to think I'm commenting on her instead of him. Despite how tough she acts, she is fairly sensitive about some things. Almost reflective.

"Ew. Gross, Dad, you're not cool." She rolls her eyes, pushing me with her shoulder, and I finally feel like I've done something right. Something soft and happy crosses her face for a moment, maybe enjoying this easy conversation as much as I am. Too soon, she's interrupted by her ringtone blaring. She pulls away, wiping at her eyes, before looking at the screen. Her face scrunches and a small frown forms.

"Everything okay?"

She pulls the phone to her chest, her eyes widening as they look up at me. "Yeah. Everything's great. I need to take this call real quick. I'll be back."

Unfortunately, I doubt she will, but it was nice while it lasted. I sit back down, staring at my hummus, doing my best not to think about it too much. Not Angel. Or Eli. I dig a pretzel into the hummus, causing it to break into a hundred tiny pieces. Fuck. Why does this feel so lonely?

"Dadddddd," Angel calls again, though she's much closer this time.

My mouth drops open. She's seeking me out two times in one day, on purpose? I don't know if I should take that as a good sign or bad. "Angel, you don't need to yell. I'm right here."

She giggles. "Right. Yeah, no, of course. Um, would it be okay if a few people joined us for dinner tonight?"

Crossing my arms, I take a moment to assess my daughter. Something seems off about the request. "Sure.

Which people? Do I know them? And… you want me to join?"

She shrugs noncommittally. "A friend. Some of them. And yes."

My brows pinch. "Which friends?"

"Not Tom, I promise. Make enough for five." She smacks a kiss on my cheek and runs off before I can question her further. So weird. I won't look a gift horse in the mouth by calling her back. She wants to spend more time with me, so I'll take it.

***

The kitchen smells amazing from the garlic, oregano, and basil wafting through the air. When I went to the store earlier, I was a little overeager. I bought all the fixings to make homemade lasagna. Even the noodles are from scratch. I also stopped at a local bakery and got fresh bread, which is heating in the oven with a garlic butter sauce. To start the meal, I made a salad with balsamic vinegar and olive oil dressing.

Angel hasn't come downstairs since this morning, but I hear her as she runs from her room to the bathroom upstairs, no doubt getting ready for her friends.

I take that as my cue to shower and get changed so that I don't have tomato goop and flour all over me when they get here. I'd rather not smell like sweat and pasta, not that Angel would care. She's probably going to kick me out right after we're done eating, anyway. I shower quickly before toweling off my hair and slipping into a pair of jeans and a t-shirt.

My phone vibrates on the nightstand where I left it, but I hear the doorbell ring so I ignore it. I step out of the hall, where I catch sight of my daughter, wearing the world's tightest dress. She doesn't see me as she touches up her makeup in the hallway mirror. She slips a light sweater over the dress, giving the illusion that it's more modest. I don't have enough time to comment because she's opening the door and I freeze.

This has to be a fucking nightmare. That's the only thing that could explain why Eli and his parents are standing on the other side of my door. Jesus fucking Christ. Eli's hazel eyes seek mine out, registering the shocked look on my face.

There are dark circles under his eyes, his skin paler than it should be, nothing like the healthy, bronzed tone from before. Even his eyes lack the luster I saw only days ago. I want to look deeper, ask him what's wrong and why he's here. I know I can't and I shouldn't keep staring at him like I want to. I stand there, frozen for a few minutes.

It's too painful, so I break first, looking away.

"Angel, *mija*. I've missed you so much. It's good to see you," Eli's mother, Sophie, says.

Angel gives a sweet smile. "I've missed you too, Mrs. Ruiz. How have you been?"

"Oh, I'm much better now. Thank you for asking."

Sophie looks up, catching me in the hall, so I plaster on the most pleasant smile I can fake, and prepare for a truly fucked up evening. Her face sours the longer she looks at me. "Noah."

"Sophie. Emanuel. It's been a while. I hope you're doing well." I look at Eli again, something in my chest squeezing tightly. "Eli. It's been a bit." He doesn't look at me, but I notice his shoulders tense.

Sophie sticks her nose up like she's too good to converse with me, but deigns to let me hear her speak. "As long as you can help us convince your daughter to give Eli another chance to win her over." I'm sorry. What?

Angel laughs. "Oh stop, Mrs. Ruiz. You're going to make me blush." She smirks at Eli, who's practically hiding behind his parents, doing his best to ignore his mother and Angel's chatter.

It's not lost on me that I'm ten feet from where Eli threw up all over me all those months ago, and I feel like I'm about to do the same. They're here to get Angel and Eli back together? Why the fuck would they want that? More importantly, why do they think I would help? "Uh, eh-hmmn, excuse me. I need to check on the food. Angel, take our guests to the dining room. Dinner is almost ready." Running seems like the best option.

She leads them away, happily doing my bidding, trying her best to rope Eli into a conversation. Instead, he watches his shoes, shuffling behind his parents. Nothing like the confident man I've come to know. It makes me want to take him away from here, hide him until that uncertainty, that defeat, is wiped away. It stirs something within me that's been missing for days now. I still want him. I want all of him, which means I need to talk to him alone.

Later tonight, I promise myself. First, I grab the lasagna from the oven along with the garlic bread. I pull the salad from the fridge and I call for Angel to help carry the dishes out. Usually she refuses to help, so it's almost like I'm asking for Eli because he used to pick up her slack.

To my disappointment, and I should really get that in check, my daughter pops into the kitchen. "What were you thinking inviting them over? And what are they talking about? You and Eli? I thought that was over."

She fidgets before letting out a small squeal. "Dad, I'm excited about this. You were right. Tom sucks, but Eli always treated me right. I should give him another chance. He's kind of a buzzkill, but he could be good for me. I thought you'd be happy about him being here." She glances over her shoulder before lowering her voice more. "I didn't say anything because I know you and Eli's parents don't get along. But they want what we want, for Eli and me to get back together. I thought if we all reminded him it was a good idea he couldn't say no. It worked out perfectly. You want what's best for me, don't you? What kind of dad would you be if you didn't support me?"

God. I am the worst, most despicable father. Person. Something deep and animalistic is telling me to snap, bite, claw at anything that stands between me and Eli. I check myself. He's not mine, and I shouldn't want that. For fuck's sake, my daughter wants to date him again. And all

I can think about is how she doesn't deserve him. It's a nasty little thought, and I try to shove it down so far it will never see the light of day again.

She can't seriously want him back. She's doing it to get my attention… for some reason. I don't know. All I can think about is Eli. The person I can't get out of my mind, whose mouth I still vividly remember wrapping around me. And worst of all, I want it to happen again. If Eli told me he still wanted me, even if it was just for sex, I couldn't tell him no.

I can't get through this dinner. I won't watch him avoid eye contact with me all night and pretend like he wants to date Angel again to make his parents happy. Swallowing a few times to clear my throat, I ask, "Are you sure that's what you want? What Eli wants?"

"What does that matter? He'll say yes."

As if our conversation summoned him, Eli stands in the archway, not quite meeting our eyes. "My parents sent me in to help grab the food."

Angel strides over to him, pulling his arm. "That's so sweet, hun. You always were the best. So helpful. I know my dad always appreciated that." She looks at all the trays, then at me. "I'll let you all handle this." Flipping her hair, she walks out of the kitchen and makes a beeline for the dining room.

Eli grabs a set of tongs from a drawer, placing them into the salad bowl, all while purposefully avoiding me. I walk over to him, slowly, doing my best to make sure I don't startle him. I'm pretty sure he's as aware of my presence as I am of his. I place my palm on his shoulder, turning him toward me, the only reaction a small flaring of his nostrils.

"Please tell me you're not actually considering dating her again." I may not have the best of intentions, I may selfishly want him for myself, but even if I can't have him in my bed, I don't want to see him hurt. To anyone listening, the words might sound like concern for Angel, protecting her from an ex-boyfriend, and maybe that should have been my first thought, but no one needs protection from Eli. Eli needs to be protected from everyone else.

He shrugs my hand off his shoulder without a word.

I try to pull his chin up, make him meet my eyes, give me even a portion of his attention, but he pulls away quickly, skirting around the side not pinning him to the counter. He races out of the room.

Maybe he actually meant what he said Thursday night, that it was only a fuck, nothing more. It's what we committed to, but it felt like more. Was our connection all in my head? One time must have been enough for him. Good. That's good for him. That's what was supposed to happen. It should make me happy. I got caught up in the moment, which means I can move on now. I have my answer. He can move on, find someone who will treat him right. As long as he doesn't date Angel again.

I grab the dishes and make my way to the dining room, ready as I'll ever be for the dinner party from hell. I can already envision the copious amounts of whiskey I'll consume later to unwind from the Ruiz family. "Dinner's served," I call out as I enter the room.

The meal is awkward, tense. Emanuel attempts to make conversation with me, asking about my work at the university, but Sophie shuts the conversation down quickly.

About three miniscule bites in, she calls out, "Eli, don't you have something you'd like to say to Angel?"

"No."

She pins him with a venomous stare. "About cutting out the distraction of others."

"I told you I'm not going to stop being friends with Violet. I agreed to come to dinner, that's it."

Pride warms my chest as Eli speaks up for himself. It's so strong that I have to hide my smirk behind my water glass. Though I feel like I'm missing an important part of the conversation. Of course, I know Violet. She's been a good friend to Eli when he's needed one the most. I just don't know why she would be a concern.

Sophie goes on like Eli never spoke. "He promised to cut that girl out of his life. He realizes he was wrong to focus more on her than your relationship. I know it's up to you darling, but would you consider taking him back? I'm sure your father would be happy to see the two of you together again as well. My boy, while stubborn, knows how to treat a woman with respect."

Angel purses her lips as if she's thinking about it, as if those words came out of Eli's mouth instead of his mother's. "Maybe Eli and I should have a moment to talk alone. Would that be okay with you, Mr. and Mrs. Ruiz?"

I want to scream at his parents. Reprimand my daughter. Instead, I clench my fists under the table. Can't they see how miserable this is making him? He doesn't want this. They are treating him like his happiness doesn't matter, as if he's a good, loyal dog ready to listen at the first command.

Clearly he didn't tell his parents that Angel cheated on him. Or, I hope for his sake that they don't know. The alternative—that they do and they're still pushing him—is unbearable to think about.

I know I shouldn't, that it will cause another rift between Angel and me, but I can't hold my tongue. "Eli's made it pretty clear how he feels about the subject, but why don't we ask him?" I direct my next words to Eli. "Would you like a moment to speak to her alone?"

No acknowledgement comes in word or action. He stares at the wall across from him, jaw clenched, unhearing. Whatever happened since we last spoke seems to have shut him down.

My daughter shoots daggers and I can see the fleeting truce we had this morning burst into flames. "Dad." Her tone is stern, slightly venomous, and eerily similar to Sophie's earlier. I put my hands up, surrendering. I said my piece. If he doesn't fight back now, then there's only so much I can do. I'm not his family, or his friend. I'm barely a fleeting memory.

Emanuel and Sophie follow me to the kitchen where we gather around the island and all silently agree not to speak.

The minutes tick by in tension-soaked silence. I strain my ears, hoping to hear the conversation. Even hours ago, I would have known without a doubt that his answer would be no if anyone ever asked him to get back together with Angel. But now, the silence, the lack of response, has me worried. He loves his family. He would do anything for them. Maybe this has nothing to do with how he feels about me and everything to do with his family's control.

"You weren't much help in there," Sophie snaps.

I have had it with this woman. "I'm sorry, but I don't appreciate being ambushed with this. Neither of you asked how I felt about the matter before you started trying to sell your son to the highest bidder like a hog at market."

"Watch how you speak to my wife," Emanuel hisses.

"I don't support this."

Sophie seethes. "If Debbie knew how you were handling her daughter, it would appall her." Yes, Debbie. The paragon of virtue and morality. I wonder what they would think of her if they had known her while she was in high school, or even now, living with her boyfriend, considering they were of the mindset that you only lived together after marriage.

I don't remember if this is the one she slept with before leaving me. My fault, she had told me, because I didn't love her enough to fight for her anymore. I shake my head, not wanting to get lost in those poisonous thoughts.

"You can tell her the next time she's in town if you see her. If she'll take your call. I'm sure Angel would love the chance to spend some time with her too."

Emanuel gets in my face. His over-inflated ego running away with him. "I told you to watch how you speak to my wife. Show her some respect or I'll teach you a lesson." Ah, the words of a fine, church-going man. Threats masked as lessons. Anger masked as respect.

My filter disappears. "If you were concerned about respect, you'd stop your wife from making your son miserable. You certainly wouldn't relish his misery."

19

Everyone leaves the room because I don't respond to Noah. I can't respond. Talking to him would be too hard. It's already painful looking at him. He's a reminder of how far off the rails I've gotten, how close I came to losing my family—a temptation I don't need. A reminder of how much he makes my heart pound and my stomach flutter as he voices his concern on my behalf. He's the only person in this room who seems to care what I have to say or think. The one person who should be a stranger to me, the one person I can never have, who shouldn't care about me, is the only one fighting for me. I laugh bitterly.

"What's so funny, handsome?" Angel rounds the table, trying to pull my attention, unaware of the anger threatening to choke me.

I clench my hands against the table needing something to ground me. "What the fuck is this, Ang? You're with Tom. Why are you humoring my family?"

She sits in the chair next to me and clutches my hand, trying to pull it to her chest as if she's going to comfort me. "No, hun. I was wrong. You're so much better than him. I made a mistake, but I'm willing to work on it. We are better together."

"You've got to be kidding me."

"Honey. Come on. I know you miss me. Vi can't possibly be as much fun as I was." She glances down at my neck, where the faintest hint of Noah's bite marks remain. She flicks her eyes back to mine as she continues to touch me. I watch in a detached sort of way, wondering how this ever worked on me before. Not a single thing attracts me to her anymore.

"*¡Dios mío! No mames.*"

She hums. "That's so sexy. I always loved when you spoke Spanish to me."

She puts her hand on my chest, and I jerk out of my seat. "Angel, we're not getting back together."

She inches closer and closer to me. For each step forward, I take one back, until I run into the wall. She crowds into my space, her hands wrapping around my neck, pushing her breasts against my chest. "You don't mean that. Why else would you make your parents come here?"

I'm speechless for a moment. Am I actually speaking? Because every conversation I've had lately seems like I've been shouting and no one can hear me. I speak, but no one listens. I fight for myself, but no one cares.

I hear my mother scream from the kitchen and I respond instinctively, pushing Angel off of me and racing toward the sound. "What's going on?" I shout over the noise, not knowing where to look first. Noah holds my father's fist in the palm of his hand, my mom looks like she's about to pass out, and my father looks as red as a beet, his chest heaving.

"He's trying to hurt your father," my mom screams, pointing a finger at Noah.

Angel runs in behind me, wrapping her arms around my shoulders as if she's hiding behind me. I step away, but she follows the movement. I watch Noah as he tracks us, momentarily distracted. Enough time that my father lands a punch to Noah's gut, causing him to wheeze, before moving to block additional punches.

I throw myself between my father and Noah. Glaring at my dad, I shout, "What are you doing?"

"None of your business, *mijo*. Go finish your talk with Angel."

I blurt the words without thought. "You can't just punch someone. Are you crazy?"

My father turns, the force of his rage transferring to me. "I have said it once, and I will say it again. Watch your mouth. You don't disrespect your mother, and you do not disrespect me."

Noah places a hand on my back, and he's so close I can feel his body heat. That simple touch, offering me support, makes wetness build behind my eyes, and I lean into it, my strength crumbling.

I want nothing more than his arms around me, blocking out my father's rage. I know Noah did it to reassure me he was okay, that I didn't need to make things worse, but I'm so tired of trying to bite my tongue. If they loved me and wanted what was best for me, they would listen to me. They would love me for me.

Angel steps in then. "I think we should all take a breath."

Mama nods her head. "You're right."

It's the first thing I've agreed with Angel about all night. "Yes. We should. I'm sorry I took a tone, Papa. I just think it's time to go. Angel and I talked." Noah's hand tightens in my shirt, pulling me imperceptibly closer to him, his broad chest brushing against my back.

Goosebumps break out along my skin. I don't think he realizes he's doing it and I don't know if it's from anger that I'm giving in or indignation on my behalf, but it brings a hidden smile to my face. The first one in three days.

She moves around the island then, sliding into my side, wrapping her arms around my waist, effectively making Noah fall back. I miss his touch immediately. "We're back together. Isn't that great?" She beams at my parents and their demeanors change, smiles breaking out. My mother claps and my father pats me on the back. None of that matters. As far as I'm concerned, it's all background noise.

I watch as Noah stumbles, catching himself on the counter, his face going momentarily blank before he plasters on a fake, mild smile. *It's not true*, I want to yell. *Can't you see she's making my skin crawl?*

That look on my parents' face, no matter how much I don't want to care, is exactly how I want them to look at me, always. They seem so proud.

I'd never have that with Noah. Even if he wasn't older, or a professor at my school, or my ex-girlfriend's father. I force myself to stay in place, even though it hurts. I was right when I said we could never mean anything to one another.

I was wrong about one thing. It's not because he doesn't want more, it's because they will never allow me to be me. I will never allow myself to be me. Like I told Carmen, I'm not gay and I'm not queer. Those desires… they belong to someone else entirely.

My mom leaps forward, pulling us both into a hug. "Oh, Eli. I knew you two could work it out. I'm so happy for you." She smacks a kiss on my cheek. Then she turns to Noah, a smug grin twisting her features into something nasty. "No thanks to you."

"I'm kind of tired, can we go home?" I whisper, losing my voice along with the will to fight. Even if the thought of us together makes them back off, I should correct the misconception. I don't. All I want is to go home, curl up on the top bunk since they won't let me go back to the dorm until tomorrow, and go to sleep.

"Yes, *mijo*. You were up pretty early today. Let's get you home. Get you to bed." She turns to Angel. "I hope to see you at dinner next Sunday, Angel."

"You got it, Mrs. Ruiz." The smile she gives my mom is so sweet, so similar to the one I used to know so well. Was it always a lie?

My father puts his arm around my mom's shoulders as she pulls me out of Angel's grasp. He leads us, all attached, toward the door. He doesn't acknowledge Noah or thank him for the meal.

I haven't said a word to Noah tonight. Too numb, too stubborn, too stupid to enjoy the one spark of light in this terrible darkness. His steadying hand and whispered words telling me I didn't have to accept this. Pretty words, even if they aren't true.

I can't leave without saying something. I need to let him know he meant something, no matter how fleeting it was always going to be.

"Noah." His head snaps from my parents, his full attention on me. His name seems to wrap around the two of us and I refuse to look at anyone else. "Thank you." For dinner, for being my only friend, for being more.

20

Noah

Unlocking my office door, I throw my bag, papers, and keys on the desk. It's Thursday, early evening, and I've finished my only class of the day. I slump into the chair, running my hand through my hair. I haven't been sleeping well the past few nights, and the students were trying to subvert the lesson more than usual. It's left me tired and out of sorts, but I'm not ready to go home yet.

Angel's been on the phone every night this week and I'm afraid it's Eli. When he left and he said thank you, a little ember of hope sparked in me that we might reconcile. I knew better. I thought I knew better. I hoped anyway. I've only heard bits and pieces of each phone call, but she keeps telling them how much she misses them. If it's not Eli, then who? He took her back to appease his parents, and I was fucking stupid. This is exactly why we shouldn't have done anything. I was supposed to be the responsible one, the one who could control this before it got out of hand. I've spent the last fifteen years of my life trying to regain a sense of control. He puts that to the test every time we're around each other, and I need to make it stop.

I slam my palm against the desk. *Stop thinking about him.* Every thought leads back to him, whether or not I want it to. It's not healthy.

The perfect distraction materializes in the form of a phone call. Tony's been AWOL lately, lost in his own writing world, but it's exactly the distraction I need. "Hey, it's been a while, man. How have you been?"

"Oh you know, conquering bastard overlords and journeying through Hell. The usual. How have you been?"

"It's hard having a nineteen-year-old. It's even harder having sixteen eighteen-year-olds in class. I should have taken the summer off and spent it writing like you."

"Yeah, Hell sounds preferable. Thank God I never got the itch to teach. Instead I get to be a poor, starving artist."

"You've sold hundreds of thousands of copies, Tony."

"Starving, Noah. Starving. My wife doesn't feed me." The last he yells, the smile radiating through his voice, teasing his wife, Beth.

I hear her voice muffled through the phone. "Excuse me, if you have two hands to type, and enough brain cells left to write that swill, you can clap those hands together with two pieces of bread and a bit of meat in the middle."

"Swill? You take that back."

I laugh, feeling lighter. Being around them always makes me feel better. They've been married for fifteen years, together for twenty, and they're still in love with each other. It's something I want again someday.

It was something I thought I had with Debbie when I was young and dumb, not realizing how toxic we were. The four of us were inseparable at one point, but then Debbie got pregnant. She wanted to give Angel up for adoption, though I told her I'd take the baby. She said no, and I wanted to respect her wishes, so she started the process before her parents told her she was keeping Angel. I proposed five days later. Married ten after that with our parents' approval, though mine begged me to wait until I was older. They told me I could support her, and they would help us, without the marriage. Debbie's parents wouldn't hear of it.

All the while, Beth and Tony had a front-row seat to our shitshow. And, as predicted by my parents, it didn't end well. So we divorced, and I got to keep Tony and Beth. "I don't know how you two can stand to love each other so damn much."

Beth must pull the phone closer to her as her voice blares in my ear. "Don't worry, Noah. You'll find the one someday." I hear a resounding smacking noise, followed by an exaggerated kiss as Beth lands a very loud and wet kiss on Tony's cheek.

I grunt in response. "To what do I owe the pleasure of this phone call?"

Tony must put the call on speaker because his voice sounds tinny now. "Well. I think it's time for a break. I finished writing, and it needs to cool its heels. Plus, the wife said she was five seconds away from kicking my ass out of the house because I smell like farts and old socks. And I'm talking like a madman so I need human lessons."

"You've definitely been in the writing phase."

"I'm going to pretend like I don't know what you're insinuating. Anyway. You, me, pizza, snacks, and beer. Showing of *Lord of the Rings* in the town square. Eight o'clock sharp. Whatta ya think?"

I think it's the perfect distraction. "I'm in. Beth, please join us. You know I love having you there to keep him contained."

"Not fair. You two are ganging up on me. Aren't you supposed to be my friend?"

She chuckles. "I'll be there too."

"Great. I'll see you both soon."

I disconnect the phone, sighing as tension rolls off my back. As it turns out, all I needed was some friend time and a movie. Honestly, doesn't that fix everything?

When I get home, I jump in the shower, moving through my normal routine as quickly as possible. I know Tony and Beth will beat me there to find the perfect spot, but I don't want to make them wait too long. I dress, comb my hair, and I'm ready to walk out the door twenty minutes later.

The plaza usually sells snacks and drinks, but it's required that you bring your own blankets or lawn chairs. Beth is a firm believer that we can only enjoy movies in the plaza on a blanket, so I decide to grab one from the living room.

Angel walks in as I grab the blanket, her face glued to her phone. She hasn't noticed me yet, and I watch as she waddles forward, perilously close to colliding with an armchair. "Angel."

She startles. "Crap, Dad. Stop sneaking around."

"Sorry. I'm headed out to meet up with Tony and Beth. Do you have any plans for the night?"

She rolls her eyes. "I'm not going with you."

"That's fine. Were you planning on doing something with friends tonight?" I will not ask about Eli.

"Yeah. I might hang out with a few people."

"No date night with Eli?" Shit.

She flops into the chair dramatically. "No. That was dumb, I don't know why I thought I'd give him a second chance. I don't understand why he made his parents call me if he was going to ghost me. It's like he's turned into a total dick. And it's not hot on him."

I should parent this. This is a situation where I should sit down and talk about what's going on, right? She wants me to ask more about this. I think. "You think he asked his parents to call you?"

"Yeah. Why else would they call? They don't like you and they never seemed fond of me."

I subtly check my watch again. It's seven now, I should still have plenty of time to get there. I sit on the couch across from her. "Honey, we should have talked about this sooner, but can you try to understand his perspective? He might not be ready to talk to you yet."

"I told him I messed up, and that I was sorry. He should have forgiven me already."

"That's not how feelings work."

She crosses her arms. "Like you care how 'feelings work.' You were a shit husband and a shit father. You don't care about anyone's feelings."

Fuck. On some level, I knew she thought that, but she's never said it to my face before. That's going to play on repeat for a while, a reminder of how much I'm failing as a father. "I'm sorry you feel that way."

"It's the truth. You were a shit father and most of the time you still are."

"Where is this coming from, Angel? I thought we moved past this when you moved in."

"It's just a fact, Noah."

"What can I say to make it better?"

"Admit that you're a shitty father. We both know it."

I stand, done with this conversation. Fucking hell, I feel so unprepared as a father. How did I turn out to be so shitty when I had the best parents? I wish they were still here so I could ask them how to make things right. "I was. You're right. I've been trying, though. When you're ready to have a proper conversation, I'll be ready to talk. In the meantime, lock up when you leave. I'll be home late. I love you and stay safe."

***

I make it with fifteen minutes to spare and I can't help but let out a sigh of relief. Knowing I'm moments away from seeing my friends keeps my mood light, even with that minefield of a conversation with Angel. I text Tony and he tells me he's in line to get snacks and Beth's at the front holding down the spot. Probably best to go help Tony. He always orders an obscene amount of snacks.

"Hey," I maneuver around a few people standing nearby, coming to a stop at Tony's side.

He laughs, lines fanning around his face. "Hey, buddy." I'm wrapped in a tight embrace and the last bit of tension melts away. This was exactly what I needed. A good movie, good friends, and a quiet night away from home.

"So, what are we getting you tonight?"

"Popcorn, 'cause you gotta. Buncha Crunch. Swedish Fish. A couple of hot dogs. I've already got beer and pizza over by the blankets. Aaand I'm feeling nachos too. You in?"

"Would it change your order if I said no?"

"Nah."

The crowds disperse as they find their seats, only a few stragglers still floating around. I peek at the screen, noticing Beth way in the front when Tony leans in close. "Hey, is that one of your students? He looks so familiar."

I look around, doubting it because I have no idea how Tony would recognize any of my students. But I catch his line of sight. Standing a few yards away is the exact person I've been trying to get out of my head. Tony doesn't give me a chance to respond. "No, that's Angel's boyfriend, right? What was his name? I've met him, what, twice now?"

It's obvious Eli intended to get snacks, cash in hand, Violet right behind him, but they spot us staring. Shit. I look away. Then I peek through my lashes. It looks like they are arguing. Whatever it's about, she must win because too soon, they are standing directly behind us. Eli behind Violet as she glances around pretending like we don't exist. Tony is watching me, expectantly, probably waiting for me to confirm his suspicion.

I lean into Tony's side, doing my best to whisper, "Ex."

Eli tracks my movement while acting like he's extremely entranced with the back of Violet's head. "Oh, that's great," Tony says at normal volume, and I watch in horror as he turns to Eli and Violet. "Hey," he catches Eli's eye, then looks at me to fill in his name. He must have thought I said yes, not ex.

"Eli."

"Hey, Eli. Remember me? I'm Tony. It's been a while. How are you?" He does an awkward thumb point back at me as if they can't see me standing here. Both Eli and Violet stare wondering why my friend is talking to them.

"Tony, let's leave them alone. They're busy."

"Nonsense, we're all waiting in line. Is Angel joining you soon?"

Violet glares at me, affronted, as if any of this is my fault. "I'm sorry, sir, but your friend is right. We're busy."

"Vi, it's okay." Eli's voice lowers, mumbling something that I can't quite make out.

Tony looks at me questioningly. "Uh, Eli and Angel broke up a few months ago." My friend's eyebrows shoot up, before glancing between all of us, like the world's biggest train wreck of a tennis match.

He rubs the back of his neck before glancing at Eli. "Ah, sorry, bud. I'm good at sticking my foot in my mouth. And sorry, miss...?"

"Violet."

"Violet, sorry for interrupting your evening."

She grabs Eli's arm and gives it a light squeeze. "Do you want to go back to the chairs and I'll get the snacks?"

He shakes his head no, his voice low. "I'm fine. Really. No—uh, erm, Mr. Baker had nothing to do with that shitshow of a dinner."

I flinch as he awkwardly tries to cover that he almost called me Noah. My friend, being the nosy shit he is, overhears that they are sitting in chairs. He also completely ignores or misses the tension. "Oh, where are you guys sitting? You know you can't enjoy a movie in the square with lawn chairs. It kills the ambiance."

"Tony." I shoot him an annoyed glare. *Shut the fuck up and leave them alone.*

Eli looks at him, amusement dancing in his eyes. My chest squeezes involuntarily. I've missed that smile. But he still sounds hesitant when he answers. "Right over there." He points in the general direction of the very back of the plaza, where they won't be able to see anything.

Tony slaps a hand against his chest. "Oh, no, no, no. That won't do. We have plenty of room up front. Come and sit with us."

"Wouldn't that be weird?" Eli asks.

Violet chimes in. "I think we're okay. Mr. Baker already sees me enough in classes."

Tony, always the optimist. "No. We're adults. You're adults. And really, you need to appreciate *Lord of the Rings* from up close. It won't be weird." Speak for yourself, Tony.

Violet looks at Eli, and Eli stares at me, trying to gauge how I feel about it. "I owe you an apology after that dinner, anyway. The least we can do is share our good seats if you're comfortable with that. Both of you." Then, I point out where we're located and Violet looks at them longingly.

She bounces on the balls of her feet. "Say no, Eli. Tell me no."

That has him outright laughing, sending a flash of heat pulsing through my chest. "I know you want the good seats, Vi. It's fine. I can run the chairs back to the car before the movie starts."

"Oh, I can help with that," Violet responds.

I shouldn't, but I want a moment alone with him, it's been too long. Too many unpleasant emotions since then. "Actually, how about you help with the snacks? I'll get the chairs with Eli. It'll give me the chance to apologize."

He doesn't seem to like that idea, and why would he? But Violet is so eager to get to the good seats that he caves. "Yeah, that works. I'll see you up there, Vi."

She throws her arms around him. "You're the best."

He chuckles, his cheeks turning pink. He watches me again, so I motion him forward. "Lead the way."

21

Eli

We are halfway back to my car, the lawn chairs slung across Noah's back, which I can't seem to stop staring at. I look up, and I notice he's caught me, but doesn't say anything and looks away, which makes me nervous. I can't tell what he's thinking. Plus, there's so much that I want to say that I have no idea where to start. But sorry might be a good place.

"Noah," I say at the same moment he says my name.

He peeks at me, again, through his long lashes before looking away. "You go first."

"I wanted to say that I'm not actually dating Angel again. Also, I'm sorry." The words slip through my mouth like water through a sieve. I couldn't keep them in if I wanted.

"I know. And sorry for what?"

Of course he knows. Angel's probably been complaining to him since I haven't responded to her many calls and texts. "If I were to list all the reasons we'd go well into the night. I'll start with that dinner. I… They… It's been a pretty rough few weeks, and it just seemed easier to let it happen. When I heard we were going there, I didn't think you'd agree to it, so I thought we wouldn't have to deal with it."

"You don't have to apologize. I'm only sorry I made things worse for you at home."

I shrug, kicking at a stray rock on the sidewalk. He's not wrong. This week has only seemed to top the previous one in the waking nightmare category.

Carmen's been calling me every day, my parents kept me at home because of my disrespect, and Miguel keeps asking who's calling me. I changed Carmen's name in my contact list because he's taken to peeking over my shoulder before scurrying off to my mom.

They've also been acting like everything is fucking roses, asking about Angel and what we talked about on the phone. "You're the only one who's willing to listen to me. It's a fucking joke that you have to apologize for that. You shouldn't need to do it. They should listen to me."

I swallow, trying to get my emotions under control again. I really try to stop, but my hand reaches for him, never quite making contact. I can't. I'm sending mixed signals, and it's not fair to him.

Sympathy shines in his eyes as we continue to watch each other. "I hated seeing how much you were hurting."

"You're too nice. You should be mad at me."

"What do you mean?"

"Thursday night. When I freaked out on you. I'm sorry about what I did before you left. It was cruel."

He glances around before grasping my upper arm to pull me along. I step closer to him, needing the warmth and caring that he so naturally provides. Before he lets go, he uses his thumb to rub the inside of my bicep, goosebumps spreading at his touch. The comfort is too short. His voice lowers, sounding rough, affected. "That doesn't have to be how we leave things."

I swallow again as we arrive at my car. Instead of answering, I unlock the trunk and mumble, not wanting to say the words aloud. I want nothing more than to give into that voice, throw myself into his arms. I can't. "It can't happen again."

"What?"

"It can't happen again."

He passes the chairs to me. "I know it's not smart. But…"

"That's not the point. It won't happen again."

"Are you actually getting back together with Angel? Is that why?"

I slam the trunk. "Of course not."

"I don't understand."

I look away, doing my best to pretend the volume of the crowd is intriguing to me. More interesting than this conversation. The movie speakers blare loudly, different commercials playing before the start of the show. There's enough noise, but I hiss the words, anyway. "I'm not gay."

His eyes turn stormy in the low light. "I didn't say you were."

"I'm straight." The words hold less conviction this time.

Mouth turning down, he places both hands on the edge of my car before bowing his head. He looks like a defeated man and I want to tell him everything will be okay. Instead, I cross my arms tight to ensure I won't do something stupid.

For a few seconds, he stays like that, his eyes closed, head tucked to his chest, panting short breaths in and out. Then his eyes pop open as he zeros in on me. He stands once more. "I see."

"I mean it."

A deep, deep sorrow fills those dark eyes and I take a step back as he moves into my space. I can't have him touch me. If he does, well, I can't think of the consequences because it will make me want something I can't have. He just can't touch me. "I know you do, Eli."

"I have to be."

He nods his head. "I know."

I nod my head.

"I'm still here if you need anything. Tony was right, we're adults. We can be… friends." It feels like a kick to the ribs hearing him say that, but I agree anyway. What else can I do? He wants me. He made that clear. But I'm straight. "Let's get back to the show, they've probably rifled through all the snacks and left us with the shit treats."

"You don't want me to leave?"

He sticks his hands in his pockets as he turns toward the plaza, retracing our steps. "No. Friends do movie nights in the plaza. I've heard it can even be fun."

"Right."

The walk doesn't take long, but where there were stragglers before, now it's completely deserted. We walk side by side, and I sidestep to put some distance between us. He moves closer, our shoulders brushing, steps falling in sync. We steal glances at one another, and I feel each one like fire under my skin. I take another step and his fingertips brush against my knuckles. It's pure, divine torture. I don't understand what he's playing at, but it seems like he's winning. My hand balls into a fist to resist the temptation to take his hand in mine. I won't cross this line again.

"I feel like I should tell you..." He waits until I turn toward him. "As a friend, just to make sure you're okay with it... I am very not straight."

I have to clear my throat a few times before I can string words together because it's as dry as a desert. "How do you know? No. Don't answer that. Um. Why? What? Why? Uh? Why are you telling me?" Just about the dumbest fucking question I've ever asked but I can't be blamed. My brain isn't functioning right now.

"How do I know? Well, I had hot sex with an extremely attractive man. I liked it. I know if given the chance, I'd do it with him again." He shrugs, meeting my eyes. "He doesn't want to and I'm respecting that boundary. Why am I telling you? Because I thought it was important for you to know."

"Why?" I whisper. "It was one time. You can't know for sure."

He pops an eyebrow. "I suppose you could be right."

"But you don't think I am."

"Not in my case, no." He shrugs his shoulders like it's the easiest thing in the world.

I wish it was. If he wanted to tell everyone he knew right now, he could. If he wanted to go to the plaza with his friends, with a man by his side, he could.

He's free to date another man. The realization hits me hard. I fucking hate it. "Well, as friends, I should say that this other guy sounds like a lost cause. Maybe you should try dating another person."

"Another man, you mean?"

I grind my teeth. "Yes."

He gives me another disarming, subdued smile, then squeezes my arm. He takes a few steps to the side, putting distance between us. It's what I want and what I need, but out of everything we discussed and every small gesture he made tonight, it's the hardest to bear. I feel like the conversation isn't over, like I need to say more, but we arrive at our spot.

The opening scene of the movie starts and I duck down so I don't obstruct the view. They must have been here extremely early to get such good seats, and Vi is enjoying every second. She's lying at the front of the blanket, propped up with a pillow, popcorn on one side and Swedish Fish on the other. To the left Tony and his wife, whose name I can't remember, lie together, cuddled under a cozy-looking comforter, propped up by no less than four pillows.

Their focus is on the screen as his wife slowly plays with his hair, her head tucked under his chin. Unfortunately, there's no spot near Vi. There's only one small chunk of blanket left in the back right corner, with three pillows thrown haphazardly for anyone else to use. I'm sure if I asked, Vi would sit up. There's not enough room left for two people to squeeze in the back corner without being extremely close. I don't know who picked this arrangement, but I can't imagine they realized how tightly Noah and I would have to sit. The smart thing would be to tell Vi to sit up, or offer to sit on the grass.

Without looking at Noah I pick the very corner of the blanket and take a pillow to prop behind me so I'm partially reclining. My head and back are against the pillow and I tuck my knees up so I don't brush Vi. Noah takes the other pillows, propping them behind his back as he sits with his legs crossed. The movement has the whole of his thigh pressed firmly against my side. I readjust, trying to find the most comfortable position, and I end up with my arm partially draped over his leg near his hip.

Only then does he pull out another blanket, draping it over his lap and the upper half of my body.

I glare at the blanket, then look up at him as his face hovers over mine, too close for comfort. "Why didn't we lay this one down?" I whisper accusingly.

His expression is one of complete innocence. "I didn't want us to get cold."

I push myself up, ready to demand he lays the other blanket out so I can get further away from him, but his left arm slides under the blanket, pinning me to the spot. "Shh, you're ruining the movie."

My mouth flops open and closed a few times, and I'm sure I look like a fish. Why am I fighting it? Friends, as he keeps pointing out, can touch. I scooch down, my shoulder digging into his hip, his thigh plastered to my side, and it's not comfortable.

To get comfortable, I'd need to turn on my side, but I'm frozen in place. I put up boundaries and told Noah what they were, and the first thing I do after establishing them should not involve violating said boundaries. But no one is looking our way and I don't recognize anyone outside of this group. The blanket is covering us. It's risky, and I really shouldn't, but I think I've established I'm not always the smartest when it comes to Noah.

I unlock my body, inching closer so my shoulder and arm can drape over Noah's thigh, my hand resting on his knee, my head against a small part of his chest. His arm tucks around me, settling on my stomach just underneath the blanket. Everywhere our bodies touch, sparks flash along my skin. I keep my eyes glued to the screen, my breathing shallow as I fight my body's reaction.

I wait, wondering if he'll call me out. I should know by now—he fights for me, not against me. My muscles melt, relaxing into the touch. Noah lifts the blanket higher, brushing a knuckle against my neck as he adjusts it. I let out a heavy breath, wanting more. Just one more night. I need one more night of his comfort. Then I'll work harder on letting it go. On being good.

22

Eli

"Elias," my father calls up the stairs. "Come watch your siblings. Your mother needs to go grocery shopping and I have to get to work." I grab all of my coursework and make a hasty path downstairs. My father looks at the books as I slide into the kitchen. "You won't need your books, Elias. You'll need to drive the kids to their summer activities and then help Emanuel and Adriana with their homework."

"But, Papa, I need to do my homework. I'm falling behind in classes."

He looks down his nose. "You should learn to manage your time better."

I fight the urge to roll my eyes. "Yes, sir."

"How about we make a deal? You watch the kids today and tomorrow, you stay the night Sunday, and you can go back to campus Monday morning. Focus on your classes then."

"Just for the day?"

"No. You've been grounded long enough and your mother and I think you've learned your lesson about respect." My grounding comprised attending classes, spending time at home, going to church, or going on "dates" with Angel. The movie night was meant to be a date with her, but they didn't call to verify. I think they were too happy about getting their way to ask too many questions.

"Yes, sir. I have. I'll run my books back upstairs before you go, if that's okay with you?"

He nods his head, and I race back up to throw my books onto the top bunk. I only have to make it three more days and then I'm free.

By the time I get back downstairs, he's gone, so I head to the kitchen, where we keep a detailed calendar of all the activities my siblings are involved in. Miguel goes to swimming class, Alex to soccer at the local boys' club, and Dani and Valeria to a training session for their swim team.

Once I've bussed everyone around to their different sports, all starting at slightly varied times, I feel exhausted. It's one thing getting them there, but the struggle of forcing them to get ready is a whole additional battle, alongside making sure they packed everything they need.

I slump into a kitchen seat as Manny and Adriana pull out their coursework. Thankfully, they haven't fought me on getting it done. It might be because I bribed them with ice cream if they got their work done quickly, as long as they didn't tell the other siblings. Manny sits at the coffee table. It's always been his place to complete coursework, in the middle of chaos, and I don't know how he does it. Adriana doesn't have a favorite spot, so she sets up across the table from me.

Whenever it's the two of us, she switches to English. I've never asked why, but it feels like it's our thing. And I like that. She diligently works on the problems and I contemplate grabbing my books and laptop, but she cuts through the silence. "So, who are you actually dating now?"

That has me sitting up straight. "Uh."

"Is it Violet, the girl we met at lunch?" She peeks up, her pencil barely slowing.

"I'm still dating Angel."

She sets her pencil down, giving me her undivided attention. "Eli, do you think I'm stupid?"

"I think you're nosy, not stupid."

She swats at my hand, and I snort. "Come on, you've gotten a million calls from some random phone number while you've been here."

Shit, she's talking about Carmen's phone calls. It's been three weeks, and she's still reaching out to me. "That's not what you think. It's…"

"Don't lie to me."

"I wasn't going to."

"I know the face you make when you're about to lie."

I gasp. "I do not make a face."

She nods her head rapidly. "You do. It's super obvious."

Panic rises, clamping down on my throat. Crap. I don't make a face, do I? She tilts her head. "Don't worry, Mama and Papa have no idea what it looks like, and I'm not going to tell them."

I cross my arms, watching her warily. She's too damn perceptive. "Why not?"

"Because you're my brother, and I don't think Mama and Papa are always right. They certainly aren't right about Angel. She's not good for you. I mean, you were so much happier after you guys broke up."

The comment startles me. I don't know where to begin—her not thinking Mom and Dad are always right, that she's supporting me with the whole Angel thing, or how she knew I broke up with Angel two months ago instead of the lie I told my parents. "Um, I don't know what to say."

"You're a good person, Eli, and you deserve to be happy. They clearly don't know what that looks like because they would ask who was making you so happy after Angel. Plus, the hickeys were like, super obvious. But you're sad again. Did you break up? Are you trying to work things out with Angel instead?"

"Woah. Woah. Back up. How do you know what hickeys are?" My older-brother instincts kick in.

She rolls her eyes. "Just because I've never had one doesn't mean I don't know what it is, Eli. Don't change the subject. Is that why you've been so sad?"

"I'm not sad, Adriana. I've been busy."

She crosses her arms, mirroring my posture. "At least tell me you're for sure not getting back together with Angel if you won't tell me about the other stuff."

I lean back, making sure Manny is still in the living room. When the coast is clear, I flop back down on all fours in the chair and hiss, "No, I'm not getting back together with her and I never will."

"Good, she was always trying to make you into something you aren't."

"What's that supposed to mean?"

She shrugs. "You did a lot of stuff to make her happy that seemed to make you unhappy. You should be with someone that makes you better, not worse."

A lump chokes me as I swallow. I had no idea how much she saw, how much she cared… about me. I lean across the table and grab her hand, giving it a squeeze. "Thanks, Adriana. How'd you get so wise?"

Squeezing my hand back, she replies, "With this many kids around, the oldest and youngest getting the most attention, you learn how to watch."

"You know I always want you to be happy too, right? I love all of you and I'd never do anything to make life harder for any of you. I'd never leave."

A knowing expression crosses her face, but she says nothing. It's been three years since anyone's said Carmen's name out loud. It's an unwritten rule, something to ignore and bury, but maybe that should change.

I open my mouth to say something, but Manny comes bursting through the door. "Eli, I need help with this math problem."

"Sure, buddy. Let me look." It effectively ends the conversation with Adriana. I make a promise to myself then and there. I need to stop thinking of my siblings as a unit—they have their own thoughts and feelings and they might not have a place to express them.

I've neglected that, thinking physically being here was enough, but maybe it's not. If I can have problems this big in my life, who's to say that Adriana isn't experiencing the same, or Alex, or any of them?

***

I sit down at my desk in my dorm to finish my research paper, but I'm exhausted. Being the kids' personal chauffeur and balancing school has been a struggle. I already have half the essay done. Maybe a quick nap is what I need. I also have the rest of it outlined and all the quotes I want to use, it's just a matter of typing it up. The bed is practically calling me.

Yeah, alright. I'm doing it. I stand up, collect my textbooks, and shove them on my bookshelf. As I'm re-shelving, my eyes fall on Noah's books and I pause, remembering he wrote dedications for me in each book.

He told me to wait until I had the time to read them again, so I probably shouldn't read it now… but one won't hurt, right?

My hand rests on the well-worn spine of the first novel before I run my fingers over the second and third. Out of all of his books, the third is the smallest. I remember when it came out. Critics bashed him for months, calling it a pointless waste of paper, unnecessary to the plot. Fans posted how disappointed they were. "After all," they said, "we waited a whole two years for a new book, and he gave us this garbage. It didn't even add to the plot." It was my favorite. I grab the first book and crack it open. There, in his cramped writing, he starts his note.

Dear Eli,

Do you remember the flashback scene where Dante was trapped in Ananta in the middle of the third book? He watched his men as they were endlessly tortured, the enemy trying to break him. They knew he wouldn't talk if they inflicted pain on him. But others, he would always fight for others. While writing this book, I was alone, facing my demons. I thought no one could understand what I was going through and no one tried.

This scene always stood out to me because it embodied the torment I went through every day. The torture, it manifested on the page like it was me. I was the story. No hope in sight. Dante, the beautifully tragic hero, was the only thing to pull me back from the edge. He was steadfast, loyal to his people, and brought them out of the enemy's grasp at the expense of his own happiness, as you saw by the end of the book. And I'm sure you know I haven't mentioned him since.

The message ends without a signature and in the middle of his story. What? I… No, he must have finished writing on a different page. He wouldn't just stop. I flip a few more pages, finding nothing but blank space and the beginning of the story. I flip to the back of the book, and nothing. Then, I glance at the second book.

I rip it from the shelf. What happened in Noah's life to make him feel like that?

My worlds and the characters within aren't real, but they are a manifestation of all the wishes and dreams I've always wanted to see in this world. I write what I know, it's why the emotions from his captivity came to me so easily. It's why I knew what Dante's downfall would look like. What I couldn't see was Dante's future. He was too good, too precious to me.

My editor told me to write him out. The fans asked me to kill him off. I knew I couldn't. He was, and is, more important to me than any character I've ever crafted. When I had nothing, he was my hope. He was the light in my darkness. I wanted him to be that hope for every reader, I just couldn't see how to save him. I couldn't see how his story would end. Why?

I set the second book aside delicately, as if I'm setting a piece of Noah down. A flutter of butterflies riots through my stomach. I have to keep reading. I need to know more.

Because I've never known anyone like Dante. Someone who inspires, loves deeply, protects those around him without hesitation or worry of recompense, and is loyal, so fiercely loyal. A man who would see that list and shrug it off, saying anyone would do the same. How could I authentically finish his story, knowing how much he meant to me, if I didn't have hope of ever meeting someone like him? Someone who might bring us all into the light. I needed that person to show me how his story should end.

I grasp the last one, my hands shaking as I try to open the cover, my fingers fumbling the pages.

Well, a few days ago I wrote how it will end. Thank you.

Yours,

Noah Baker

23

Noah

I'm in the garage working out when the doorbell chimes, so I grab a towel, wiping the sweat from my brow. Maybe Angel forgot her keys before heading to work? I don't think I'm expecting anyone. I make my way to the front, searching for keys, and pull the door open, not prepared to see Eli standing on the stoop, his expression raw, beautiful.

It's been too long since I've seen him, so I can't help but take in every inch of his tall, hard body. He's wearing tight dark blue jeans and a threadbare band tee, his hair mussed in this sexy way only he knows how to pull off. God, those jeans. My eyes snap up, remembering that I should say something instead of ogling. "Eli, what…"

He launches himself into my arms and sends us crashing into the wall, nipping at my lower lip. His tongue swipes across it, asking for entrance, making me moan. His hands wrap around my neck, tugging at the ends of my damp hair.

My brain acknowledges that I should set him aside and ask what's changed within the past three weeks. I know why he wanted to stop, and it's a valid reason to him, so I should ask. As quickly as I register the thoughts, I push them from my mind as his mouth moves over mine.

"*Mierda*, Noah. I've missed this so much," Eli says as he breaks away from my mouth to plaster kisses along my chest. He licks into the concave of my collarbone, sending a shiver down my spine.

"I missed you." I grab his hair and give it a light tug, pulling him from my neck.

He looks up, his eyes pinched as his mouth turns down. "What's wrong?"

"I was working out and I'm gross. I need to shower."

Tugging out of my grasp, he licks a path up my neck, my cock stiffening at the sensation. He grins, fully aware of what he's doing to me. "I think it's hot."

My chest vibrates with silent laughter. God, I've missed him. "You are such a tease."

"Me? I'm not the one trying to waste time with something stupid like a shower."

I pull him closer, running my hands down his back and under his shirt until I meet skin. He's solid and warm under my touch and I'm just as eager. I need to see every inch of his bronzed body. I stroke him, my fingers gliding over his pecs and back down, tracing the ridges of his abdomen. "Join me."

He hums, lost to the sensation of my fingers. I repeat the pattern, feeling every gasp and twitch as I get my fill of his body. It's been too long. Finally, he finds his words. "Yes. Yes. A shower. Great idea. So smart."

I can only imagine how foolish I look as a broad smile splits my face. I don't care because I get to watch Eli sprint to my bedroom, glancing back at me every few steps to make sure I'm there. I stalk closely behind as I watch his firm ass tense, too hidden by those tight jeans for my liking. They need to go, along with the shirt.

He strips it off in my bedroom doorway, the muscles of his back flexing as he reveals inch after enticing inch. It's unfair how sexy he is because I can only lick so much of him at once, and every bit deserves to be worshiped. He thumbs the hem of his pants, so I lunge forward, snatching his hand away. "That's my job."

His head falls back onto my shoulder, his hazel eyes taking me in lazily. From this close, hooded with lust, they look more golden brown and it's the most beautiful thing I've ever seen. I place a soft kiss on his cheek, his shoulder, his neck.

"Fuck. Noah, please. I need your hands on me."

I flip the button open on his jeans and take my time dragging the zipper down, my knuckle grazing against his length. I watch his eyes flutter shut and his chest heave as I slide my hand under the material, palming him through his boxers. He moans, the sound echoing through the room as I nip his neck and step away.

"Wha—Why'd you stop?"

He's not the only one who knows how to torture. Instead of answering him, I walk into my ensuite bathroom, flipping the shower on to a tolerable heat. I strip out of my clothes, leaving only my boxers. He's behind me in seconds, tracing every inch of my skin that he can reach. "So fucking hot."

We take his pants off together as we stand there, tracking every part of the other, waiting to see who will act next. I can't wait. I slide my boxers off, my dick curving high on my stomach, a small bead of pre-come leaking into my happy trail.

Eli palms his cock through his boxers, eyes riveted to my shaft. And that heated look, it makes me lose control, so I tell him to lose the boxers. "Get naked. I need to see your cock."

He rips them off, tossing them onto the pile, his erection bobbing with the movement. I'm slightly above average, impressive enough, but every time I see Eli's cock I can't help but stare. He's long and thick, and at the moment, leaking from his tip—painfully hard for me. "You have two seconds to get in that shower and clean yourself. Then, I want you facing away from the spray, hands planted on the wall. Do you understand?"

I watch his throat bob as he swallows, already nodding yes.

"Use your words, Eli."

Those hazel eyes blaze with fire, his tongue darting to wet his lip. "Yes, sir."

"Hmmm. Good. I like hearing you say that."

He opens the glass door, leaving it ajar as he walks through the water, droplets cascading down his hard body. I thought watching his ass flex in jeans was a marvel, but I was wrong. I need him naked in front of me day and night for this alone.

He grabs the soap, quickly washing his body and hair. Then, he slicks the dark strands of his hair back and places his palms against the back of the shower. In true Eli fashion, he bends the rules and glances over his shoulder, his back arching slightly, pushing his ass out on display.

Climbing in behind him, I shut the door and grab my soap. I readjust the showerhead so the water falls on both of us, keeping him warm. "If you're good, and stay just like this while I clean myself, I'll give you a reward."

His eyes close and his nostrils flare. "Noah?"

I drag the soap leisurely over my body, and each brush pushes me higher. "Yes?"

"What's the reward?"

"You don't like surprises?"

"No, sir," he lies.

"Hmmm… I don't think that's true. I think you're being greedy." I pet his stomach and stroke his cock before letting go to continue my shower.

He whimpers, then leans forward, resting his cheek against the wall like he needs something to ground himself.

His eyes pop open, searching for mine. "You're right. I just wanted to know what I'm going to lose out on for disobeying your orders."

I frown. "Why would you do that?"

"Because I need to fucking touch you."

An uneven breath slips past my lips and I take a moment to collect myself before stepping forward. I take him back in hand and pump once, loosely, not giving him any real satisfaction.

Leaning into his ear, I say, "If you wait for me like you're told, I'm going to lick every inch of you. I'm going to eat your ass until you beg me to fuck you. Then, and only then, I'll let you have what you really want."

He lets out a strangled moan, his fingers clenching uselessly against the tile.

I step away from him to rinse the soap from my body, then move on to the shampoo. "I think you like that idea. You want my tongue and fingers in your ass, Eli?"

The length of his body shivers, his control hanging on by a thread. His "Yes" sounding more like a growl than an actual word.

I rinse my hair, my cock screaming at me, calling me a fool ten times over for waiting so long. When the last of the soapy suds are gone, I drag one finger down his spine. "You did such a good job, babe."

As promised, I kiss a path down his body, running my hands everywhere I can reach. Each touch a tease of what we both want, but I need him wild before I give in.

"Noah, please."

I chuckle before falling to my knees. I spread his cheeks, licking a line across the hole with the flat of my tongue.

"Fucking hell."

I bury my face, tracing the rim, pushing against the muscles.

He clenches, pushing back.

I knead his ass, needing him to relax for this to be fully enjoyable. I pull back. "Take a deep breath."

He nods his head, his eyes squeezed shut. "Right."

I brush my hand against his thigh, then his back in long, soothing strokes. "Hey, I don't have to do this. I can stop."

"No." The word comes too quickly. "I, uh, obviously haven't done this before. It just feels… too good. But wrong. Like I shouldn't like it."

I nod in understanding. I stroke his side again. "That makes sense. It's not wrong if we both want it, though. And I'll very much enjoy fucking you with my tongue."

He looks at me, surprised, as if he thinks I'm doing this to humor him. I could stay right here all day. Without warning, I flex my tongue, pushing into his ass, the muscles loosening.

"Fuck." His hand switches to a fist, slamming into the tile wall. I take that as a promising sign and do it again, picking up speed. I slide into him a few times before circling the ring of nerves with the tip of my tongue.

"Need more," he cries out.

"Turn around," I demand as I grab the lube I keep on hand in the shower.

He does as he's told, and I admire him once more. His back pressed against the tiles, his gaze unfocused, cheeks flushed. "Do you still want my fingers in you?"

It takes a minute for the words to process in his lust-drunk mind. He blinks down at me, a bashful smile adding to his beauty. He tilts his head up and down, but that's not good enough. "I want to hear you say it."

"Say what?" His voice sounds like smoke, caressing every part of my body. I stroke myself, unable to hold back. That lustful timbre is too much to handle.

"Tell me what you want me to do to you."

He takes it for the challenge it is, the haze clearing, replaced by a heat so scorching I know I'll never come out the other side alive. "I want you to swallow my cock while you fuck me with your fingers. Stretch me so good that I can take every inch of you."

"Fuck, Eli. Look what you do to me. Do you know how hard I am for you?" His gaze falls to my hand, where it involuntarily squeezes my poor, neglected cock.

His smile brightens as he leans down, getting close to my face. He places a wicked kiss on my lips before tangling his fingers in my hair. "I know."

I laugh, my whole body flooding with this lightness I can't quite name. As requested, I swallow his cock, gagging as I go. I pull back and lick down his shaft, my left hand sliding over the length that I can't quite manage with my mouth. I get a rhythm going, following the pattern of Eli's hisses.

Grabbing his hip, I bob up and down as I wrap my hand around, the movement awkward. Adjusting, I throw his thigh over my shoulder, giving me better access. His hands tighten in my hair, forcing him further down my throat.

I look up and see his head tipped back against the wall, his eyes shut, and his expression one of complete bliss. "Noah. Oh, God. Noah."

I hum at his praise and his dick twitches in response, liking the vibrations.

"You're too fucking good at this."

Once my fingers are fully coated, I rub a finger around the circle of nerves. His gasp is loud, his fingers tightening painfully in my hair. I push against the puckered skin, his cock hardening in my mouth. Then, I slide in up to the first knuckle.

"Oh," he breathes.

I feel the muscles clench and release around me in protest, unused to the intrusion. I give him a minute to adjust. When he sighs, I move in an inch further, and again, until his body relaxes around me, letting me all the way in. His hips buck, making his cock hit the back of my throat. I swallow at the unusual sensation, feeling him everywhere.

He lets out a long, low groan as I pump in and out of the tight heat. With each thrust, his body adjusts until he's grinding against my finger. He rolls his head around to watch me as I keep working his hard length. "I'm so fucking close. Another one, please. More."

I pull out and push a second finger in, this time meeting more resistance. Looking up, I catch the wince on Eli's face. I pull my fingers out and take my mouth off his cock. He whimpers at the loss, so I kiss his hip, then slick more lube onto my fingers. "Don't worry. I'm not going anywhere."

"Thank God," he says in a light, teasing tone. I slide into his ass once more, scissoring slowly, doing my best to stretch him without pain. I pull his wet cock back to my mouth and match my sucking with the rhythm of my hand. His ass clenches around the touch and I curl my fingers, reaching for his prostate.

"Fuck, Noah," he shouts. "Fuck, I'm going to come." He tries to pull away from me, but I dig my left hand into his ass cheek as the first rope hits the back of my throat.

His face is the sexiest thing I've ever seen as he comes undone, spasms rocking his body. I withdraw my fingers and lean back so I can watch him catch his breath. "That was the hottest thing I've ever seen."

He peeks at me through his lashes, his whole body flushed. He clears his throat, trying to rid it of the gritty lust still clinging to him. "Thanks."

I stand, leaning into him as I pin my hands on either side of his head. "Thank you for the show." I place a feather light kiss on each cheek, and one on his lips.

As reality creeps in, I feel the cold water pelting my back and I see Eli shiver. I shut the water off and grab towels for both of us, but he doesn't move when I hold it out for him.

"Everything okay?"

He chuckles. "I don't know if I can move yet."

That brings a satisfied smile to my face. "God, you know exactly how to sweet talk a man."

Another pretty blush colors his tanned cheeks. I run a finger over his flushed skin, happy to know it's because of me, hoping I can make it happen several more times before he leaves tonight. "Do you need me to carry you to the bed?"

He scoffs. "Shut up."

I turn away to wipe myself down as he moves, wrapping a towel around his waist. The normally soft material feels like sandpaper against my dick, given how painfully hard I still am.

Eli takes in his fill before asking, "Need help with that?"

It's my turn to groan.

"So dramatic."

I am not dramatic. It might fall off if it doesn't get relief soon. I grab Eli's hand and pull him into the bedroom with me before flopping onto the bed. He tumbles, draped halfway over me, his chin propped on his arms. He watches me with a soft look in his eyes and I can't resist leaning in to kiss him. "I hope you had fun."

24

Eli

Is he joking? "You have no idea." More like it has blown my mind to bits and I will ride an orgasm high for days to come.

I slide my leg up between his thighs, subtle enough that it could be for comfort, not to get him worked up. He gives me a withering look as he does his best not to rub his hard cock against my thigh. The restraint causes a slight tremor to rock through his body.

"Eli." He's always so controlled. For once, I want to see it shatter completely. I want him to come undone in my hands like I've done in his every time. I slide my leg against the hot length again.

"What?" I ask, widening my eyes in innocence.

"I know what you're doing."

"Hmm…"

"This is about you, not me."

"Says who?" I sit up, pulling my towel off and straddling his waist.

He groans as he takes in my body. His hands dimpling my hips with the force of his hold as he grinds us together, his cock begging for attention. Jesus, that feels good. Our mouths clash, tongues fighting for dominance. I know he won't give in easily—it's not in his nature—but I need to push him. "Noah."

His hips buck, searching for more. "Hmm?" He stares at our cocks where they're touching.

"I need you inside me."

At my panting plea, he meets my gaze, biting his lower lip unconsciously. "Are you sure? That's…"

"Yes."

"Eli."

"I want you inside of me. To feel you as you come. I want your body on mine, any way you'll give it to me. I'm sure."

He assesses me, noting every rise and fall of my chest, every caress of my palm on his body. "Grab a condom and the lube from the nightstand."

I don't waste time, following Noah's command before it's fully formed. My hands fumble the handle of the drawer, my heart hammering, egging me on. I toss the condom at him and jump back on the bed.

He growls, "Put it on me."

I rip the packet open and grab his hard length, only struggling a bit as I roll it down his erection. Then, I put a generous amount of lube in my hand and give him a few more strokes. "You make me feel so powerful. Seeing how much you want me, it's so fucking sexy."

His eyes pop open, and a sweet smile crosses his face, crinkling the corners of his eyes. "I always want you." I can't help but wonder if his words mean more. They shouldn't. Best to ignore that for now.

He bucks his hips, impatience setting in. "Eli, stop teasing me, I can't take it anymore. Not if you want me inside you."

That deserves a wicked response. "I'm in control now." I give one last harsh tug before I lean down and capture his mouth for a bruising kiss.

I push onto my knees, straddle his waist, and line up his cock right at my hole. I sink down, but he pulls out and flips us, pinning me under his body.

I cry out, beyond frustrated. "Noah. Put your goddamn cock inside me."

He chuckles before sliding his fingers back into me, three all at once, and I feel a slight burn as heat creeps into my cheeks. The pleasure is all-consuming, my eyes falling shut to compensate for the overwhelming sensation. He isn't gentle fucking into me like he'll never get another chance. I try to pull at his hips in a last-ditch effort to get him inside me, but he won't budge. He leans close to my face before saying, "Look at me."

My eyes don't want to open. But slowly, almost painfully, I push them open. That devilish smile is back on his face. "Who's in charge?"

I let out a strangled cry. "Noah, please. It's too much. I need you."

"Who's in charge?"

"Fuck. You are. Always."

At my desperate plea, he finally removes his fingers and lines up his cock. "You're so good for me, babe." He leans down for a scorching kiss. "And so stretched, ready for me. Fucking gorgeous."

My heart races at the endearment. It's the second time he's called me that and it's doing weird things to me. I want to hear it more. I never want him to stop saying it. He joins our mouths again as he slowly eases into me. A small whimper falls from my lips, devoured by him. As if each noise is his to own. Fuck, he's so big. A slow burn builds as he pushes in inch by inch.

He notices, breaking our kiss to look down at me. "Hey, if this is too much, I can stop."

"No. Don't stop." I breathe in a lungful of air, then exhale, letting my body open for him. His words reassure me, though I already knew the truth. Noah would never hurt me.

He takes my cock in hand once more, working it over, causing the flush from my cheeks to travel lower. My neck, chest—everywhere is red for him.

Soon I'm bucking my hips, wanting and needing more of him. His tongue trails up my neck before nipping at my ear. "It's so sexy when you blush for me. And fuck if it's not sexier knowing every part of you does the same when I'm inside you."

"You're going to be the death of me."

Twisting down on my shaft, he thrusts forward one last time, completely seating his entire length inside of me. A slight pain grips me as I adjust to his size, but it fades as he jacks me off, lust shining bright in his dark blue eyes. I try to get some relief, to rut against his stomach, but he holds me down. "I think I like the sound of that."

He doesn't give me a chance to retort because he pulls out and slams back in, eliciting an embarrassingly loud moan as he quickens his pace. I grab his back, holding on as tight as I can before pulling him into a kiss.

He adjusts the position and starts pounding my prostate. "Oh. Oh, fuck. Noah." He hit it with his fingers before, but I've never felt anything quite like this. I'm making so many noises that I know I'll be embarrassed later, but I'm out of my mind enough not to care right now.

I dig my nails into his back as I spiral higher and higher. Moments later I slide my hands to his ass as I grind against him harder, leaving crescent shaped nail marks on his hot skin. I'm not going to last much longer. He feels too good, and he's hitting that spot just right. He seems to like my nails digging into him, and he surges into me with renewed force.

"*Me vengo*. Fuck, I'm coming, Noah." My orgasm rocks through me, over my stomach, and lands on Noah's chest, which sets off his own release as I pulse around him.

Thrusting a few more times, I feel him twitch before collapsing on top of me. He has just enough energy to roll us so I'm draped on top of him, all while his cock remains in my ass. The thought has my erection taking interest again, impossibly. How? This man does crazy things to me. I'm spent and yet I want so much more.

He must catch the movement because he groans. "Dear God. Haven't I worn you out?" I look up at his face, worried that he might be upset, but I only see a wide, sleepy grin on his face. He's teasing me.

I can't believe I'm about to say this. "Uh. Well. You are still inside me."

He cups my jaw with his hand. "I am. But unlike you, I'm an ancient man, and I can't go again yet."

"Yet? Again?" I ask hopefully.

Securing his hand around the condom, he pulls out of my body, and I feel the loss even while being sore. I roll off his side so he can sit up and throw it out. He walks to the bathroom and turns the faucet on. Then he's back, crawling onto the bed, pushing me back onto the pillows so he can wipe the come off my stomach.

"I can do that," I say. I reach for the towel, but he brushes my hand away before moving between my legs. He wipes up the lube, despite my mortification. "I, uh, can do this myself."

"You can, but I want to."

My face must look like a flaming red tomato. His tongue and fingers and cock were all just there… and I'm worried about him washing me. I know, priorities and all, but it feels excruciatingly intimate.

When he's done, he tosses the rag onto the nightstand. "Are you sore?"

I shrug. I am sore but not in a bad way. "Not much."

Giving me a nod, he lies back down and pulls me into his arms, my head resting on his chest. He pulls the covers over us as his other hand runs through the strands of my hair.

We lie there in silence, and it's the most peaceful I've felt in months. I never want to leave, though I know I should soon. With each moment that ticks by, the real world comes into focus. This was a rash decision. Not one that I regret, but coming to his house during the early evening when Angel could have been home was not smart.

Noah interrupts my racing mind. "I can hear your mind in motion. Penny for your thoughts?"

"I was thinking about how stupid of a decision it was to come here unannounced. I should have called beforehand. Or done something other than show up on your doorstep. What if Angel was still in the house?" He stays quiet, so I continue. "But I don't regret the decision. It was amazing. I had to see you."

He slides his other hand over my body until he reaches my arm, lightly squeezing it. "It was a very nice surprise. Why did you have to see me?"

"I saw your note." I add for clarification, "In your books."

The hand that's brushing through my hair stutters before picking up where it left off. "I see," he says.

"I hope his story ends happily."

He turns my chin up so that I'm looking at him, his features unreadable. "That depends."

"On what?"

The pad of his thumb traces along my lower lip before gliding across my cheek as if he's trying to remember every part of my face.

I run my hand down his chest in response, leaving my hand below his navel in his happy trail. I wait for an answer, feeling a vise grip around my. Suddenly, it feels like the most important thing in the world to know the answer.

He changes the subject. "I hope you don't regret this. What happened between us."

Those weren't the words I expected or wanted to hear, and disappointment ripples through me. Maybe I read this wrong. Was Noah not talking about me when he wrote that note? Was I wrong in thinking he believed I was all those things… that I could be his hope? That he wanted our story to end happily. But, no matter how many times we sleep together, how many times we give in, this will always have to end. And it won't be happy. There's no reality where we end up together. It might be easier if he didn't mean it.

I hold him tighter, determined to drop the subject. "No, I don't regret this."

25

I wake in increments, my mind fuzzy and slow to function, only noticing how hot it is in my room. I throw the covers off, trying to get a cool breeze from the small AC unit that seems like it's not working. The motion causes me to shift and I wince as a dull throb hits me. Noah. Last night. The memories come flooding back and I groan as my morning wood intensifies. I stretch to assess the rest of my body and my hand hits something solid. At my touch, it seems to shift closer. Rolling over, I pop an eye open and promptly bolt upright.

Shit. I fell asleep at Noah's. How the hell did I let that happen? My rustling must wake him because a moment later he's staring up at me, happiness written in the lines of his face. "Morning."

"Hi." I can't help the giant grin that spreads across my face. He's being sweet, and I can put my freakout to the side to tell him good morning.

His eyes rove my body, which makes me acutely aware that I'm fully naked, the sheet barely covering my painfully hard erection.

That absolutely cannot be the focus this morning. On top of leaving my phone at the dorm, and who knows how many messages from my parents, the likelihood that Angel is home is very high. To highlight my point, down the hall, I hear a cabinet bang on its hinges before thundering feet move down the hall.

Chinga. She's not coming to his room, is she? I scramble off the bed, and Noah follows suit, running to his dresser to grab clothes. I look for my own but only seem to find my pants. "Noah, where's my shirt?"

He pauses, glancing around. "Bathroom?"

I race in there, closing the door as he gets his shirt on in time to hear Angel yell from the other side of the door. "Dad."

I also don't have my boxer briefs, but I'm past caring. I yank my pants up, not wanting to be naked while I hear Angel whining from the other side of the door.

What the hell are we going to do? This is bad. I rest my head against the bathroom door, listening. If this is going to happen again, we need to be a lot smarter about it.

The bedroom door clicks open, and I hear Noah's voice, muffled through the wall. "Hi, sweetheart. What's up?"

"There is no food in this house. I thought you said you were going to go grocery shopping yesterday. I'm starving." Oops, that's probably my fault. Not sorry.

"Yeah, I sat down to write after I finished my workout, expecting to spend ten minutes on it, and I ended up losing track of time. Sorry, honey."

I can't see her, so I can't say with any certainty, but I bet she's rolling her eyes right now. "I don't need excuses. What am I going to do about food? I'm so hungry I might die."

"How about I take you out to breakfast? Then we can go grocery shopping together. You're always saying how I don't pick the right things for you." How did I ever think it was a good idea to date her? She's such an asshole to her dad.

I hold my breath, waiting to hear her response. It's a fifty-fifty chance she will say no. "I'll go to breakfast as long as I get to pick the spot."

"Of course."

"Also, my boss is being a real bitch. She's making me increase my hours from once a week. So I'm going to have to go into the store on Tuesdays and Fridays now. Are you sure I can't quit the job? Working at a nail salon cleaning up all that shit is so nasty."

"Angel." I hear the reprimand in his tone. "Do you not want money to go out with your friends? Do you want to pay to get your nails done yourself?"

She scoffs. "No."

"Then you should probably work it out with your boss. I'm going to jump in the shower real quick. I'll meet you by the car in fifteen."

"Whatever."

I hear the door close, then Noah's standing in the bathroom doorway looking troubled. I open my mouth to say something, offer some support, when he silences me with a soft kiss. Then he walks to the shower, turning it on. "I am so sorry about that. I was going to wake you up last night but then I fell asleep. You're not mad, are you?"

"No. It wasn't your fault. I'm just glad she agreed and we can sneak me out of here."

"Your car isn't out front?"

"I parked a few blocks away."

He strips out of his shirt and shorts before turning away from me, my whole body lighting with interest. This man is so fucking sexy. I wince as I take in his back. "I scratched the shit out of you. Sorry."

He steps under the water, droplets cascading down his body. He must be trying to kill me. Again. He smiles lazily as the water pelts him. "I'm not sorry. It was hot."

And there's my blush again. Thank God he likes it because it's embarrassing as hell to me. I grasp the counter behind me, forcing myself to stay rooted to the spot. His cock grows under my attention and I groan.

"Can I see you again?" he asks.

"I'd like that."

He opens his mouth to say something, but closes it, running his hands over his body to rid it of soap instead.

"Good." He shuts the water off and wraps a towel around his waist.

"I don't think you could get rid of me if you tried."

He makes his way over, crowding my space. "Well, it's a good thing the only things I want to try involve making you come."

I swallow. "Jesus. You can't say stuff like that when you have to leave."

His mouth takes mine in a wet, heated kiss. Too soon, he pulls back, but not before he takes the time to run his thumb over my bottom lip. "So perfect. I wish I could stay."

***

Back at the dorm, I check my phone and sigh in relief when I don't see any messages from my parents. I head to the shower, feeling the grime still on me from the night before.

Once I'm clean and back in my room, I see a message flash across the screen from Vi asking what I'm up to. I let her know I'm headed to the library to finish a paper, and she asks to tag along.

Thirty minutes later, we're seated at a table in a private conference room that I reserved, two steaming cups of coffee in front of us courtesy of Vi's job. We work quietly, only commenting on something every once in a while.

"Hey. I've been kinda distracted lately, if you couldn't tell. I almost forgot to ask, how are things going between you and Cade?"

She flops over the back of the chair, letting out a devastated sigh. "They aren't. After that party when we went back to my place I tried to kiss him. He told me no. He said he wanted to get to know me a little better. But come on, I was looking for fun, not another serious relationship. So I found a random hookup on campus. And it's been fine. We haven't talked much, which is fine."

Clearly it was not fine at all. "Why the dramatics then?"

She doesn't bother denying it. "'Cause I still like him. He's sweet. But now he's doing his best to friendzone me. Really though, it's like, I don't want a guy friend, I'm not looking for a serious relationship, so what's the point? I'm in college, I should have fun."

"I don't know. If that's what you want then, I guess. Just because Tom was a dick doesn't mean every guy will treat you the same way."

"We dated for a year. I shouldn't be seriously dating so soon after, right?"

I shrug not knowing what to say. She may differ from me, but I don't feel any sort of obligation to Angel anymore. "It might be time to move on. He certainly doesn't deserve your consideration. It's up to you."

"You're right." She changes the subject. "Does that mean this mystery girl has snatched you up and you're dating now?"

"What?"

"The sudden insight into moving on. Have you moved on? Is that why you're being all optimistic and shit?"

I don't want to lie to Vi. It doesn't seem right, but there's no simple answer to that question. "I'm not dating anyone, it's just a hookup." The words taste bitter.

"You want it to be more?"

My knee-jerk reaction is to say no. It's what I should say and the only reasonable answer because it won't go anywhere. It can't. "I don't know. Whether or not I want it, there's an expiration date."

"Do I know her?"

Shit. "You don't know them." This is getting way too personal. Avoid, avoid. "I need to go to the bathroom. I'll be back."

I run away like a coward, as if she'll drop it when I get back. I hate lying to her, she's my best friend, but no one can know. What if she looks at me differently? I couldn't stand it. I run water over my face and try to collect myself. Looking in the mirror, my eyes look crazed, my hair only adding to the madman look. Ugh.

When I feel confident enough that I won't fall apart, I make my way back to the table. Vi is staring down at her screen and I can't tell if she's upset or giving me space. Either way, she doesn't wait long. She leans over, grabbing my hand, and whispers. "Do I know him or them?"

Damn it. "What?"

"I'm sorry. I just realized. Every time I asked about 'her', you said them."

I feel my stomach drop as I stare at Vi.

She sees my face and it must look concerning. "Hey. No. It's okay, Eli." She moves to the seat next to me and takes my hand in hers. "I shouldn't have asked. It's not my business."

I swivel in my chair, praying that no one else is around to hear this conversation. When it's all clear, I continue, my words halting, "Do I, uh, um, do I seem… that way?"

Her brows scrunch up. "What way?"

"Like, um, into, not women. Is there something about me? Do I scream… you know, that?"

"No. Not that there would be anything wrong if you did. You just didn't say she. I assumed, and I was wrong."

I squeeze her hand, a lifeline keeping me tethered. "And… if I was… into someone who wasn't female? A, um, guy."

"I'd say you're still you, and you're still my best friend. You just also like guys."

My voice goes quieter still. I watch our hands, unable to meet her eyes. "You don't hate me? Think differently of me?"

"Hey. Will you look at me?" She waits, and I know her well enough to know that she won't budge until I do. I peek through my lashes first, only seeing concern, no hate or disgust. It's a relief and makes the muscles in my shoulders relax, if only incrementally. I meet her steady gaze with a little less trepidation as she says, "I do not hate you and I don't think differently of you. I'm sorry I pushed it instead of letting you come out on your own terms. That wasn't cool of me."

"I wouldn't have." The words hold more conviction than I mean them to and she flinches, making me wince. I didn't mean to hurt her. It has nothing to do with her and everything to do with me. How others might see me.

"Then I'm even more sorry that I forced it."

I rub my hand along the back of my neck, hoping to ease the tension from my muscles. "Sorry, I didn't mean it like that. It's not because of you. Are you sure you're okay with it?"

"Yes."

"Why?"

"Well, I should hope I'd be okay with it. I'm bisexual. I was worried about how everyone would look at me too, at first. But love is love. It's beautiful when there's more of it in the world. We already have too much hate. Who cares who it's with as long as there's goodness and love?"

"My parents."

Understanding lights her eyes. "I see. Is that why they were trying to force you to get back together with Angel?"

I shrug. She's not the first person who's thought that. I can't exactly ask them, though. "See what I mean about the relationship being doomed? I can't be this way, so eventually it will have to end."

She pulls me in for a hug. "Eli, that's not… You can't choose this. It's part of who you are. You can't turn it off like a light switch."

"Well, we're not serious, anyway. And I dated Angel. I'll find another girl to like. I just need to get him out of my system. That's what we're both doing, anyway." The thought sends a stabbing pain to my heart, but I continue, committed to showing how unaffected I am. "Maybe we can help each other. I'll be your wingman, you my wingwoman, and we'll find different people. No Cade, and no No… my person."

Her skepticism is obvious. She doesn't believe me, but that's okay. Noah and I will have fun, as promised. No strings attached. When it's done, I'll find a girl and be happy with her.

"Fine. Tell me about this hookup. You said I don't know him. What's he look like?" She wiggles her brows, lightening the mood.

"I don't know. A person?"

"Oh, come on. Give me more than that. What's he like? Is he a student on campus?"

The questions loosen me up, making me certain we'll be okay. Vi loves to tease me, and if she's doing it now that means she doesn't look at me differently. I know she said she's bi, but it's different for men, right? Or is it? I don't know. I shift, getting comfortable again now that I know she's okay with it.

The change in position reminds me of last night, the dull ache surfacing, and I feel wicked delight from the fact. If Vi is okay with it, and Carmen, maybe it's not something I should be ashamed about.

Noah treats me well and I feel good when I'm with him. Maybe I can just enjoy it for what it is, for however long he's willing to have me. "Okay, okay. He's not a student.

He's a bit older. Vi, honestly, he's perfect. I've never had someone make me feel as good as he does by just being around. He makes me laugh and when I'm with him I feel cherished, protected. We have so much fun. And the sex…" My eyes widen, I did not mean to mention that part.

"Damn, Eli. Lucky bastard. The sex is so good you're speechless?" She fans herself dramatically. "If only you could send some of those good vibes my way."

I lean in. "He's so sexy too. Abs and biceps and shoulder muscles and his ass. Oh my God, his ass."

"Fuck, I think you have a bit of drool right there." She motions at the corner of my mouth and I smack her arm playfully.

"Smartass."

"I think I might have a little drool too. Mind sharing?"

"Ha, ha. You are hilarious." I know she's joking, but something deep in my bones screams "mine."

Clueless to my possessive thoughts, she continues. "So what's wrong with him? He wouldn't be worth coming out for? Sounds like you like him a lot, among his many other sizable qualities." She winks at me then holds her hands a centimeter apart, slowly widening the gap. They widen until they are beyond her shoulders before giving me a dirty look and starting again. Oh sweet lord, is she trying to ask how big his dick is?

I swat her hands away. "I'm already regretting telling you. Did you seriously ask me how big"—I lower my voice more—"his dick is?"

"I did. Yeah. I gotta live vicariously."

"Please, you said you're hooking up with people on campus. I'd say you're doing plenty of living."

She sighs and leans back against her chair. "Yeah, but I don't have feelings for any of them. Not that I really want that. But sometimes it makes it better."

My smile slowly drops. Feelings? No, it can't be that obvious. I need to get anything I feel for him in check. Neither of us can get attached to more than each other's body. And even that only for a short while. We're just extremely attracted to each other and using one another. That's all. "We don't have feelings for each other. It's completely no strings."

She eyeballs me, not saying a single word, and I squirm in my seat. A devious tilt to her lips signals her victory over me. "Is it fun living in denial?"

"You're frustrating."

"But you love me."

"No."

She pushes my arm. "See, complete denial of all feelings. It's okay. You can't be both pretty and smart all the time."

"Hey." I flip her off. She's such a smartass, but she's the same smartass she's always been and it's comforting. I wouldn't have made it through the last few months without her and I'm glad she's the first person I told about Noah, even if I didn't use his name. "In all seriousness though, you're okay with it?"

Her smile turns softer. "Yeah, Eli. I'm more than okay with it. I'm happy someone is making you happier. Can I meet him?"

"That wouldn't be in the spirit of keeping things casual."

"Mmm, I don't think I like that answer."

"I didn't think you would. Also, I'm okay with it too. I know you didn't ask, and I'm sure you don't need the reassurance because you're a badass… but I do love you. Just the way you are."

She shoves my shoulder, giving me a beautiful, wide smile. "Obviously. What's not to like?" She winks, sassy as ever, before speaking again. "All jokes aside, thanks, Eli. It's always nice to have people in your corner. And I know we have each other's backs."

"Definitely."

26

Eli

Noah and I fall into a rhythm as summer school ends, our time opening up significantly. I've been preemptive with my parents, offering to babysit twice a week now that classes are out and attending church and family dinner on Sundays. What they don't know is that my RA is letting me stay on campus without telling the university. He said it was the least he could do after the whole Tom debacle and not getting him kicked off the floor. That means more free time for me and I'm loving it.

That also means more time for Noah. He's spending most of his time writing, except for the days when Angel is out of the house. She leaves around ten in the morning and doesn't get back until seven every Tuesday and Friday. Those are our days.

Unfortunately, all of our schedules will change soon. The school year is fast approaching and I'm not ready for it. Something about it seems so final. And right now, it's perfect. Or nearly. The only thing getting under my skin is Carmen, who still tries to call every day. I haven't called her back, but I know I need to. I want to talk to her but something's holding me back.

This thing with Noah, it's exactly what I need. It's Tuesday afternoon, and I'm lying in his bed, the sheet draped over my waist. He's out in the kitchen, making us paninis. He'd thoroughly fucked me and I wasn't able to string enough words together to tell him I needed a minute. Thankfully, he picked up on my daze, gave me a kiss, and told me he was going to get me food. I think I sighed internally. It might have been out loud.

I pull out my laptop to put a show on, our routine consisting of sex, food, watching TV, and hopefully more sex. Each time, one of us picks the show, and it's been fun arguing about which is better and why.

He walks into the room balancing a couple of plates on one arm, with two water bottles and a bag of chips clutched in the other. I stop to appreciate the rippling muscles and low-slung gray sweatpants, my eyes trailing the V cut off from my sight by the low rise of his pants. It's hands down the hottest thing I've ever seen. Everything about him is.

I kneel on the bed, reaching out for the plates to help lighten the burden and he watches me with fire in his eyes. "Fuck, I love coming back in here and seeing you naked, babe. Like you belong in my bed." He's also taken to calling me that whenever I'm around. Neither of us has mentioned it, but I can't imagine him calling me anything else. I like it. A lot.

"I love you feeding me while I get to lie here, naked, in your bed." The sassy remark makes him smirk, so I smack a kiss on his mouth, careful not to upset the food. He comes around to his side of the bed and strips out of his sweats, crawling under the covers.

I hit play on the screen as we sit side by side, eating sandwiches. It has turkey, mozzarella, fresh tomato, and basil as well, and it's currently giving me life after Noah tried to kill me with his cock. I moan, relishing the first bite. "This is exactly what I needed."

Noah chuckles, before leaning over and rifling through his pants on the ground. He produces two napkins and hands one to me. I scoff. "It's like you think I'm a messy eater or something."

He pokes me right between the ribs, where he knows I'm ticklish. I drop the sandwich onto the plate, frantically swatting his hand away, but that only eggs him on. "That's because I know you're a messy eater."

"No! Oh, fuck. Stop. That's… so… ah-ha-ha… Stop." I cry out, trying to get away from his grasp, but he tightens his hold. He does it a few more times but finally relents. He pulls me close to his side again as he munches on a few chips. "Really? Gonna just act like you weren't torturing me? Everything is fine, just eating chips over here."

"Yep. Pretty much."

I flip him off and that only makes his smile grow. "I already did that, babe."

"Fucking comedian." I suddenly hear a phone vibrate. "Do you hear that?"

He tilts his head, listening for the sound. He pauses the movie, and the noise gets louder. I usually leave mine on campus to be safe. I wouldn't want my location tracked here. So it can't be mine.

"Is that your phone?" he asks.

"I rarely bring mine."

He walks over to his dresser and picks up his phone. "Not mine." He shows me the black screen as proof.

I couldn't have brought mine with me. I search through my bag and find it empty. The room goes silent as the missed call ends. It rings again, making my heart drop. That has to be mine. I scramble to my clothes, and sure enough, I find it in the pocket of my jeans. I turn the screen to face me and see Carmen's number pop up.

"Everything okay?" he asks.

I shrug then power down the phone. "Yeah."

"You sure?"

"No."

He nods his head as if he understands. I wish he would shine some light on it for me because I don't. I've forgiven her in my head. After that talk with Adriana, I did some soul searching and realized my being angry at her wouldn't fix anything. She's human, and she stuck up for someone she loved. It's not like she wanted to leave my siblings.

Our parents didn't give her much of a choice. But after how ungrateful I've been, what do I say?

He walks over to me, resting his arms on my shoulders, pulling me close. "Do you want to talk about it?"

"Maybe. I don't know. I don't want to bother you."

He tips my chin up so that I have to meet his gaze. "You could never be a bother. My ears are at your disposal. Well, anything of mine is at your disposal, but especially my ears." He emphasizes the comment with a salacious grin.

I crack up, which seems to make him happy. He kisses my cheek, then the corner of my mouth, and finally my lips.

Kissing him back, I disengage from his arms so that I can steal a pair of shorts. If I'm going to talk about this, I definitely need to be dressed. He seems to get the message because he shuffles over to the bed, slipping his own pants on.

We sit down again, Noah propped against the headboard, and I curl into his side, seeking comfort and avoiding direct eye contact. Somehow it seems easier to say if he can't see me. I talk. I tell him who called, and all about how I thought she abandoned my siblings when we were younger. How mad it made me to know that she could just leave us.

Then the night of the fight where she came back into my life. How poorly I'd treated her, how she told me she wanted a relationship with me again. And how we talked on the phone that one night, my panic attack, and how she was there for me. Again.

And now, I haven't answered a single call. "I've forgiven her for abandoning them. I understand it wasn't her fault… but, I've sent such mixed signals. What if she's calling to tell me she's done trying? She might walk out again."

Unwanted emotions clog my throat, threatening to spill from my eyes. Shit, the last thing I need to do is cry in front of Noah. Who does that? He didn't sign up for a weepy hook up. I sniff, then clear my throat, trying to hide the sound.

He readjusts us, tightening his grip around my body, showing me silent support. "Is this a listening problem, or a solving problem?"

My brows pinch. What an odd question. "What?"

"I'm more than happy listening, Eli, but do you want me to share what I'm thinking too?"

I bury my face in his chest, inhaling his scent. It goes a long way to calm me, enough to prepare me for this conversation. "I want you to be honest with me."

I feel him shift as he acknowledges my statement with a tilt of the head, before pressing a light kiss over my curls. "I think you're mad on behalf of your siblings. You're right about that, but you're more upset because she left you. When you needed her the most, trying to figure out who you were going to be, she wasn't there to guide you or offer support. And you're worried if you truly give her a chance, if you let her in, she'll leave you again. Or she won't like who she sees if you do. It's not about you being ungrateful, you just want her around, and you're afraid of making her leave because some part of you feels like you did in the first place."

The words, falling from his lips, seem so simple. As if they were sitting in front of my face this whole time, shining in bright neon lights, screaming, "Hello, idiot. Obviously this is how you're feeling." The simplicity stuns me into silence.

"Babe?"

I sit up so that I can look at him. "How do you make the most complicated feelings I have seem so simple? For weeks I've been trying to figure out why, and there it is. Summed up in a few sentences."

"Well, unfortunately, I have experience with something similar. Did I upset you?"

I lean forward and kiss him, lacing his fingers with mine, offering my support, for what it's worth. "No. Not at all. Thanks for listening to me."

"Do you know what you're going to do about it?"

"I'm going to tell her what you said. That's how I'm feeling. I'm afraid I'm going to lose her again and I don't know how I'm going to get past it, but I'm willing to try if she is. I wouldn't think about it this much if I didn't want her in my life. She left me. I am mad about that." I pause, really thinking about it. "She didn't want to, and she's trying to fix it now. I should forgive her."

"Good."

"You make everything better. Thank you."

His gaze drops like he's embarrassed. "Same to you."

Conversation over, we snuggle under the covers and finish the episode we started. Normally, we'd start fooling around again, but this time we lounge in the bed, talking about anything and everything.

He tells me about the time he went on a ski trip with Tony and Beth. The disastrous outcome, Tony knocking himself out with a ski, cementing Noah's resolve to never try again. Or the time I went on a day trip white water rafting with the university and saved some girl from falling in. I'd caught her life jacket by hooking my finger into the end of the strap, reacting on instinct. We talk about how we take our coffee. I drink mine black. He likes a lot of frothed milk, a double shot of espresso, one pump of vanilla, and a little sugar, which sounds nasty.

We talk about so much that I easily lose track of time, happy to be in this moment with him forever. Too soon, six o'clock arrives, so I get dressed and we make our way to the front door. Each time I leave, it gets harder. I want to stay with him again, wake up in his arms, get those lazy, wonderful morning kisses.

He holds me in his arms when we get to the front door. "I don't want you to go." His words mirror my thoughts, and it makes the ache worse.

"I don't want to either."

"Classes start next week," he adds.

"How are we going to see each other?"

He kisses me, the movement desperate, like he won't get another chance. Too soon, he breaks away. "We'll figure it out. I promise."

27

Eli

I sit on my bed and power my phone back on, staring at the notification that says I have a missed call from my sister. It's long past due that I reach out, but I want to talk to her face-to-face, on neutral ground. And I might need backup to make sure I don't chicken out. I text Vi, asking if she works at the coffee shop tomorrow.

> Vi: Yeah, 1–5. Why?
>
> Eli: I'm going to need you to force me to sit down and talk to my sister. But I don't have enough faith that I won't go running before she shows up.
>
> Vi: Well, I'll be there. You sure you want to do it in public?
>
> Eli: Yeah. It'll help me freak out less. I don't need the same thing happening to me as last time.
>
> Vi: Ok, see you tomorrow, bud.

I like her message, then pull up my sister's number. I click to connect, thanking Noah for making me brave enough to make this call. It rings once before the call connects.

"Eli?" Her voice is unsure, and a little worried.

"Hey, Carmen."

"Are you okay?"

I nod my head, then remember she can't see me. "Yeah. Yeah, I'm fine. I'm ready to talk. Would you be willing to meet me on campus tomorrow? If you have the time."

"I have the time," she responds immediately, almost tripping over her words. "Where at?"

"The coffee shop, attached to the bookstore."

She hums in confirmation. "I remember where it is. What time?"

"Four?"

"I'll be there."

I hesitate. Should I say more? Does she want to say more? I pull the phone away from my ear and look at it like it might have answers. None appear. "Thanks, Carmen. I know I haven't been easy the last few months."

"You don't need to thank me, *hermano*. I'll see you tomorrow."

The phone disconnects and I lie back, sending a text to Noah. We normally try to keep the texting to a minimum—not that Angel would care enough about her dad's life to look at his phone.

> Eli: I did it. I called her. I'm going to meet her tomorrow to talk about it.

Noah: That's amazing!

Seconds later the three dots pop up again, and I wait for the second message to come. It happens twice more without a message, so I decide to respond.

Eli: Thanks, I asked her to meet me at the coffee shop near the bookstore at four.
Noah: I could be there at another table, offering moral support.

I re-read the message three times. He… he would do that for me? God, I want to say yes. It feels like I need him there more than anything, but wouldn't that be crossing the boundaries we put in place? He's not meant to be that for me.

Eli: No, I couldn't ask you to do that. That's very nice of you but I'm sure you're busy. I wouldn't want to take up more of your time.
Noah: If you don't want me there, that's ok too.
Eli: No, I didn't mean it like that. I don't want you to feel like you're obligated because of… well, you know.

Whatever we're doing. Casual sex doesn't seem to describe it anymore, but neither does friends with benefits.

Noah: Well, good luck tomorrow, Eli. I'm sure the conversation will go well.
Noah: Feel free to text me after, if you want.

I can't tell if he's upset. The words are nice. There's no hint of tone. But I feel like there's more I should be reading. It's not him, though. I'm the one who needs these barriers in place, I need to stick to our plan of light and easy, no strings. He's older and more experienced than I am.

I'm sure he's good at putting boundaries in place and blurring them without feelings getting involved. I haven't learned how to do that yet. I… I don't want to nurse a broken heart, even if I might be on my way there already. So, boundaries it is.

***

I arrive at the coffee shop ten minutes early the next day and I'm already dreading it. My palms are sweaty, and no matter how many times I rub them on my jeans, the sheen sticks. I glance around, looking for Carmen, but I don't see her yet.

While I'm looking, I notice Noah is nowhere to be found. I try my best not to be disappointed. I hop in line behind a couple clinging to one another's sides. They take ages to order, but finally step away to wait for their coffee. Vi stands there, giving me a sympathetic look. "How are you feeling?"

"Like I want to throw up. Thanks for asking."

That gets a snort of laughter from her, which helps lighten things. "You know, I can't imagine it will be that bad. She clearly wants to spend time with you, Eli." While she talks, she enters my usual coffee order.

A few weeks ago, Noah made me try his sickly-sweet concoction and a clingy, needy part of me takes over. I need his comfort, even if he's not here. "Actually, Vi. I want to get something other than my usual." These are boundaries, right?

"What?" Her complete shock is obvious.

"Dark roast with frothed milk, double shot of espresso, a pump of vanilla, and a little sugar?"

She blinks at me a few times before entering the order and writing it on a cup for the barista making the drinks. "That drink sounds familiar."

"It's, um, his drink."

She quirks a brow. "Mr. No Strings? His drink? You have it so bad it's sickeningly sweet, just like that coffee order."

"It's coffee, Vi. I think you're reading into things too much." I'm a fucking liar.

"Mhmm. Sure."

Before I get the chance to respond, Vi's gaze sharpens over my shoulder, so I glance back and see Carmen step forward. She gives me a tentative smile, so I motion for her to come up to the counter. "Hey, I put my order in but I haven't paid yet. Get whatever you want."

Her smile grows a little. "Oh, thanks." She looks at Vi. "Hi, Violet."

"Carmen. It's nice to see you again under better circumstances."

My sister looks between us, a shy expression crossing her face. Something out of place for her. "I hope it is."

Order placed, we grab a seat at a booth in the back corner. I'm able to see the entire shop from my seat, but it's secluded enough that we'll be able to talk without being overheard. It's not extremely crowded since most students aren't on campus yet.

"Eli, I'm glad you asked me to meet you."

Butterflies erupt in my stomach at her words. Should I be this nervous? This is my sister, and she says she wants to be a part of my life. I give a terse nod, unable to find the right thing to say.

Vi walks up with our drinks, putting mine down first, then Carmen's. As Carmen tells Vi thank you, the door opens, catching my attention. Noah steps through the doors looking tantalizing in his usual on-campus professor garb—nice black slacks and a button-up shirt—hair tamed except for a single brown curl falling into his eyes.

Observing me, Vi follows my gaze to the door, her eyes going comically wide. She turns to me, waiting for my reaction. We may have spent that night at the plaza with Noah and his friends, but she probably still worries it's weird for me. If only she knew.

When I say nothing, she asks, "Should I get rid of him?"

I glance at him again and he's trying his hardest not to watch us. He moves to the front of the line, where Vi should be taking his order. I shake my head. "No, we're cool. Besides, you can't kick a customer out, Vi." That seems like the lamest response, but what else can I say? That's my boyfriend, Noah? Surprise.

I pause, startled. Boyfriend? Where did that come from? This is a no-feelings zone. Besides, I have another pressing matter and she's sitting in front of me watching this exchange with a scrutinizing gaze.

Vi looks back at me. "I can do what I want. And if that's getting rid of people you don't want here, I'll do it." We both know that's not true, but I appreciate that she's looking out for me.

She hesitates for another moment, but makes her way back to the counter. She calls over her shoulder, "Let me know if you two need anything else."

I can't seem to look away from him. I told him I would be fine, that I didn't want to bother him, but he came anyway, knowing how much I needed him here. It tightens something in my chest, making it hard to look away.

He smiles at me, a quick, private thing, and all the nervous energy I had fades. Carmen sits there, assessing me, so I clear my throat, hoping to start this conversation. "I asked you to meet me because I had something important to talk about and I didn't feel like we could do it over the phone."

"Okay." Her voice sounds wary, afraid of what I'll say next. Though I don't enjoy hearing the uncertainty in her voice, it brings a calm rationality to my thoughts. Maybe she's as nervous as I am.

"I realized I was afraid to let you back into my life."

She opens her mouth, but I rush on. If I can't get it all out now, I'll never say it. "No, please. I need to say it in one go. I don't want to chicken out." She tilts her head, then motions for me to continue.

I tap my fingers on the tabletop, take a sip of the sickeningly sweet drink and it calms me. This is something I can do. "I am mad that you left our siblings. But I wouldn't let myself think about how betrayed I felt that you left me. I was fifteen, all alone, trying to navigate the world outside our home. Mom and Dad put all the responsibility on you, and I didn't realize that until you left and I had to fill that void.

"One day, I had a sister who loved me, and the next, I was the oldest, responsible for all the younger kids, and my sister was gone, and I was told she never wanted to speak to me again. I know that's not your fault, you shouldn't have to feel guilty for that. But." I swallow, trying to fight back tears. "I lost you and I had to learn how to do it all on my own. To cope, I buried anything and everything I needed to. I'd do anything to be the brother they need, even if I'm too distant sometimes. I'm still mad I had to do it on my own. You were the only one I talked to when we were younger. I thought you would understand and be there for me when no one else was.

"The worst part is, when you came back and you told me you loved me, I didn't know if you were being honest. If you could even answer honestly. You say you want to be in my life, but you don't know who I am anymore. What if you don't like who I've become? What if Mom and Dad have gotten so inside my head that everything you hated about them is everything within me? I can't lose you again. I won't. What I need to know is that I have a sister who will love every part of me even if I don't love every part of myself. Especially when I don't love every part of myself."

My words trail off, everything feeling like it's too much. I told her I'm still mad at her, and I don't know how to get over it. Who in their right mind would want to deal with that? She's going to decide this isn't worth it, turn around, and walk out. I'm preparing for her to do just that, focusing on the cup sleeve instead of her reaction. I don't know if I can handle rejection again.

Her fingers twitch, as if she wants to reach out for my hand but thinks better of it. Instead, she mimics my movements, pulling the sleeve off her cup and worrying it in her hands. "Thank you for telling me. I know my word isn't good enough, but I hope you give me a chance. If you do, I'll do my best to show you I want to be in your life, how much I still love you, and that you will always, always have that, unconditionally. For who you are. And I hope someday, you'll be able to do the same. I'm not perfect, and I won't pretend to be. I know there will be things I'll do that will piss you off, there are things you'll do that will piss me off, but you have a safe place with me, Eli. Full stop. No conditions."

I grab her hand in mine and give it a light squeeze. "I believe you. Maybe we can start with phone calls and getting together for coffee or lunch once a week?"

"I would love that. Can I give you a hug?"

The tears seem to threaten again, so I stand up and bury her in my arms. The conversation turns lighter as we chat for a few minutes, simple things to get reacquainted after all this time apart. She tells me more about her roommate from college, Jess, who she still lives with. I tell her about Vi and school. I want to tell her about Noah, badly. And, as if his name alone controls me, I glance at the table he's taken. He has his laptop open, working on something, but it's like he can feel the heat of my gaze, he glances up, locking those beautiful, stormy blue eyes on mine. Warmth tickles my skin as it flushes under his appraisal, and I know I have to look away, but it feels impossible.

He grins, the lines around his eyes crinkling, then turns back to his work, releasing me from the spell he had me under. And I blurt out, "I'm bisexual. Or gay. I don't know." I'm so fucking obvious it makes me sick. She turns back to me, having followed my line of sight.

"Is that an ex?"

My brows furrow, before replaying the conversation Vi and I had about Noah. I suppose that assumption would make the most sense. I think about playing dumb, like she didn't just catch us staring. Obviously, that won't put us on the best foot to start over. Would telling her about my thing with Noah be better than flat out refusing to tell her? "Uh, no." Simple. Perfect answer.

"But you know him?"

"I do."

She sighs, exasperated with my one-word answers. "Eli."

"Carmen," I say back, mocking her.

"Who is he?"

"Aren't you going to ask me about the fact I told you I'm bisexual or gay? Like actually said the words out loud. That's now the second time. Ever." God, never thought I'd use my first official coming out as an excuse to get out of talking about something else uncomfortable.

"Sure. I'll ask about that. Are you bi-horny for that guy, whoever he is?"

I sputter, my eyes widening and my mouth flopping open. Her face is a perfect picture of amusement as I continue to stutter. My sister literally said the word bi-horny to me. "Did you seriously say that?"

"I did. 'Cause I think it's true."

I groan and slouch in my seat. "You are as bad as Violet."

She only smiles, not taking the bait. I sober, leaving the joking behind. Even if she's fine with me being bi—and I will definitely have a freak out about finally admitting that out loud later—confessing about Noah… It's a minefield. "If I said I don't want to tell you who that is?"

She senses my change of mood. "I would say that I'll stop asking, but you can trust me. I'm obviously not in a place to judge. After how I left you, all our siblings. No, I'm not here to judge. You're an adult and you can make your own decisions. That's true about talking to me or choosing who to date."

I don't think our parents would agree with that sentiment. "He's not my boyfriend."

"Okay."

"I don't know what we're doing." It's like I can't stop myself. When did today become spill my guts day? Every pent-up emotion and secret spilling from my mouth feels cathartic, but scary.

Her head tilts to the side. "Do you want him to be your boyfriend?"

"We're casual."

"That didn't answer my question."

"It would never work."

"You have feelings for him."

"How are you doing this? I don't talk to anyone about anything." Except for Noah, I almost add. I peek at his table again, and he must feel it because he turns to me again. This time, a small frown plays at his mouth when he looks at her, then me. Carmen catches him and gestures to come over.

I lean over the table and swat her hand down. "No, Vi doesn't know and she can't know."

"Why?"

I lower my voice. "That's my ex-girlfriend's father, and one of Violet's English professors."

She keeps her expression neutrally blank, and it's somewhat disconcerting how well she plays it off. The only sign that she's surprised is that she stops fighting my hand where it's pinning hers down. The silence stretches on as I wait for her to say something. This can't be good. I already scared her off.

"Say something, please."

She scrunches her face, like she's debating what to say. "That's not what I was expecting. That's… complicated."

"You don't approve."

"It's not for me to approve or disapprove, Eli. I meant it when I said I'm not going to judge you."

"You made a face."

"Only because I can imagine you've been freaking out about it all."

"I didn't cheat on her."

She grabs my hand across the table, both of us needing the confirmation of touch. Until Noah, it wasn't something I thought I needed, but it always seems to settle whatever turmoil I feel. She does the same now. "No, she cheated on you. I remember you telling me about that. Want to talk about how you two started dating?"

"We used to talk whenever I would wait for Angel. We always had a lot in common. He also listened to me. As you well know, that doesn't happen a lot with our family. It didn't happen with Angel either. And his mind is brilliant. He's an author—one of my favorites. He creates whole worlds with diverse characters, breathtaking landscapes… Just, such beautiful stories. I've always admired him. It was hard after the breakup because it felt like I lost more than Angel.

"I went to get my stuff one day, and he apologized for what she did and told me I deserved better. He was being friendly. He always is because he's a good person like that. I kissed him and he put a stop to it. Then, I continued to pursue him. I don't want you to think he took advantage. I pursued him. He tried to stop it. But then we ran into each other again and he was worried about me because I got my ass kicked protecting Vi and Angel from this guy. Tom. So he stopped by to thank me and things got out of hand. Then that awful dinner happened, and he was the only one who was on my side. He refused to let Mom and Dad push me around.

"I promised myself after that it would stop. It did, for a while. I told him I wasn't, uh, you know, that way, and I was determined not to be. I'm bi, so I could shut down that side of me, right? It probably would be the best thing to do. But he wrote me this note in his books. And I had to see him. So I did, and it kept happening."

"Eli."

I take a deep breath and keep going. "And I know it's still wrong, I shouldn't have done anything with him because it puts him in a terrible position with his daughter and the university. He's a lot older than me and our parents would never approve even if he was a woman. They hate him. I mean, I'm probably super fucked up for starting this. And it's an impossible situation which is why it isn't anything serious. We have an attraction and once that's over we'll move on. School's starting soon and Noah will probably tire of me."

"Eli." My sister raises her voice, cutting me off. "Please, stop."

I snap my mouth shut and instead of looking at her like I should, I glance at Noah. He stands as if he's going to make his way over here. "You okay?" he mouths. I give a sharp nod and he returns to his seat, completely giving up the pretense of working on his laptop. He's ready to step in if I need it and it only makes me like him more. God, I'm going to have so much explaining to do. There's no way Vi hasn't noticed this shitshow.

Carmen lets out a long sigh. "That was a lot."

A strangled laugh falls from my lips in response.

"I'm going to try to address all of that." She gestures toward me with an open palm as if she's encompassing all of my word vomit. "First, if I ever see that piece of shit who hurt you, ugh. Just tell me if he gives you trouble again. We'll leave it at that. Second, you're not fucked up. You're both adults, and everything you've done sounds consensual?"

She pauses and waits for confirmation, so I nod my head yes, then grab my drink taking a long gulp of the now lukewarm liquid. "Good. And last, but most important, none of that other stuff matters if you love him."

I choke on my drink, coughing heavily. "Fuck." My eyes water as I continue to clear my lungs. She comes around the table and thumps me on the back.

"Sorry, I should have waited. Didn't realize you were that deep in denial."

"I am not in denial."

"Did you not hear that monologue you gave?"

"I black out most of what I say when I ramble because it doesn't actually mean anything."

"Come on."

"You come on. You're being ridiculous."

She crosses her arms. "Eli, he came here to make sure you were okay after our talk. You've spent years getting to know each other. You love his brilliant mind? And he supports you and cares about you. If it was only sex, you wouldn't care what I think, or what Vi thinks, and you certainly wouldn't worry about what Mom or Dad think."

"Of course I would care even though it's only casual. You know how Mom and Dad are."

"If it was casual, you wouldn't worry because there would never be a chance that someone would find out. You don't want to hide him. You want us to know. Me and Vi. I mean, for God's sake, you haven't even noticed that Violet's been eyeing the three of us this whole time."

"Shit, really?" I turn my attention to the register, and sure enough Vi is watching us like a tennis match. "Fuck. Vi's one of his students. This is not good. I don't have time to debate this. I need to talk to Vi. I'll text you to set up our next lunch date?"

"Yeah, of course. I'm sorry, but now that we know, invite him to lunch next time."

I laugh, completely losing it. "That's not how we are. We don't go out. He might not even talk to me after this… Anyway, I need to go. Vi is not going to be happy with me and she won't have a problem bitching him out."

28

Noah

I'm in love with Eli.

I think I've known for longer than I'd like to admit, but I was blissfully living in denial because he doesn't want anything serious. When I asked if he needed me there and he told me I shouldn't feel obligated, it became so glaringly obvious. I want to be there for him. In every happy memory, every loss, each moment of his life. When I'm with him, everything seems better. It was such a small thing, over a simple text, and I thought I would know in a bigger, crazier way. But there it is. Plain and simple. I love him and I want to be with him… as long as he'll have me.

It's a gift to be by his side. I want to be in this chair, watching him talk with his sister animatedly, the excitement and relief on his face bringing both of us joy.

I sip my coffee as I turn to my laptop, the drink a perfect mixture of coffee and sweetness. I ordered it about ten minutes ago, and Violet brought it out to me, reading the order back twice. When I told her yes, it's my favorite drink, she gave me an odd look, reminding me of all the issues keeping me and Eli apart.

It's complicated being in love with him. I'm older. He's my daughter's ex-boyfriend. He won't come out to his parents. I'm not the type of person someone would do that for.

My mind continues to spiral, never finding a solution. I know a few things, though. I'm in love with him. He's not in love with me and never will be. I don't want to stop what we're doing.

It's too late to save myself from a broken heart, and I know I'm not strong enough to stay away. All that leaves is continuing to fall, with no hope of Eli catching me.

I wipe a palm over my face and look at my screen, pretending to write. I know I'm not being subtle enough, but I need to know he's okay. They're still talking, and he tenses before glancing my way.

His sister turns and waves me over. Fuck. She must think I'm some old pervert who's taking advantage of Eli. He distracts her quickly, so I don't move, but I give up the pretense of work, ready to act if necessary.

A few minutes pass, the conversation heated. His attention moves to the register, and my gaze follows. Violet is staring at the three of us, an accusatory expression boring into me before flicking to Eli. I wonder how long she's been watching us. He stands abruptly, throwing his sister into a hug before racing over to Violet. I follow him.

He calls out to Violet. "Can we talk? I can explain." Her sharp stare darts between the two of us a few times. She doesn't look angry, but she's not happy either.

"Is Mr. Baker joining?"

"Yes. Can we go to the back office, please?" She nods, then glares at me again. She raises her voice and shouts to the other barista who's wiping down tables. "Hey, I'm going to head out if you don't need me anymore." The other woman waves her off.

We head to the back, away from prying eyes, so I grab Eli's hand. I worry he'll pull away, but he tightens his grip. It makes me smile despite the situation. We take a seat on a dingy old couch as she sits in the chair across from us. Her undivided attention pans to Eli.

Eli, however, turns his undivided attention to me. "Noah, I'm so sorry. I know we agreed to keep this quiet. I'll understand if… if this needs to stop."

Pleasure swells in my chest that he spoke with me first. He doesn't care about saving face. He only wants to make sure I'm okay. It makes my stupid heart flip, and a small ember of hope blooms. I know it's stupid, but it's there. "It's okay, babe. I shouldn't have come. I know you said not to, but you were nervous, and… I don't know. It felt like I needed to be here for you."

And right there, in front of his best friend, he leans in and plants a light kiss on my lips. I return the gesture, greedily. We break apart and there's a calmness in Eli I wasn't expecting given the circumstances. A small, warm smile meant just for me lights up his face before he turns to Violet. "I'm sorry I didn't tell you it was Noah."

"Noah?" I feel kind of bad for her. Her eyes bug out, mouth hanging open. It's odd to see her stunned. Violet's a smart, witty student in class, always ready with a well-thought-out point. This is a change of pace, but I don't think that's good.

"You know, the guy I've been seeing." Eli hitches his thumb in my direction, which makes me laugh. It's such an endearing gesture, and so out of place in this serious conversation. I might be a tad hysterical.

He looks back at me, then Violet, and me again. "I think she needs a minute to process." He shifts so he's facing me once more. "So, I told my sister I'm bi. She obviously figured out I've been, um, well, whatever we're doing together. She was shocked, but she invited you to join us for lunch. I told her that wasn't what we did, but I'd tell you, anyway."

I'm disappointed and excited in equal measure. I want him to say we're partners. I can't expect that when he doesn't know how I feel. It's unrealistic. I can't tell him. I can't believe his sister wants to meet me. Is that hope growing larger?

I don't have time to respond because Violet finds her voice. "I'm sorry, but really, Eli? This is the guy you've been sleeping with and you let me frickin' ask how big his dick is?"

My eyes pop open at the declaration. "Excuse me?"

Eli laughs uncomfortably. "Do you hate me?"

Violet flops her head back against the chair. "Oh, God. I jokingly asked you to share him with me. Um, can I retract that statement? No offense, Mr. Baker. You're, uh, good looking? Not my type though."

I cringe. "None taken, Violet. For our future sanity, though, I think I'd rather not hear what else you two talked about. You still have a few more courses with me, and… that statement's already going to haunt me."

"At least you're not the one who said it."

"Touché."

Eli clears his throat, refocusing us. "So you're not mad?"

"No. Like I said a few weeks ago, anyone that can make you this happy is good in my book. I'm sure I don't have to tell you I'm the least of your worries."

A possessive, deep-rooted part of me flushes with delight that others have noticed how happy I've made him. It shouts "mine." Mine to please. Mine to love. I try to tune it out because none of those things are true. Especially because he's currently glaring at her, mouthing, "Shut up."

Now that I know he doesn't need me, I think it's best to leave. I would have gladly taken the brunt of her anger because she should aim it at me. Thankfully, she's not mad, which means I should go. "Should I give you some time to talk?"

"Yes," Violet chimes in.

Eli looks at me, refusing to let go of my hand as I stand to leave. "Can I see you tomorrow?"

Tomorrow isn't one of our days, but I want to see him too. "Yeah. Text me when you're home, babe." The words "I love you" almost slip past my lips. I clamp them tight, knowing I absolutely cannot say them. That fiery feeling in my chest won't go away. With each step I take from the room, it screams louder. Eli is mine, and he was always meant to be. Just like I'm his, if he wants me.

29

Eli

I sigh as Noah leaves, grateful that he didn't shy away from Carmen and Vi finding out. Yet again, he had my back without my having to ask for it. It makes my heart ache thinking about how quickly he came to my rescue, willing to take the brunt of everyone's anger to shield me from it, simply because he doesn't want me to face it alone.

I'm still looking at the door where he left when Vi interrupts my musings. "Babe? Wow. You two are as smitten as a kitten."

I turn back to her, annoyance coloring my voice, though I have no right. "What does that even mean?" I'm a little on edge. Hopefully she'll forgive me.

"Oh, don't be grumpy."

"I'm not."

She laughs as if it's the most amusing thing she's ever heard. "So tell me again how you don't have feelings for him?"

I hang my head between my legs. "I don't."

"Eli, you ordered his froufrou-ass drink. You hate sweet coffee. And instead of doing damage control when you both got in here, you made googly eyes the whole time. Then kissed each other!"

I lift my head, barely meeting her eyes. "I'm so fucked, Vi."

A sympathetic expression crosses her face. "I'm sure I don't need to tell you how complicated all of that is. Even if you didn't have feelings for each other."

"I know." Flopping back on the couch, I cover my eyes with my arm. "I like him a lot. I don't know how this happened. It was supposed to be casual."

I lift my arm up and see her hesitate, her mouth opening then closing a few times. Her words are halting. "Was this some revenge sort of thing? Did you do it to get back at her?"

"No." I recap everything that happened between us up to this point, only leaving out the sex. I know it's a legitimate question, and anyone who knows our circumstances, if it ever came out, would ask the same, but it stings.

"You know I had to ask. If it was revenge, I'd say it's best to stay away and move on. But, come on, you like him and he likes you. If you started things honestly, why stop?"

"You know why. He can't have feelings for me. I'm already in too deep and someone needs to be smart about this."

"He calls you 'babe.'"

"It doesn't mean anything."

She claps a hand on my shoulder giving me a pitying look. "Are you sure?"

"If it means something then it has to end."

Her head tilts to the side as if her thoughts are jumbled and it will give her a new perspective. "I get it, your parents wouldn't approve, but they won't approve even if it's someone your own age. Not as long as he's a he. If you're going to go behind their backs to date a man, then why does it matter if he has feelings for you?"

"Because it's one thing to let my emotions get trampled. I get to decide how much I get hurt. If his are involved, I'd have to end things before it could hurt him more. And I don't want it to end. I don't want to lose him."

Her nose wrinkles and I can't tell if it's because she thinks I'm dumb, or if she doesn't understand. I hardly understand myself, I just know that if I have to walk away now, it will be crushing.

"Then you're right and I was wrong. I don't think he has feelings."

I know she's saying it to make me feel better, but I'm pretty sure she's right. Which means I need to end it. "So, you really don't care? You don't think it's weird?"

She shrugs. "I get it. Honestly, you two make sense… Also, I was totally joking about the whole size thing earlier. I still want to know."

"That is your professor," I say, scolding her.

"Mmm. I bet you play a lot of student-teacher scenarios, don't you?"

"You're disgusting."

She only smirks before changing the subject, asking about Carmen and how the conversation went. I fill her in on some of it before we go our separate ways.

***

I text Noah when I get back to my room, letting him know we have nothing to worry about. Vi won't say anything.

> Noah: That's good, though I wasn't worried. I like
> that they know.

My fingers hover over the message. This is the furthest thing from temporary. God, I sound like a broken record. All I know is I don't want to stop, I can't. He makes me feel too good to have it ripped away this soon. Another message pops up from Noah.

> Noah: Can I come over tonight? You said your
> floor is still empty?
> Eli: Won't Angel ask questions?
> Noah: She doesn't care what I do. I want to see
> you.
> Eli: Ok. Text me when you're here.

282

I switch to my dad's contact and click the number to connect the call. I'm supposed to watch the kids tomorrow, but I want to spend as much time with Noah as possible before school starts. There's this deep, troubling sensation making me paranoid, making it feel like this arrangement is ending, despite what either of us wants. I can miss watching my siblings once.

My dad answers on the fourth ring and says hello.

"Hi." I fake cough into the receiver. "I don't think I'm going to feel well enough to watch everyone tomorrow. I'm really sick."

"Did you go to the doctor?"

"I'm going to go in the morning around nine. I'll call you after and let you know what they say."

"Okay. Feel better. I'll let your mother know."

"Thanks, Dad." That was surprisingly easy.

A few minutes later, I get a text from Noah saying he's here. I open the door and he steps inside smelling like soap, his hair wet, and it makes my mouth water. He's wearing jeans that hug every muscle in his legs, and I know from previous experience that his ass looks exquisite in them. His shirt hugs his biceps and I watch them flex as he closes the door behind him.

I cage him in against the door, running my hands through the damp strands of his hair. Taking a moment to examine every part of his face, our breath mingles in the close proximity. "I can't believe you came to the coffee shop for me. You're amazing." I place a light kiss on his mouth, tugging his hair exactly how he likes.

I kiss a path down his neck, biting at the juncture between neck and shoulder. It's not my typical move, but a small part of me wants to mark him like he marks me. I want him to be mine despite our problems. If it was a possibility, I would, and I wouldn't take no for an answer.

"You're not upset that my being there outed you?"

"No, Vi already knew I was seeing a guy, and I told my sister before she figured out it was you. Want me to show you exactly how happy I was to see you there today?" I rub him through his jeans, knowing the response will be yes.

He shifts us around, pinning me by my neck, his thumb brushing against my jaw line. Squeezing my throat lightly, he grinds his cock into my palm, pushing into me. I shudder at the touch, my erection growing painfully hard. He hovers over my ear, licking the shell before commanding me in his deep timbre. "Get naked."

I swallow, feeling the press of his palm, and I shiver. My body heats as I think about how much I like what he's doing to me.

"Hmmm, what's this pretty flush for?" Noah asks, running a finger down my cheek while he holds me at his mercy.

His words seem to fluster me more. I can't admit how turned on I am. But it's Noah. Of course I can trust him. "I like your hand around my throat. It's making me so fucking hard. I… I want you to choke me. A little. If you're okay with it."

The response is silent—a wicked smile and a tightening of his fingers. The pressure goes right to my cock, making my hips thrust, but they have nothing to grind against because he's still too fucking far from me. "I believe I told you to get naked, Eli."

My head swims from the heady excitement of Noah's hand on me. Naked. I want that too. I start with my pants because I don't want him to let me up. It's hard maneuvering my body while I'm still pinned, and he knows it too. He licks his lower lip as he watches me squirm, my breathing heavy and uneven. I slide one leg down as far as it will go, then switch to the other, shimmying until they fall to the ground. By the time my pants and boxers hit the ground, I feel lightheaded, and it has nothing to do with where his hand is, and everything to do with how unbelievably hard I am. I would happily spend the rest of my life naked and in his bed if he asked.

My dick bobs under Noah's scrutinizing gaze, examining my handiwork. He drags a knuckle down the length of me, feather light, before saying, "The shirt too."

I need him to touch me so badly that my hands are moving before he finishes speaking. I pull it over my head and off my shoulders until it can't go anywhere else. Noah moves his hand long enough to rid me of the shirt, but pins me the second it's free. His other hand slides down to my waist, pushing the whole of my body into the door, causing the hinges to rattle. "I'm supposed to be showing you my appreciation," I say, panting breathlessly.

"I don't think you understand how much it turns me on to see you following my every command, at my complete mercy." He licks a stripe down my neck, over my pec, and sucks my nipple into his mouth. I moan helplessly as he thrashes it with his tongue. My hands travel to the hem to pull his shirt off, but he swats them away, giving me a hard stare. "Hands on the door. Don't move them until I tell you."

My hands follow the path of my body, slamming hard against the door. He gets back to work, licking and sucking a path down my chest, over my stomach, and places hot, wet kisses everywhere but where I need him. "Noah."

He gives in, rewarding my needy tone, licking a teasing stripe from the bottom up before swirling his tongue at the cockhead. But that's all it is. A tease.

Standing abruptly, he backs away, watching me as I shift under his attention, desperate for relief. He runs his hand over the bulge in his pants, his gaze heavy-lidded. "Go to the drawer, take out the lube."

I race to the drawer, following his instructions to a T. "Good, Eli. Now, I want you to go to the end of your bed." He waits again as I follow his words. My gaze riveted to his hand where he flicks his button open, diving below the material.

"Bend over the bed." I shudder at his tone, my body folding over, my chest lying comfortably against my soft sheets. "Lube up your fingers." The crack of the lid and my heavy breathing are the only sounds in the room. It makes me hyper aware of my dick shifting over the sheets, pre-come leaking from the tip. I look over my shoulder to watch Noah as I coat my fingers, and I catch myself in the mirror—the one spot in the room where I'll be able to see myself the whole time. Legs spread, cheeks flushed, open for him.

Walking closer, he pulls his shirt off, dropping it to the floor. He takes my mouth in a slow caress, then shifts back, catching my eye. "Now, fuck yourself and don't take your eyes off the mirror. If you do, you won't get my cock."

"Fuck. I need you inside me." I'm completely his to control. As if I want it any other way. I spread my legs wider, sliding my slick digit through the crease until I find my puckered skin. The first finger slides in easily and I watch as it disappears. I see Noah in the mirror, his gaze zeroed in on my hand, enthralled by my actions.

I wait for further instruction. "Stretch that ass for me. Three fingers. Now." I pull out, ready to dive back in when he leans forward, spreading my cheeks wider, putting everything on display. I fuck back onto my fingers, taking three in at once, a slight burn the only sign that I'm stretching myself faster than normal. "See how open you are for me? That pretty, tight hole is all mine, isn't it?"

He pushes my hand away and makes me watch as I clench uselessly, missing the stretch of my fingers. I cry out, needing relief, his hand making it impossible to move, only allowing me to feel everything I'm missing.

"I said, it's all mine, isn't it?"

"All yours."

He rewards me with his fingers, a victorious, filthy smirk dancing on his lips. "Good. Now get on the bed. On your back."

I scramble up, watching as he sheds his pants and boxers all in one go. I spread my legs, my dick twitching under his examination. He crawls over me, dropping kisses sporadically, then tracing each one with his tongue. He brushes against my lips, our tongues tangling as he thrusts against me, grinding hard, his shaft sliding along my lubed ass.

We break the kiss, and he lets out a long groan. "Eli, you feel so good."

My hands run down his back, the nails grasping his ass, pushing him down so that we can get more friction. "So good."

His slick cock continues to torture me as he tilts my head up, placing a long, wet kiss on my neck. He grinds down, his hips shifting, changing the angle, and his head slides past the ring of muscles. We both pause, the sensation overwhelming enough that his hips thrust forward again, sliding him further into my ass.

"Fuck." He grits between his teeth. "I... Condom. We need one." His hips thrust again, shallowly, like he can't control his movements.

It's the smart thing to do. I should get one. My hips buck, needing him. "I'm clear. I've never gone without before."

At my words, he lets out a long, tortured groan, burying his face in my neck. "I've been tested, but..." That's all I need to hear before I'm thrusting my hips up, taking his whole length inside of me. He hits my prostate, and that, combined with his hot, bare length, has me on edge.

He doesn't give me time to adjust or calm down. Instead, he pulls out and slams back in, hard—exactly how I like it. "Fuck. Noah. I need a minute. I'm too close."

"You won't come. I've got you." He growls. Being the avid listener that I am, I take my cock in hand and squeeze the base, praying I can hold out.

His thrusts are fast and wild, becoming increasingly sporadic. Each beat lands on my prostate and I can feel my balls tightening, only held off by the pressure in my hand.

My ass clenches, which sets him off. "Fuck. Come with me, Eli." I release my dick, exploding into a blissful orgasm as he fills me with his come.

"Noah, that was…" Words fail me. It was everything.

He rolls off me and pulls out, but tugs me close, running his hand down my back. My legs are splayed across his body, and I can't imagine moving anytime soon.

"We should probably talk about not using a condom," he says.

I groan. "I don't know if I have enough mental energy to keep my eyes open, let alone talk about that."

He snorts, amused by the comment, and I can't help but appreciate how relaxed and handsome he is, lying there, watching me. Even if he is trying to ruin the post-sex bliss. This—us together—it's so easy. I turn my upper body to the side and kiss the first part of him I can reach. His shoulder. The shift makes other things apparent. I squirm as his come leaks from me. "I can feel your come running down my leg."

He stands from the bed, and I ask him where he's going, the words garbled in the sheets. Fuck, he wore me out. I think I might… I doze off, too exhausted to wait for an answer. He doesn't respond anyway, but I feel the bed dip under his weight a minute later, stirring me awake.

My muscles feel weightless and I don't stir as he cleans me, then pulls me to his chest under the covers. He whispers something, but the alluring pull of sleep takes me under, his voice too quiet and soothing to register the words.

30

Eli

We woke up two more times in the night. Hands, mouths, bodies everywhere and long, sensuous, pressing kisses. It was unlike anything else—something I want to do every night. And I'm not going to let that thought scare me anymore. I have feelings for him. Full stop.

I sigh, stretching out, feeling every sore muscle protest. Noah makes a noise, so I look back to make sure I didn't wake him. His eyes are closed and I stop to admire his chest as it rises and falls with each breath. I turn slowly in his arms to get a better view. I've only woken up with him that one other time, and I didn't get to appreciate it. He looks so peaceful asleep. I reach out, running my fingers over his shoulder, down his arm, then over his stomach. He's so beautiful, and it hits me all over again how lucky I am that he's with me.

Too soon, his eyes flutter open, putting an end to my perusal. A grin plasters his face as he takes me in. "Morning."

"Good morning."

He yawns. "I didn't know if it was okay to spend the night. I was going to go back, but I must have fallen asleep. Sorry."

I run my hands through his chest hair as I move closer. "I'm glad you stayed. I wish it could happen more."

"Yeah?" His smile grows impossibly wider.

"Mhm. I enjoy having you around. In fact, I think I'm way too obsessed with you and I might never let you go." It's the closest I've ever come to admitting feelings, and my stomach dips at the realization—I may be in love with Noah. I like him a lot, but all those feelings, denying it so staunchly, has it all been my way of coping with the realization that I love him? Instead of filling me with happiness, I feel heavy, the realization a double-edged sword. I bury my face in his neck, inhaling everything that is Noah, and it calms me.

"I hope you don't let me go," he whispers so softly I'm not entirely sure that's what he said.

We lie like that a while longer before a buzzing interrupts the quiet. I push up onto my arm and lean over his body to grab my phone. I look at the time, realizing it's already ten in the morning. Noah looks at me expectantly as I groan in frustration. "It's my mom. If I don't pick up…"

He nods his head, well aware of how my parents are. I answer and he pulls away. I glare at him and he refuses to make eye contact. Does he think I won't want him touching me just because my mom's on the line? That's unacceptable, he needs to know I always want him next to me. I grab his arm, and pull it over me to press my face firmly against his chest, the phone propped between us. He lies stiff for a moment, but melts into the touch, slinging his arm low on my back, our legs intertwined.

"My poor baby, I heard you were sick."

"Hi, Mom. Yeah, I just got back from the doctor's. Thankfully, it's only a bad flu, but they already said I'm not contagious, so I should be able to watch the kids soon. I'll definitely be home for family dinner."

"You need me to bring you food? I don't like the idea of you eating that disgusting food at all, but especially not when you're sick."

I'm reminded how much she cares about me and my brothers and sisters. She will drop anything to make sure we're taken care of. It's hard to reconcile this loving behavior with everything else, even with the very real, solid reminder lying under me.

That love, this level of care, would change in an instant. If she was here, if she saw I was with a man, I'd never see my siblings again. And why? Because I love him. What's so wrong with that even if it's not traditional?

My thoughts choke me, and my voice sounds raspy when I say, "No, Mama. They recommended rest and fluids. I'll be okay. I need to get back to sleep. I'll talk to you later, okay?"

"Okay, if you're sure. I expect updates. Feel better."

I toss my phone back onto the nightstand and bury my face in his side, trying to hide from everything that stupid conversation brought up. He runs his hands through my hair, and it does a lot to soothe the raw edges. He breaks the silence first. "Have I ever told you that your voice gets so deep and sexy when you speak Spanish?"

My lips tilt up, a ghost of a smile. "Yeah, faking sick and convincing my mom not to come here is so sexy."

He pokes me in the side, right between the ribs. "You're such a brat."

I swat his hand away. "You love it."

"Hmm. Maybe."

"It's ten now. Do you need to leave soon?"

He moves his hand from my hair to my back, rubbing slow circles, and it makes me feel like a damn cat, stretching into his touch.

A long-suffering sigh parts his lips. "I don't want to, but I'm pretty disgusting. I should probably go home and shower."

"Shower here." It's a truly terrible idea. "After, you can take me for food. I'm starving."

His hand pauses along its path, making me stop to think about what I said. We've never gone out in public before and it sounds like I asked him out on a date. I hold my breath, not sure if I want him to agree or not.

"I know the perfect breakfast place."

***

We get a table at a diner about forty minutes from campus. At first, when he told me about it, I thought he was hiding us, which hurt more than I care to admit. But he told me it was closer to his friend Tony's house, and they frequent this place. That left me glowing, proud that he wanted me to go somewhere important to him. Though, it might also have been the hours of mind-blowing sex.

"So, what do you two usually get here? What should I order?"

"Do you want breakfast or lunch?"

"I'm more of a lunch guy, though I won't turn away breakfast if it's good."

Noah looks through the menu, contemplating the question seriously. "How about I order for you? Make it a surprise."

"Really? Even here you have to control everything?" I cross my arms and quirk an eyebrow to let him know I'm teasing him.

"Don't pretend you don't love every minute of me telling you what to do."

"You're right. I can't. I love it." And there's that word again. Love. I've been saying it too much this morning, and I'd be mortified if he found out exactly how I'm feeling. He'd probably laugh in my face. It's too soon to talk about love, especially given our circumstances.

A middle-aged woman comes over, and my first instinct is to hide, worried she'll sneer at us, ask us why we're here together.

A kind smile crosses her face as she pulls out a notepad. "Noah, you brought us some new meat. Who's this? Tony and Beth are going to be awful jealous." Her voice has a slight Southern drawl, so out of place here, but it's charming. That, and the teasing, put me at ease.

"This is Eli." He turns to me. "Eli, this is Cara. She's been stuffing me full of food since I was, oh, how old, Cara?"

She doesn't look older than fifty, so I can't imagine it's been that many years. "I think I saw you running around here at thirteen? Always getting into trouble."

He scoffs. "I was never the one causing trouble. That was Debbie."

"You're right. Never did like that girl. Wasn't sad to see her go. You had bad taste back then."

My eyes widen in shock, and I peek at Noah. He clutches at his chest. "That hurts."

"Don't worry, hun. You'll find what Tony and Beth have. What me and my Ray have." I have to force myself to stay still as she looks at me from the corner of her eye. She can't know about us. She probably isn't even looking at me. "Speaking of trouble, how's that daughter of yours?"

"Angel's alright. Like you said, trouble."

"Hmm. Hopefully not too much. Anyway, I'm being rude. Eli, what can I get for you?"

I clear my throat. "Actually, Noah said he wanted to order for me." I sound extremely sophisticated. Oh, gee, uh, he's going to order for me. Like I'm five, ordering off the kid's menu. I cringe at the image that pops into my head, wishing I could get out of my head.

Noah orders two of his "usual," saving me from having to say anything else. When she steps away, I catch the full brunt of Noah's attention. He asks, "You okay?"

"Yeah."

It makes me nervous that he knows me so well that he can tell something is wrong. He makes a noncommittal noise. "Cara may be a tad involved in my life, almost like a second mom, but she's not going to ask questions about us. You can relax."

"I am relaxed."

"Come on. Your shoulders passed your ears about five minutes ago while we were talking. They'd probably be floating about a foot above us if they weren't attached to your body."

Despite the truth in his words, I can't help the snort of amusement that falls from my lips. "Fine. I'm surprised."

"About?"

I shrug my shoulders, not quite meeting his eye.

"You think she'd have something to say if we were on a date." It's not a question.

I want it to be a date, but it's obvious to both of us that what I want conflicts with many other feelings circling inside me.

"Because we're both men, or because of our age difference?"

I sit up straighter. "It doesn't matter. We're not on a date. Besides, you bring friends here, so she's used to seeing you with other people. She knows you were married, so I doubt she's assuming anything. I'm fine. I promise."

"You sound fine."

I clench my jaw, his sarcasm obvious. I don't know what to say. I like being with him, but I've had years to think about what it would mean if I wasn't straight, even if I wouldn't admit it to myself at the time. Given how much my parents brushed things under the rug, all the little comments they would make if we were out and about and came across someone who had "that look," even if they thought I wasn't listening… It left me wary of where I stood with them. Always. That instinct isn't something that will go away overnight.

"I'm sorry. That was mean. I get it, I don't like the idea of people thinking I've taken advantage of you because I'm older. I don't want them to think I'm coercing you. And I know that's what some will see. Just like some will see two men sitting here, assume we're on a date, and hate us for that alone. I should be more understanding. That need to protect yourself isn't going to go away." I hate seeing pain flash across his face, especially knowing I put it there. "Do you want to get out of here?"

"No, no. I'm sorry. I know I shouldn't care. So many people are out now. Why should I care what strangers think about me? Let's stay, enjoy our breakfast."

31

Noah

For every step forward, it feels like I take two steps back. But being frustrated with Eli isn't fair. I know it's difficult for him, embracing this part of who he is, knowing how much he has to lose. Just look at his sister. Without ever having come out, he knows what his family life will look like.

If he came out, the two people who are supposed to love him would turn their backs on him. My parents are long gone, but I know without a doubt that they would support me with this like they supported me in raising Angel. They might not have been happy at the time, but they supported me through it all. Both helped me raise my daughter so I could finish school, attend university, and pursue my dreams. Eli's parents… I have no words. Love, given conditionally, is bullshit. He doesn't deserve that.

Thinking of my parents makes me nostalgic, and I spend a few minutes daydreaming about if they had the chance to meet Eli. They would have loved him, after the initial shock of his age. It still makes me sad sometimes, though they lived a long, happy life.

My mom was forty-five when she had me—their miracle baby. The time we had would never be enough. Which makes it that much worse for Eli, because I know he loves his parents as much as I loved mine. I don't know the right move here. I want to support him, scream at his parents to love him and never let him go. But those things can't happen. They won't while he's with me, which makes it even more precious that he chooses me.

He might be right—this isn't a date—but I know he cares, which is why I had to bring him here today. Somewhere special. He might not realize how important this is, but I wasn't going to waste this opportunity he's given me.

Cara brings our food out in record time and I sigh as the delicious, greasy aroma wafts through the air. It's by far the best thing on the menu, though it's not healthy by any means. Homemade waffle fries topped with fried tenders, marinated overnight, smothered in their secret hot sauce. It's delicious.

His eyes bug out when he catches sight of the pile of food, as if he isn't constantly eating when we're together. I swear he can inhale food indefinitely and still complain that he's hungry. "Come on. We both know you're going to eat the whole thing."

He looks at me, then Cara, who's standing to the side watching him with amusement. "I'm going to die, right over this plate."

"You had a nice, hard workout yesterday. You'll be fine." I let the words slip before I think better of them, that pretty flush creeping up his neck, landing on his high cheekbones.

Cara gives me a calculating look as Eli glares daggers at me. Oops. She quirks a brow as I smile at her, but all she asks is, "Can I get y'all anything else?" Her southern accent thickens on the word y'all, and I give her a look, daring her to ask, knowing she wants to.

"Some extra napkins, please." His words are soft when they're aimed at her, but I know I've riled him. It's in the way his hand twitches. He can't wait for her to leave so he can reprimand me for the comment, even though we both know he's not actually mad.

As soon as she's gone, he turns on me. "I'm going to murder you."

I laugh, my head tipping back. "I bet I can make you forgive me."

It draws the attention of a few other patrons and Eli shushes me, then shakes his head, completely exasperated. This is the most fun I've had going out in a long time. Any moment with Eli is my favorite, but I like that we're out with each other, like a couple.

We dig into our meals, and he sighs with pleasure.

I give him a smug grin. "It's good, isn't it?"

"Exactly what my 'workout' called for."

As predicted, he inhales most of his meal before I make a dent in my own. It's messy, and I'm glad he asked for the extra napkins. We sit in companionable silence as I continue to work on my plate.

He rubs a palm over his stomach in the universal gesture that he's full. So at odds with his next words, which fill me with dread. "So, there's something I wanted to talk to you about."

I drop my fry. "Okay?"

"School starts on Wednesday. That means we have Friday and Tuesday left to spend with each other before everything starts back up."

"Mhm." God, please don't tell me this is over.

"I was thinking… I don't want this to end. But how are we going to see each other? I mean, that is, only if you still want to as well."

My head falls back against the top of the booth as the tension drains from my shoulders. "Thank fuck. I thought you wanted to break up with me." My mouth snaps shut. Shit, shit, shit. I did not mean to say that out loud. Insinuating that there's something to break up with your very flighty love interest is not ideal. I don't want to look at Eli, afraid of what I might see written on his face. More than likely, he'll want to end it now. I have to know. I glance at him and his normally open expression shutters, his guard up.

Fuck. Me. "I didn't mean it like that. I meant…" No. I'm not going to lie anymore. I'm going to put it on the line. "No. No. I meant it exactly like I said. Eli, I know what you want this to be, and I know how impossible this is, but for me, it's more. It's been more for a while. You're the only person I've been with in a long time and the only person I want to be with. I want to date you. Officially."

He opens his mouth, and I know it's going to be a rejection, so I speed on. "It doesn't have to be out in the open. We can keep going how we're going, but I don't want to lie anymore and say I don't have feelings for you. We don't have to come out. I mean, Violet and Carmen already know. It wouldn't even be that different."

"What exactly are you proposing then if we don't change anything?"

Fuck. It's not a no. I expected an emphatic no. That hope that I barely wanted to acknowledge goes from an ember to a crackling fire. "We're partners. We're committed to one another. You're mine and I'm yours."

I expect him to pause, ask for time to consider. What I don't expect is a small, hesitant smile to bloom. "Yes."

"Yes?"

"I want that too."

I want to jump out of my seat, round the booth, and take his mouth with mine, but I wait, asking for permission. "Does that include a public kiss where no one knows you?"

He glances around, but says, "Yes. If you're okay with it."

My ass is across the table in seconds as I pull him close for a sweet, chaste kiss. I push back, staring into his beautiful hazel eyes, trying to remember everything about this moment. It feels unreal.

"You can do better than that," he teases.

That bratty tone that he reserves for the bedroom comes out full force and I tug him to me again, exploring his mouth like it's the first time. I should probably care that I'm making out with Eli like a teen in the diner, but the only person I care about here is Cara, and she won't mind. She won't kick me out, so anyone who might have a problem can fuck off. I pull back and his cheeks flush, his expression content.

His words are slow, muddled from the kiss. "Uh, hopefully we don't get kicked out."

"Cara owns the place. We won't get kicked out."

"She won't care about us?"

I shrug. "Not at all."

"Why?"

"Well, for starters, she's pretty open-minded in general. But, Ray, her husband, is thirteen years older than her. He was actually the manager here when she started at eighteen. Both families disapproved, but they fell in love and got married anyway. So, she recognizes that a relationship may look different, and it's okay."

"I think we still have them beat."

I grab his hand in my own, curling our fingers together because I can. He said yes to dating me and I'm still reeling. I've never felt luckier in my life. "Yeah. On paper we don't make sense. But everything feels so right when we're together. Yeah?"

He nods his head as Cara delivers the bill. She winks at me, then pats me on the back. "Ray's ready to ring you out up front whenever. No rush."

We pay, then walk out to the car hand in hand. I drive him back to the dorm and give him a kiss on the cheek with a promise to see him Friday.

He's about to step out of the car when I make a snap decision. "Hey, would you be okay if I told Tony and Beth about us?"

"You want them to know about me?"

I do. Other than my daughter, they are the most important people in my life. Telling Angel is out of the question… for now. While this is still new and fragile. I'm happy and proud to be with Eli. I want them to know. "Yes. Only if you're comfortable with it, though."

"Well, I mean, Vi and Carmen already know. It's only fair. I should be okay."

I run my thumb along the back of his hand, a shiver pebbling his skin under the simple touch. "Should and actually are, are two completely different things. If you're not comfortable with it, I don't have to say anything. Take some time and think about it. It's okay if you say no."

He shakes his head. "No. I don't need time. Tell them. I'm okay with it."

"For real?"

"Yeah. Totally fine with it. If you trust them, I trust them."

***

Tony and Beth invite me over to their place Saturday afternoon for burgers, brats, and football. I could take or leave the sports, but the food is to die for. I'm nervous, but excited to tell them, and I know they've picked up on that.

Yesterday, while lying with Eli, watching reruns, we talked about how I was going to tell them today. He reminded me he was fine with it, but if I wasn't ready, I didn't have to say anything. I'd pulled him tighter in my arms and told him I wasn't going to hide him anymore.

We grab plates and sit down in front of the TV, the volume low as we talk about Tony's book and Beth's latest project at work, and then the conversation turns to me. We talk about the start of the school year, but as the minutes tick by my answers become shorter and more distracted.

Beth's the one to say something first. "Out with it, Noah. What's going on? Something's wrong."

"Nothing's wrong."

Tony shakes his head before leaning back on the couch.

"That is to say… I, um, nothing's wrong with me. I have to talk to you. Tell you about something."

"Okay," he says, waiting for me to continue. Beth grabs my hand.

"I'm worried you won't react well."

Tony sits forward, giving me his full attention. "We're your best friends. Rip the Band-Aid off. It can't be that bad."

"I'm seeing someone."

They both sit up straight, the expressions on their faces almost comical as they yell, "Congratulations," at a level only dogs can hear.

Beth adds, "Why wouldn't we be happy about that?"

I wince. "Well, you know the person."

"Mhm. And who might that be?" Tony motions for me to continue.

"I'm actually seeing a man."

Beth slaps Tony's arm, then speaks directly to him, "I told you so."

"You did, dear. Looks like I was wrong." He kisses her on the cheek.

"What?" I ask, confused.

Tony answers. "Since high school Beth always thought you might like men."

"I… I want to ask why, but that's not important now. There's more." I wave my hand, brushing the topic away, if only temporarily.

That seems to pique their interest because they don't interrupt again.

"I'm in a relationship with… God, this is harder than I thought it would be."

"Spit it out," Tony says, even keeled despite his usually sporadic behavior.

"Eli."

Their faces stare at me blankly. They look at each other, seeing how the other reacts, then at me again. "What?" one of them says.

The other says, "Who?"

"From the movie in the plaza. Eli."

Tony's look is incredulous and I can't blame him. "Your daughter's ex-boyfriend?"

"Yes."

"Fuck," he sighs, rubbing a hand over his face.

She adds, "Is it serious?"

"It is."

"He's twenty."

"Yeah."

My amazing mood from the past few days evaporates as I'm confronted with the reality of the situation.

"Buddy, I love you, but are you sure this is a good idea? Does Angel know?"

I'm feeling defensive, and I know I shouldn't be. They haven't said anything bad, but I want them to be happy for me. Excited, like I am. "Yes, I'm sure. I-I love him. I know it sounds insane and it shouldn't have happened… He brings me peace. I'm lighter when I'm with him and he makes me better. Ever since Debbie left and took Angel with her, something's been missing from my life. When Angel refused to see me for a few years after the divorce, screamed whenever she saw me, when she was so afraid of me she couldn't look me in the eye… I was lost. And then I lost my parents."

They both nod solemnly. Tony whispers, "You were in an awful place."

"I was. I never thought I'd claw my way out of that depression. Then, to the world, I got over it, and I functioned again. I thought I was functioning again. Is functioning enough? I've always wanted what you two have and I've found it. He makes me happy. I feel right when I'm with him."

Beth moves to my side, pulling me into a hug, and I let out a deep breath. "I don't get it, not fully, but I want to. If you say he's your person, I believe you. Maybe we can meet him. Officially. As your boyfriend?"

I squeeze her hand, thankful for the support. We both look at Tony, who sits on the other couch, worrying his lip with his teeth. "If it's actually this serious, you need to tell Angel. You'll never be able to move forward with that hanging over your head."

"I know."

"You're sure? If you end it now, she won't have to know. It would be the smart thing to do."

Beth stares down her husband. "Tony, stop."

"I'm looking out for our friend, Beth. I'm trying to be realistic. What does this look like ten or twenty years down the road? They can't hide it forever. The kid's only twenty, what happens when he meets someone his own age?"

"I'm sure about him, Tony."

"Does he feel the same way?"

I swallow, but I refuse to flinch from his gaze. The truth is, I don't know if Eli feels the same. I don't know what one year looks like for us, let alone ten or twenty. If it came down to it, I don't know if he would choose me. I wouldn't want him to have to choose me. "I don't know."

"You're being an idiot."

"Tony." Beth's voice is sharp.

His words hurt. "Right. Well, you've given me some things to think about. I should… head out. Thanks for having me. I'll talk to you guys later."

"He is, Beth. He's not some doe-eyed sixteen-year-old anymore. Debbie already fucked him over, and a twenty-year-old who doesn't have their life figured out will do the same."

She stands, giving her husband an unspoken reprimand before turning to me. "Noah, don't leave upset. Give me a minute to talk to Tony." Normally I'd do whatever I could to make her feel better, but Tony is right. I don't want to hear it, but he's right. Even if it doesn't fucking matter because I'm going to choose Eli, anyway. Even if he breaks my heart tomorrow or next week or in a year.

I make my way home and slam the front door, needing to release this energy inside of me. Tony might be fucking right, but I'm done hiding Eli. If he wants me, I'm his, and I want the whole world to know it. I walk into the living room and find Angel sprawled on the couch, Tom's hand moving to unbutton her pants, her shirt discarded on the floor.

32

Noah

My feet carry me to the couch, yanking the piece of shit up by his shirt, the hot and cold of the last hour fueling my reaction. Angel yells, getting in my face, telling me to get the fuck off him as I push him away.

"Get the fuck out of my house."

"Get your hands off me, douchebag!" he yells, instantly on the defensive.

My fists clench tighter in his shirt, but a calm clarity envelops me as I picture Eli. Even after all the shit this kid put him through, he still wouldn't lay a hand on him, and I want to be like Eli. I want to be good for the one person who expects it from me.

Tom squirms in my hold, genuine fear shining in his glassy eyes. I release him and he quickly retreats through the house until I hear the door. I turn my undivided attention to my daughter as she throws her shirt back on. "You're such a fucking asshole."

"Why was he here?"

"Because this is my house too. If I want him here, he's allowed to be here."

"Angel, he almost hit you. He's beat the shit out of Eli. Twice. He's dangerous."

She has the sense to look guilty. "He's not going to hurt me. How do you even know about Eli?"

Shit. That didn't mean to slip out. "You don't know that he won't. I love you. I just want to keep you safe."

"You don't love me. You just want to fucking control me. From the day I moved in, you've only wanted to judge me 'cause you're so fucking perfect. That way, when you decide to leave, you won't feel bad about it."

"That's not true, and you know it."

"What part?"

"All of it. I love you so fucking much, I'm never going to leave, and I don't have any room to judge you. All I want to do is keep you happy and safe."

She stomps her foot. "I'm just a disappointment to you."

"No. You're not. The only disappointment is me. I just want to fix our relationship."

"What relationship? We'd have to have one at all in order to fix it. You left me when I was ten and never looked back. And now, you're distracted all the time. If you wanted to fix anything, you'd be here." My face must give something away, because she laughs humorlessly. "Come on, like I wasn't going to notice… What? Do you have a new girlfriend? Just like Mom? Oh, you try so hard not to be her, but you're two sides of a damn coin. You're a fucking joke. You tell me you're not going to leave, but all you've done these past few months is avoid me or tell me what to do. So, tell me I'm wrong. Tell me you're not doing the same fucking thing as her. Tell me, again, that you're not leaving when you're already halfway out the door."

"That's not what's happening."

"You're a fucking liar." She shoves me, her nostrils flaring as she huffs.

"I am seeing someone, but I'm never going to abandon you, Angel."

"Who is it?"

I don't respond.

She shoves me again. "Who is it?"

Tom steps back into the hall, a smarmy grin on his face. An eerie laugh echoes around the room, a self-satisfied sound that sends chills down my spine. The blood drains from my face as I read his intent. He taps a finger against his chin, head tilted as he contemplates everything I just spilled. "I bet I could make a guess, Ang."

That catches her attention, just as surprised to see him standing there. Fuck. Fuck. Fuck. This is not good. "What are you talking about, Tom?" She looks embarrassed and confused.

I try to cut him off. "You need to leave my house, now."

His eyes light up with glee. "Oh, I'm definitely right. God. Ang, did you know your dad's a fag?"

My fists clench, my teeth grinding as I take a menacing step forward.

Ang looks between us, and must decide he's onto something. "What the fuck are you talking about?"

"It all makes sense. I thought it was Vi, but this makes sense. Oh, this is so fucking good." He gives me another smarmy grin. "You think his parents will try to have you arrested?"

Panic overwhelms me, each word landing a direct blow. He knows it too. I try to take another step forward, but I'm locked in place. Fuck. Me. Angel turns to me, looking for an answer. But I just stand there, frozen, stupid.

"You're not making any sense."

"Seems like your little ex had a taste for some daddy porn revenge, Ang." He turns to me.

She takes a moment to process his words, but when she does, she turns on me, spitting out, "You're fucking Eli?"

Her venomous words snap me out of my stupor and I move toward her, aware of how precarious the situation is. I whisper, "Come on, Angel. Why would you believe anything he has to say?"

Tom knows Eli's parents, and he's vindictive enough to do something stupid. I glance at her. I have to deal with my daughter. Do damage control. Without lying to her. Fuck. I've already lied enough.

She takes a step back. "Don't try to fucking manipulate me. Tell me the truth."

"He doesn't have any proof."

Tom laughs. "He's not denying it. Come on, Ang."

"Shut the fuck up," I yell, regretting it immediately when he gives me a victorious grin because he knows exactly how to get under my skin. I turn on him, about to rush him. Fuck my hot-headed younger years. I've tried to be good. I haven't been in a fight since I was a twenty-something, but I think that's about to change.

"Oh my God. It's fucking true. You make me sick." She storms from the room before I have the chance to say anything else. Fuck. I want to go to her, but the need to ensure Eli's safety overwhelms me.

I rush him, my hands fisting in his shirt as I shove him against a wall. "You won't say a fucking word. Leave Eli out of this."

"Get your hands off me, fag. I'm not into that queer-ass shit." His words sound brave, but I can see the hesitation in his eyes. He's afraid of me, what I might do. The slurs barely register as I battle the instinct to kick the shit out of him.

My body trembles. "Leave him out of this."

"Sure. But what's in it for me? I'm thinking it's at least worth five grand to keep my mouth shut. Otherwise, his family might hear about it. The school too."

My fist lands on the drywall near his head. "You can leave now, keep your mouth shut, and I won't have you arrested for assault and battery or destruction of public property. How does that sound?" He can't tell if I'm serious. "I see the wheels turning in your head. Yes, I have evidence, and I can make it stick."

Again, he puts his hands up as if he's being completely reasonable. "Alright, man. You win. I'll go. I already got what I wanted."

It takes all of my willpower to release his shirt and let him walk out the door. The threat will have to be enough. Even though I want to race after him and ensure he'll never hurt Eli.

When I shut the door firmly, and I know he's not there anymore, I race up the stairs to finish my conversation with Angel. I know I'll need to talk to Eli too, tell him Tom knows, but I need to be a father. Even if I've been a shitty one, lately.

I turn her knob, not entirely surprised that it's locked. I knock, and she doesn't respond. "Angel, I'm sorry, but we need to talk. Open the door."

"No." It sounds like she's been crying, and it slices at my heart. I fucked up. Long before Eli and I were ever a thing. I have no fucking clue how I'm going to fix this.

"Angel, let me in. We are going to talk about this and I'd rather it be face to face instead of through a door."

I hear stomping from the other side before she throws it wide. She storms over to her bed and plops down, so I take her desk chair, finding it hard to sit with adrenaline still racing through me. "What can I do to fix this?"

She sits up straight. "Go back in time and not fuck my ex-boyfriend. Who does that? I was in love with him."

A crawling sensation starts on my skin, hearing those words. I don't want to examine the feeling too closely. "We will talk about him. I promise, but I'm talking about us. What can I do to fix our relationship?"

"There's nothing you can do. You don't care. I don't care. It's fine. Obviously we aren't meant to have a relationship. You don't love me."

"In three years, I haven't done a single thing to make you feel loved?"

She looks away. "You don't want me here."

"Why do you think that?"

"Mom didn't want me. Why would you?"

I will always want her, and I'm a worse father than I even thought because she doesn't know that. Whenever she pushed me away, I should have done more. "I have always wanted you. From the moment I found out your mom was pregnant, I was so happy to be your father. When she took you away… I was lost. She never told me why she left, or why she wouldn't let me see you. Instead, I respected her wishes, I signed the divorce papers, as long as she'd let me see you. She agreed, but by then, whenever I came over, you'd run screaming. I thought you were mad, and I wasn't in a good place, so I didn't realize it was fear. I thought you just didn't want to see me. I thought it would be best to leave you alone. Angel, I cried myself to sleep"—I clear my throat—"every night. Hating myself for it all. It wasn't until you were older that I realized you were afraid. Did I do something? Did she—did she say something to you?"

"It's not like I actually believed it. Or, I did, but I haven't for years."

"Believed what?"

"I was ten."

"I know. I'm sorry I didn't fight harder to keep you. I should have."

She nods her head, but I don't know if it's meant to acknowledge my statement. "No. I needed to say it so you could understand. Obviously ten-year-olds believe things easily. She told me a lot of lies."

"Okay. I understand."

"She told me she was pregnant again, to save your marriage. She was… so excited to have another baby. A little boy. Or so she said."

"What?" My whole body goes numb, as I'm rendered speechless. If Debbie was actually pregnant, she never told me.

"When she told you, she said you went into a rage and demanded she get an abortion. Of course, at the time, she said you wanted to kill him, because I didn't know what abortion was."

I shake my head, unable to process the words. "Angel, I'm so sorry. I can't… I don't know why…"

"I'm not done."

I fall silent again. That alone would be enough to scare her. Why the fuck would Debbie have lied about that?

Why would she want to make Angel afraid of me? Telling her I killed her little brother.

She waits, making sure I won't interrupt. "She… she said, 'if your father had his wish, you'd be like your brother, right now.' And…"

"I would never hurt you." The words are automatic, a gut reaction to the unbelievable story. What the fuck? How? In all these years, I never imagined this. I thought Debbie might have told Angel that I used to get into fights, that I was a stupid hothead when I was younger. Debbie was beautiful, and men used to line up just to talk to her and she liked it. Frequently, she'd make out with them in front of me just to see me crack. It worked every fucking time. After, when the blood was dry, she would tell me she loved me and now she knew how much I loved her… because real men fought for their women. But this. It's so much worse than I ever thought.

She whispers, "I know."

"Do you?" Water pools in my eyes, and I fight it back, now realizing the depths of my failure. I would hate me too.

"Yeah. Now. Even as she was dropping me off she alluded to the fact that I might get abused if I stepped out of line. That your anger would flare up. After Mom left me here, saying it would be for the best, I learned it was just another way for her to manipulate me. What was I supposed to do? She didn't want me anymore. I thought you didn't want me."

"I'm sorry I failed you, Angel. I didn't know. Didn't realize."

"Was she ever pregnant with my brother?"

I want nothing more than to wrap my arms around my daughter and never let go, the broken, vulnerable rasp of her voice squeezing my chest. I answer her as best I can. "If she was, she never told me."

She nods her head, as if she assumed as much.

"I don't think there is anything I can ever do to make up for not being there when you needed me. I want to try, though. I love you and I'm never going to leave you. I want to protect you. From everything. If I could wrap you in bubble wrap, I would. If I could go back in time, I wouldn't let her take you."

"Why did you? Let her take me."

I watch her as she wraps her arms around her knees as if she's trying to soothe herself. I stand, slowly approach her, and hold my hands out, letting her know how much I want to hug her, but letting her decide on her own terms. "Any excuse I gave you wouldn't be good enough. There is no excuse."

She stands, like she wants to reach out. "Can you try?"

Anything. I'd do anything for her. "I was twenty-five. Pursuing a degree, handing you off to your grandparents or leaving you alone with your mom. I wanted an education so I could provide for you. By the time you were ten, you were already so close with your mom. You loved her, and I was barely there. I thought it would be smarter to let you go to the parent who was more reliable in your life. The lawyers seemed to think the same thing. I asked for joint custody, but your mother was against it and I didn't want you to have to see how ugly it could get, so I gave up."

"I was close to her."

"I'm sorry."

"I'm not perfect. I'm not going to change overnight… but I want to forgive you. And I hope you'll forgive me too. I know I haven't always been easy to deal with."

"Really?" I ask.

She nods, then walks into my arms. I wrap them around her, tears finally breaking, streaming down my face. "Where does that leave us now? What about Eli? I can't believe you slept with him, Dad. You're not even gay." Her voice comes out muffled as she buries her face in my shirt. I find it promising that she doesn't pull away. Maybe we can find our way. Start over.

I don't address the last comment. Eli is who I want to be with. It's that simple. "I shouldn't have, but it just happened. Where does that leave us? I don't know. I think that depends on your feelings. How mad are you?"

"I don't even know how to answer that. Pretty mad, I think. It's just so weird. Did it start while we were dating?"

"No. Absolutely not. He came over to get his things after the breakup, and we started talking like we did when we would wait for you. And… we kept running into each other, discovering that we had a lot in common. I don't know what to say. I fell in love with him. He's everything I never knew I needed in my life and he makes me happy."

"You love him?"

"I do."

"And he loves you?"

I shrug because I don't know.

"Of course he does. Eli loves with his whole heart, and if he did something like this, it wouldn't be to upset me. He's not like me."

My mouth drops. Did those words come from my daughter? "Uh."

"We were friends before we dated. I know how he is. He was always too safe, and we didn't bring out the best in each other. He didn't push me enough. I wasn't supportive enough. But he wouldn't do this out of revenge. Oh, God. Were you two dating when I made his whole family come over?"

"Not officially. But yes." This sounds so bad spelled out, but I imagine Eli's face and everything that we've shared, and I know all of this pain is worth it. He's everything to me.

"And you'd still choose me? If I made you choose…" She crosses her arms and worries her lip with her teeth.

"Yes." I mean it too.

She shakes her head. "After all the bullshit I've put you through?"

"I'll always choose you, Angel. I love you."

She tilts her head from side to side. "You deserve to be happy."

I shift under her scrutiny, not quite believing this conversation. "I can't be happy if I know my choices are making you unhappy."

"I mean… it's weird. Dad, I took his virginity."

If that doesn't make me want to throw up. "God. I never needed to know that."

That gets a small giggle from her. "See what I mean? Weird. Weird."

"I don't have to talk to him again."

It's her turn to shift. "He deserves to be happy too. Clearly I wasn't that for him. I think I loved him. Once. We were always better as friends. I… I can't say I'm cool with it. I…" She shudders. "God, this is fucking trippy. I don't want to see PDA if he's around the house. For what it's worth"—she makes a fake gagging noise—"I give my blessing. Ugh. That was hard to say. See, I can be mature too."

That sounds more like the Angel I know, and it makes me smirk despite the weight of the conversation. Her words wash over me, almost too good to be true, but even if Angel's okay with it, we still have two very real roadblocks.

She doesn't wait for me to respond, instead continuing her train of thought. "His parents are going to shit bricks. I'm pretty sure they're huge homophobes, Dad. Are you sure he's who you want? I doubt he'll ever tell his parents."

"Yeah, his parents are a big issue. I don't know what we're going to do. It probably won't end well for me. Wait, you don't want to hear about this. Sorry. I shouldn't be unloading these problems on you." I stand up, preparing to leave her room.

She reaches out and puts a palm on my arm. "No, don't go. This is actually helping, in a super weird and slightly uncomfortable way. It's not like I own Eli. You both deserve to be happy. I've been pretty shitty lately."

She holds a hand up as I open my mouth. "I know you'll deny it, but you don't have to. We know I have been to both of you. I'm going to be better. Perfect."

"I don't need you to be perfect, I need you to be in my life and I hope you'll come to forgive me. I'd like to be close again."

"I know. So, what are we going to do about Tom? He heard… everything."

I almost forgot about him after all of this. "He won't bother Eli."

"No. Dad. You don't know Tom like I do. You need to call Eli and warn him. Tom's going to do something stupid. Maybe show up at his dorm and cause shit."

"No. He won't say anything."

"Say anything?"

Unease settles in my stomach. "Yes. He said he would tell Eli's parents unless I paid him, but I told him we'd go to the police with evidence of his assault."

She shoots to her feet. "Shit. Shit. Dad, he's probably already called them. Where's your phone? You need to call Eli now." I see horror plastered on her face, and that snaps me into action. She knows Tom better than I do, and if she's this sure, then I'd better call Eli.

I run downstairs and grab my phone, Angel following on my heels. I call him, but he doesn't pick up, so I try again. Shit. Shit. Fuck. I send him a text, telling him to call me, that it's important.

I grab my keys, ready to drive to his dorm. I throw some shoes on and see Angel do the same. She notices me watching her. "I'm coming. He's going to need all the support he can get."

"Okay." We race to the car, and while I'm driving, I think of who else to call. Violet. She'd be able to get in touch with him. "Do you still have Violet's number?"

"Yes. Why?"

"Call her from my phone and put her on speaker."

Angel doesn't question it, instead entering the number rapidly and connecting it to the Bluetooth.

"Hello." Violet's voice sounds tinny over the call, but I sigh in relief that she answered.

"Violet, this is Noah Baker. Is Eli with you?"

"No, sir."

"Do you know where he is?"

There's a slight pause over the phone. "I think he said he was going to babysit his brothers and sisters tonight so his parents could go out. Probably his house. Why, what's wrong? Is he okay?"

"I think Tom is about to out Eli to his parents."

The line goes silent. It's the longest pause of my life. "How did he find out?"

Angel chimes in before I admit to my stupidity. "It's my fault, Vi. I figured it out and texted my dad to confront him and Tom saw my messages."

I'm floored. I never thought I'd see the day that Angel tried to protect me. Unfortunately, that's not the pressing concern right now. "Can you call him until he picks up? I'm going to his house now."

"I'm coming too. I'll tell Carmen. Maybe we can take some of the heat off of Eli by being there. Plus, she'll want to be there and he's going to need us if this all blows up."

I disconnect the line and step on the gas.

33

Eli

I've been driving the kids around for the past two hours, chauffeuring to the movies and ice cream. Now we're finally home, and I'm beat. I haven't even had time to check my phone, though I got quite a few notifications while I was out. At least one is from Noah because I saw his name pop up. I know I shouldn't call him because any of my siblings could overhear, but I'm contemplating it as the younger ones get ready for bed.

Another call comes in before I can decide. This one from Vi. "Hey. What's up?"

"Eli, thank God. Are you okay?"

"A little tired, but the siblings were all pretty good for me, so not too bad. How are you?"

"I'm on my way to your house."

I pull my phone away from my ear. "What? Why?"

"Didn't you see your texts?"

"No. I've been busy."

"Tom's going to out you."

A quiet hum starts in my mind, the noise gaining volume as I process her words. "Out me?"

"He's going to tell your parents that you're bi."

"How the fuck does he know?" My palms start to sweat and I almost drop the phone. None of this makes sense. I woke up to take care of my siblings today. It was supposed to be a normal, no bullshit day. I finally admitted my feelings to Noah and things were supposed to be good. Not whatever this shitshow is. And my parents. God. My parents.

"Angel told me he read her messages and confronted Noah about you."

Noah? Angel? What the fuck happened? I feel like my mind is processing at half its normal speed. "Wha… How? Angel knows? I need the complete story, Vi."

I hear a horn blast in the background. "Well, they're on their way, hopefully they'll get there before your parents. I also told Carmen. We'll be there soon. Are your parents home yet?"

"No."

"I'll be there soon."

The line disconnects as I hear a pounding at the door. I race to the front, yanking it open to find Noah and Angel standing on the other side, both of them looking frantic.

Noah rushes me, grabbing onto the material of my shirt, as if he's going to pull me in for a hug, but glances at Angel. "Are you okay?"

"What the fuck is going on, Noah? Vi said Tom's going to out me. And Angel knows?"

She creeps around Noah's shoulder and stands near us. To make matters worse, the triplets come up front, drawn by the noise.

"Eli, what's going on?" Adriana calls out in Spanish.

"Nothing, go back to your room, girls."

They hesitate, but make their way back to their room, grumbling all the while.

As soon as they're gone, Noah says, "You could deny it. Tom doesn't have proof. Say that he was jealous and lying and making shit up. We can still fix this before they get home. Say I brought Angel over to comfort you because of Tom."

Angel watches her father as he becomes more desperate, more agitated. "Dad."

He's giving me the out I need. It's believable enough if my parents want to keep their peace of mind. Stay in the bubble they raised us in. I could deny it. But… Noah's here, and he told Angel about us.

"Don't deny it, Eli. He loves you."

Noah turns to her, pinning her with his stare. "Angel."

My mouth drops open.

He turns back to me and says, "Make the right decision for yourself. This is your family and you have to live with the choice."

Everything else, all the worries and doubts fade to the background. "Do you love me?" Angel knows. That conversation couldn't have been easy. Am I brave enough to do the same if he loves me?

He nods his head. "I do. I love you."

"I love you too."

He pulls me into his powerful arms, making me feel safe and warm. He places a gentle kiss on my cheek, another on my forehead, and we're interrupted by a clearing of the throat.

"Sorry to rush you, but you need to decide quickly. Who knows when they'll be home."

Right. My parents. I could fucking lose my siblings. What if they don't want to see me after all of this? What if my parents make up the same lies?

Noah... I love him. He's it for me, which means I don't have much of a choice. Or rather, I already know what choice I've wanted to make for a really long time. "I'm going to tell them the truth. I don't want to hide who I am. Not anymore. You're too important to me to risk losing. If you can tell your family, I can tell mine."

Angel chimes in. "I'm also mostly cool with this, in case you were worried about that. It's kind of weird as fuck, but... I'll try not to gag too much."

I look at Noah, shocked by the sentiment. Something big must have happened between the two of them. Lines fan out around his eyes as he smirks, amused by my reaction. Then he mouths that he'll tell me about it later.

"Um. Thanks, Angel."

"Sure."

He asks, "Should I be here, or should I leave?"

"Stay. Please. I… I don't know if they'll let me stay." My family might not let me stay in this house because I'm in love. I might lose them. And my parents might try to cover it up like they did with Carmen. I can't let that happen. They can't think that I left them. "I need to tell my sisters and brothers while I can."

I race to their rooms, corralling them as they grumble about my agitated state. In a matter of minutes they're seated, eyeing Angel and Noah before giving me their attention. I clear my throat, their expressions ranging from confused to bored, and finally, suspicious. God, please don't let this be a huge mistake. Let them understand.

"Why are you calling us out here, Eli?" Valeria asks.

"I'm in love and I wanted you all to know."

Valeria claps. "With Angel? Yay. You worked it out."

"Obviously not, idiot. He wouldn't be calling us out here for that," Dani snipes back.

Adriana, level-headed as ever, says, "Shh. If you listen, I'm sure he'll tell you."

I smile at her gratefully. "No, not with Angel. I'm in love with Noah."

"Who's Noah?" Miguel asks.

"Angel's father," Adriana adds, her brows disappearing behind her bangs. The rest of the group gasps.

I rush on. "I'm about to tell our parents. But I wanted you to hear it from me. I love him, and that might mean I have to leave. You might not see me again."

"Not see you? Why?" Manny asks.

Adriana answers. "Because Mom and Dad think it's wrong when two men are a couple. Like them." I can't tell if she feels the same or not.

"What's so wrong about that?" Alex adds.

"Someone, somewhere, decided God didn't like it and people believed them," I say. Wow, this is a lot harder to explain than I thought it would be. Not that I've had much time to prepare.

"Is God mad about it?" Miguel asks in the way that only a young child can, completely guileless.

I don't know how to answer that. In my heart I feel like the answer is no, but that doesn't mean I'm right. I can't believe that ours is a world where the universe hates me because of something I have no control over. A universe that hates me for loving somebody. I don't know how to convey that to a seven-year-old, though.

I don't have to answer the question because Dani says, "No, Miguel. God isn't mad about it. He made Eli exactly as he should be."

"Mom and Dad just don't understand," Valeria adds.

One by one, I look at my siblings' faces—a unified front of unwavering support. Silent tears roll down my cheeks as I let out a long sigh. I didn't know how much I needed that, but it makes me ready to face my parents.

"We're with you, Eli. We love you." Though they are Adriana's words, I see all of my siblings nod in agreement. Then they rush me, piling on top until I'm sandwiched between all of their arms. The tears flow freely and I seek out Noah, catching his gaze as he smiles lovingly at me, wrapped in the embrace of my family.

But too soon, that peace is interrupted by the sound of keys clanging against the door. I break away from my siblings and wipe my face. "Go to your rooms, now." My heart thunders as it wars with protecting my siblings and facing what's behind the door.

"We're not leaving you to face them alone." Adriana crosses her arms and my other sisters follow suit.

"At least put the boys to bed, they don't need to see this." The boys grumble, but given the time constraints, they agree as Dani rushes them away. The rest stand off to the side, ready to offer support if needed. I turn to Noah, "Please don't say anything. It's going to be bad enough. I don't want the attention on you."

"Eli."

"I'm serious. Don't say anything."

The door clicks open, and my parents walk in, my mother's face a mask of rage, my father's a conflicted, more tempered anger. They see Noah, Angel, and my siblings and I can tell they're seething. They wanted to find me alone.

I start, "Mom, Dad."

My mom ignores me. "Valeria, Adriana. Rooms. Now."

They turn their noses up. "No," they say in unison.

She decides not to fight it. Instead, my mom walks up to me, close to my face. "It's true?"

"Is what true?"

"Are you living in sin?" Her eyes flick to Noah, where he wears a serious expression, his hands clenched.

Adriana answers. "We're all sinners, Mom. That's why we ask for God's forgiveness. But this isn't something that needs to be forgiven." I glance at her and shake my head. I try to convey a message to her with my eyes alone. Don't interrupt again. I appreciate Adriana wants to stand up for me, but I won't let her get in trouble too.

"If you're asking me if I'm in love with a man, yes, I am."

She slaps me across the face before reeling back as if I've done the same. It's a hard, loud crack, and I stumble back a few paces. I—Wow—I really didn't think… I hoped. Well, it doesn't matter what I hoped.

Noah lurches forward, reaching for me, his stare going deadly, but I shake my head, telling him to stay in place. If he speaks now, or touches me, it will make things worse.

She runs to my father's arms, huge, wracking sobs shaking her frame. "What did we do to deserve this?" she cries out to no one in particular. "We raised you better than this. You don't know what you're talking about. You're sick."

"I'm not sick. This isn't a choice. This is how God made me."

"No. The Devil's in you. We can fix this. You don't have to be an abomination. That man preyed on you, turned you into this. We can fix it. There are camps. We just have to get you to church." She crosses herself as if I'm an evil spirit.

My body tenses, the word abomination ricocheting through my mind. I really shouldn't have hoped.

The whole time, my dad stands there, silent. Does he feel the same? Could he possibly disagree with her? "Am I an abomination in your eyes too, Dad?"

My mother doesn't give him the opportunity to answer. "It's the Lord's eyes you need to worry about, Elias. Repent, give up this lifestyle, and He might forgive you. You don't have to damn yourself."

The door swings open, and Vi and Carmen step inside, rushing to my side. Carmen takes my face in her hand, turning it to look at the mark on my cheek. I feel heat where her fingers brush against it and I know it's going to swell.

My mom's crying stops, her anger returning full force. "What is she doing here?"

All three of my younger sisters stand there, stunned. Thinking back on it, I probably should have warned them that she was coming. It did the trick though. My mom's glower is now aimed at Carmen, taking some of the heat off of me.

While my mom looks apoplectic, my father looks devastated, his hands clenching around my mother's body, as if he wants to let go and come to Carmen's side. To my side. "I came to make sure you didn't do the same thing to Eli that you did to me."

"Both of you need to get out of my house, now. If you won't repent and ask for His forgiveness, then there's no place for you here."

The three youngest girls protest, saying that there is nothing wrong with me, but I quiet them with a wave of my hand. I already knew this was going to happen before I ever opened my mouth.

Noah steps forward then, though I shake my head, silently begging him not to say anything. "Be reasonable, Sophie. This is your son. How can you turn your back on him?" I close my eyes, trying to shut out everything. Gratitude that he wants to help, fear of what my mom will say next, and hurt. So much hurt it's suffocating.

"I should have you arrested. Did you pervert my son? Get out of my house. The police will know where to find you. I should have known better than to let you and your daughter into our life without Debbie's guidance."

He stands there, his hands shaking, devastation clear on his face. Before I have the chance to say anything, I hear Angel shout from behind him, trying to get around us, like she might sock her in the face. "Don't speak to my father like that, you bitch." Jesus fucking Christ.

Noah holds Angel back as I whisper, "Mom, we both know you're not going to call the police. I'm an adult and so is Noah. We love each other and he didn't do anything to me that I didn't ask him to."

She crosses herself again. "Disgusting. Get out. Now. All of you. This is a house of good, honorable people, and you won't taint it anymore. If you won't get help, you're not welcome here. I can't even look at you." She's shaking in my dad's arms. I watch him, hopeful he'll say something. Give me any sign that he doesn't agree with her, but he only stands there, silent.

"Can I at least say goodbye to the boys?" I want the chance to say goodbye. It might be the last time I'll see them.

Her voice rises higher. "I said get out."

Nodding, I pull the girls into a hug. "I'm so sorry, girls. I'll do my best to stay in touch. I love you. Tell the boys I'm sorry and I love them." They all nod their heads, their tears soaking through my shirt.

Breaking away from their hold, I turn, and I'm engulfed by Noah's large arms. They cradle me as he steers us toward the door. As one, I travel with Noah, Angel, Carmen, and Vi, each one acting as a protective barrier, holding me together when I feel like shattering into a million pieces.

I give my dad one last hopeful glance, that same sad look written in every line on his face. I call out to him, "If there is any part of you that disagrees with Mom, and you want to talk, I'll take your call." I don't wait to see if he responds, or to see how he reacts. We make our way into the hall and Carmen slams the door behind us.

Collectively we sigh, the tension draining from us, a wary cloud hanging overhead. Well, that's at least how I feel. We make our way down to the parking lot, no one saying a word.

I'm numb. I know I'll break down later when I have more time to think about it. For now, I'm dumbstruck. I say the first thing that comes to mind, "I don't know where I'm going to live. They paid for the semester, but it's still early enough for them to get a refund."

"Stay with me," Noah says.

I look at Angel as she winces. I don't blame her. We have too much shit to figure out. There's no way we could live together. Plus, I need to stand on my own two feet, separate from him before talking about living together. "Thank you, but I don't think we should. Not yet, anyway."

"No, you're going to stay with me," Carmen says. "Besides, my roommate moved out recently and I have a spare room." I turn to her, not that surprised by the offer. I'm so thankful that Vi forced me to call her all those months ago.

"Only if you're sure."

"I am."

I pull out of Noah's arms long enough to give Carmen a hug. "Thank you."

"No need for thanks, but you're welcome anyway."

I hug Vi next then pat Angel awkwardly on the arm, which makes everyone either laugh or cringe.

Vi gives her major side-eye before looking at me. "What should we do now?"

"I appreciate you all being here, but would it be okay if I talk to Noah alone?"

All three women nod their heads, and Carmen offers to give Angel a ride home. "I'll be around town until you're ready to grab stuff out of your dorm and head back to my place."

I thank her and they make their way across the parking lot, leaving me alone, standing in front of the man I'm in love with.

He takes my hand as reality starts to creep in. I've lost my parents. Probably for good. I might lose all my siblings except Carmen. God, how can I be so sick to my stomach from the loss, while being the happiest I've ever been? I don't regret choosing Noah… but fuck, I just can't think about the rest right now.

34

Eli

As soon as they're out of earshot, Noah scoops me into his arms, burying his face in my neck. "I'm so sorry, Eli. I didn't mean for any of this to happen."

I run my hand through his hair, doing my best to soothe him, sensing his day was more terrible than mine. "It was time. I wasn't going to give you up. We knew that this was bound to happen if my parents found out."

"We could have made it on your terms. I forced you into it, and you shouldn't have been."

My arms wrap around him tighter, thankful that I found someone who cares this much about me. He loves me. I'm still reeling from that revelation. "You didn't force me to do anything. Yeah, it's true, I wouldn't have come out like this. But it's done now. The only place to lay blame is with Tom, and I don't even care about that. I'm just worried about my siblings, but I'll figure out how to see them. Honestly, the most surprising part of this whole thing is how cool Angel's been with it."

He lets out a strained laugh. "We had a heart-to-heart that was years in the making."

"Ah."

"Yeah."

I rub his back, reveling because I can touch him openly, anytime I want. We're not a secret anymore. Anyone who matters knows, for better or worse. "Let's head back to my dorm."

"One last thing."

"Okay."

"I love you."

I hum, agreeing with that statement. "I love you too. It's unreal that everyone knows now."

"I know. That… with your family, it had to be so hard. I'm sorry. I don't deserve you."

I don't want to think about them right now. I need a distraction. What's a better distraction than losing myself in the arms of the man I love? "Not true. You know what you deserve though?"

"What?"

"For me to have my way with you. Every deplorable, indecent way I can think of." My words make him shiver, even as he tilts his head, examining me, clearly reading the thoughts plastered on my face. He wets his lips as he lets me push him against his car. I take his mouth with mine in a heated kiss and he responds eagerly, his tongue twisting with my own.

"Are you sure? We should talk about this."

I wince. "I need to not talk right now." I need something I can control, or I need Noah to control me. Something that will stop me from spiraling. Too many emotions plague me. And I want to forget, just for a little while, with Noah. I deserve to be happy and think about everything else later.

He smiles at me, then pulls my door open. "Let's go."

I hop in, not needing additional prompting.

***

We slam through the door, knocking over a lamp in the process. The clatter sounds loud in the room, but we hardly notice as we rip each other's clothes off until we're only in our boxers. I trace every line of his body with my hands, following each pass with my tongue as I walk him backwards. I shove him onto the bed, his chest bouncing back toward me on impact. My tongue searches for every dip and ridge between his neck and collarbone, down his sternum, over every abdominal muscle.

"Are you sure this is what you want? We should probably talk."

"No. Fuck talking. I need this. Please distract me."

He pulls at my hair, searching my face. I know I can't ignore everything that happened today, but this is one thing I can control, and it's exactly what I need: something that I can control. Noah must sense that because he puts his hands above his head without argument when I give him the command. I pull his boxers down, throwing them over my shoulder as his dick bobs, brushing against my cheek. I take him in my mouth, enjoying the feel of him on my tongue. He fists the sheets above his head, barely containing his need to control things. I pop off and give him another lick. "I think I should be in charge more often."

He groans before shooting me an unamused glare. "Fucking brat."

That only makes me want to work him harder, and soon he's writhing against the sheets, crying my name. "Babe, please, I need to touch you."

I swallow him again before pulling off. "Alright. If you must."

That gets an amused look. One that says, "We both know you're full of shit." And that look would be right. I'm desperate for him.

He flips us so I'm under him, then grabs the lube out of the nightstand. He turns me into a mess with his mouth, tongue, fingers—anywhere and everywhere. It's not enough. "I need you inside me."

"Then get on your hands and knees." He sits back, watching me comply as he slicks up his length. I roll over, getting to my hands and knees, and he repositions me so that I'm ass up, my face buried in the sheets. He slides a finger around the rim of my hole, drawing a moan from my lips, my cock aching for his touch.

He pulls my cheeks apart and licks a long stripe from my balls all the way back. He pushes the tip of his tongue inside me and works me over until I'm thrusting back, needing more. His tongue, while marvelously talented, is not enough. He replaces said magical tongue with a finger, but I cry out, "Fuck, Noah. I'm ready, get inside me."

"So bossy." Grabbing my hip, he positions his cock over the sensitive ring of nerves. Pushing in with a shallow thrust, tormenting me, driving me entirely out of my mind before slamming into me hard.

"You love it." The words punctuate each thrust as he drives deeper.

He pulls me up so my back is against his chest and he whispers in my ear, "Damn right, I do. I fucking love you. Every single thing about you."

I sigh, his words bringing me to the edge. "Shit, Noah. I'm going to…" I come, and his thrusts become sporadic, uneven as I clench around him. He thrusts once, twice, and comes with a loud grunt in my ear, bowing us over so I'm pinned to the bed, panting.

"I don't think I can move," he says between his own labored breaths.

"I know I can't," I wheeze, teasing him, pushing against his shoulder.

He laughs, then does his best to shimmy off me with the least amount of effort. Our limbs are tangled and half his chest is on top of me, pushing me further into the bed, but it's warm and perfect.

I have enough room to shift myself around, putting us face to face. I stare into his eyes, wondering how, after everything, we got here. What felt nearly impossible only days ago is now a reality. I'm out, and I'm in love with someone who treasures me, makes me feel special, and takes care of me. He runs his hand over my back, up my neck, and smooths my hair. It's soothing and I melt into his touch. I could let him do this forever, have him take care of me forever.

As if reading my thoughts, Noah rolls off the bed with a smile, grabs a towel, and brings it over to clean me. He parts my cheeks, wiping gently before placing a kiss on my shoulder. I feel a blush creep across my body, still not used to the intimacy. It's vulnerable enough having sex, but the acts in between, when caring and love shine through, are at a different level entirely, and I'm still adjusting to it. I'm thankful it's with Noah, and I tell him as much. "I love you."

He cleans himself, then plants a devastatingly sweet kiss on my lips. "I love you too. It's still unreal, like I'm expecting to wake up any moment. I'm sorry about a lot of it though."

I can see the sincerity radiating from his eyes, a certain sadness for me, and it almost overwhelms me, reminding me of everything I wanted to forget. I reach a hand out, needing him closer, and he comes instantly, falling back to the bed so he can take me into his arms.

It hurts knowing that my parents won't love me, that they'll act like I never existed, but wrapped in his arms, it's more bearable. "I'm sure I'll break down at some point, but right now, I'm okay. I was so afraid of what they might think of me. The worst has happened and… I'm here. I didn't lose you. Or my friends. And I have Carmen."

"That's all true. It's not easy. You were brave and I'm proud of you, babe. You're perfect." He places a kiss on my nose.

I roll my eyes. "No one is perfect."

"Mmm. Okay. Nearly perfect. You're definitely a brat when you don't get what you want." He digs his fingers into my side as I try to squirm away, pretending to be indignant. He smacks playful kisses all over my face as I attempt to break out of his hold. I might not be trying that hard. His strength is so hot, and his warm, muscled body revs me up again.

He laughs. "Fuck, Eli. Give my poor dick a break. He's a little older and needs time to recover."

"I bet I could help with that."

"Like I said. Brat." He shakes his head, his smile only growing.

I stop fighting against him, because let's be real, there's nowhere else I want to be in the world. "Fine, what should we do then?"

He looks around the room. "I hate to say it, but we should pack up your room."

Like that, reality sets in again. "Ugh. You're right. Will you help me?" I try to look innocent with the request, but he must pick up on the tone because he watches me warily. Like he knows it's a ruse to distract him, to distract me, again. He would be right, but I try to look innocent anyway. My hand slides down his back, around his hip and toward the front. I'm centimeters away when he pins our bodies together, promptly stilling my hand.

He pinches my ass, then pushes off the bed, enjoying the yelp I let out at the contact. "Get dressed. We're going to pack together."

"Yes, sir."

His eyes darken and he wets his lip, fighting what he wants to do with what we should do, before shaking his head at me. I can practically hear the word dripping from him… brat. But I'm his brat and he loves it because it's all for him.

35

Eli

The next week goes by in a blur. After Noah and I started packing my room, I called my sister, who was at Vi's place waiting for me. They both came back to help us pack, bringing boxes and pizza to make it all bearable. Each one tried to get my spirits up, but packing reminded me how little I owned. Most of it was at my parents' house—the stuff that wasn't destroyed by Tom—and I couldn't pick it up.

Everything fit in four boxes and two of those boxes were books. Despite the gloomy atmosphere that seemed to blanket me, it wasn't all bad. Vi and Noah got along surprisingly well considering he would still be her professor for a few more semesters. Carmen was a bit more reserved, but even she chimed in every once in a while, her comments sarcastic and hilarious.

I got a new phone when my parents shut mine off. That was a hard day. I didn't leave my room, despite Carmen and Noah trying. It was a stupid little thing, but it hit me harder than I thought possible. What hurt worse, though, was the last call I got before my phone shut off. A call from Financial Aid and Housing, telling me my living expenses had been refunded and if it was a mistake, I needed to pay for housing or vacate the dorm.

I'd cried late into the night, Noah holding me close and reminding me exactly why I'd chosen this path. They can do their worst, but I'll never hide who I am again. But it hurt enough, and I spiraled long enough, that Carmen and Noah insisted I attend counseling. It's... a work in progress.

One obstacle I didn't expect is that my parents changed the triplets' phone numbers to break all contact between us, which meant we had to get clever. I won't let them slip through my fingers. If my siblings decide they no longer want to talk to me at some point, I'll respect that. I know the risk they're taking, disobeying our parents, but I'll never take away their choice like our parents do. Over a long phone call one night when my mom was out of the house and my father was busy, I reassured everyone that I still loved them and I was going to be there for them. Carmen also told them they were always welcome at her house.

We've already planned on meeting them one afternoon two weeks from now, when things settle. My parents are keeping an even closer eye on them, and I told them I wasn't worth the risk of getting in trouble. Their response was to tell me I was dumb, and they'd see me for ice cream. Knowing they're on my side helps, especially knowing in the back of my mind that my parents don't care.

They washed their hands of responsibility the moment they found out about me. I could be homeless, starving, looking for somewhere safe to sleep, and they wouldn't know. They haven't contacted me or asked my siblings about me. It's like I never existed to them. I'm coming to terms with that.

One good thing that came from all of this was that I switched my major and I won't have to stay longer than necessary because I only took pre-reqs the first few years. I am now pursuing an English degree and the classes are so much better. Minus the fact that I can't take any of Noah's classes.

There isn't anything in the bylaws or state laws stating we can't be together, though it's frowned upon. The dean wasn't happy, but because we came to him before someone else did, we were able to resolve things before they became an issue. I'd originally told Noah that I didn't have to switch majors, not if it would put his career in jeopardy. He told me that if I could face my parents, he could face the university. The next day he went to the dean and told him about the situation, and I switched majors later that day.

The most awkward part about everything now is seeing Angel when I go to Noah's house. She's civil. Distant, a little cold, but civil. Much more than when she was sleeping with Tom. I know a lot of it has to do with the conversation Noah had with her the night we admitted we loved each other. He told me about it two nights ago, and honestly, that conversation was a long time coming. She never treated him well, which was on her, but he also never pushed back to learn why. Overall, it was for the best.

It also made me want to do violent things after hearing what his ex did to Angel and the lies she spread about Noah. In all the time I'd been friends with Angel, she'd never told me. It made me see things differently, made me more willing to move past our issues. Maybe one day we could actually be friends again.

I'm sitting on the front porch, my books propped open, though I'm too distracted to read for class. We're working on a set of short stories, but they can't keep my attention, my thoughts drifting through everything that happened to me in only a week's time. I'm so distracted, I don't notice when a car pulls into the driveway, or when someone gets out of the car.

"Hey, Eli."

Angel stands in front of me, the last person I thought I would ever see on my sister's porch. She looks uncomfortable as I continue to stare. "Angel?"

"Can I sit?" I'm about to say no, but the uncertainty swimming in her eyes, it's vulnerable. It makes my heart wrench because I still care about her. Even if everything's changed.

"Yeah." I shift, piling my books to the side. "What's up?"

"I came here to apologize."

"Huh?" That, I was not expecting.

She laughs at my dumbfounded expression. "I know you're going to want to interrupt, and you don't owe it to me to listen but if you could listen to everything I have to say, I would appreciate it. I don't know if I'm going to say it all unless I spit it out in one go." She waits for me to acknowledge her request. A quick tilt of the head is all I can manage.

"We were friends for so long, then we started dating. You were always so good to me. So sweet and kind. Both as a friend and boyfriend. When you left, I changed. I was alone in that house most days, thinking about how my mom left me. How my dad left first. And then you left me too." She pauses, sensing I want to interrupt, to tell her that this doesn't sound like much of an apology, but I hold my tongue.

"I felt like no one wanted me around. And then I found the friends we partied with, and they made me feel special. Or, they were there, at least. And then you came back, and you were different. Happier. Level-headed. So I thought you would realize how much better off you'd be if you left. How everyone always seems to be when they get rid of me. I refused to let you be the one to leave, so I… I sabotaged. They really know what they're talking about with that whole self-fulfilling prophecy thing, don't they? But to me, I was right. You left me too. I wanted to hurt all the people who were supposed to love me, who abandoned me instead. So I acted out, pushed everyone's buttons. I mean, I'm still dealing with my mom abandoning me and getting to know my dad all over again without all the bullshit in the way. I don't know if my dad told you what my mom said…" She trails off and I nod, letting her know he did.

"I was afraid. So I lashed out, and it got me attention… so I didn't stop. I still worry my dad will decide I'm not worth it. Anyway"—she shakes her head—"you don't need my excuses. What I'm trying to say is, I did a lot of shitty things. A lot of them to you. It wasn't fair and I'm sorry. I'm trying to be better, and I hope someday I can earn your forgiveness, but I know you don't owe it to me."

When it's clear she's done, all I can say is, "Thank you. I, uh, appreciate the apology." It means something that she came here, but even though everything is so different now, it's hard to leave the unease behind. Her words still feel like a trick, like the other shoe is going to drop at any moment.

She shrugs, looking down at her hands. "You don't need to thank me for apologizing for shit I shouldn't have done."

"True." I try to say it in a teasing manner, but it falls flat.

It gets an eye roll from her, and she shoves me with her shoulder. We'll never be the same, but we might be okay, which makes me happy. She adds, "You know, it's still fucking weird that you're with my dad."

"I know. It is weird, but I'm not going to apologize for it. He's the best thing that's ever happened to me." I wring my fingers together, debating if I should continue or not. "Though, I do owe you an apology. I recognized it too. That we weren't right for each other, but I kept pushing because we were friends and I thought it was the right thing to do. Or maybe it was just easier for me to stay. Either way, I was shitty too. So, I'm sorry. But your dad, he's it for me."

"I don't know if it will ever make me not gag. Are you sure?"

"Yes. He… understands me like no one else. Like I said, he's it for me."

She looks out across the street, turning away from me. She sniffles a few times before saying, "I hope I deserve that someday. With someone."

"You deserve it now, Angel. You're not a bad person. We were both dumb, and we did shitty stuff. That doesn't make us bad people."

She shakes herself, breaking out of her melancholy state. "I didn't come here so that you'd make me feel better. Sorry. Also, my dad said to pass along the message that he misses you and wanted to invite you for dinner tonight."

"He knows you're here?"

"Yep."

"Did he make you do this?"

"No, but we talked about it a bit."

I ask, "Do you seriously want me there for dinner? The three of us?"

She stands, then shrugs her shoulders. "Yeah, it's fine. We'll have to get used to it eventually."

"Alright, I'll see you later."

"Bye." She runs down the porch before getting into her car and driving off.

Carmen walks out the door then. "I wasn't eavesdropping. The window was open," she says, preemptively. "That seems like it could be promising?"

"I guess time will tell. Looks like I'm going to have to take a rain check on dinner tonight. That okay?"

"Sure. No problem. I have to get my lesson plan completed. If you plan on staying there send me a message so I know you're safe." It hits me then how different my life is now. No parents trying to control my life under the guise of loving me. Instead, I have family and friends who love me, and ask me if I'm safe.

"Alright. I'm gonna run these upstairs and then head over."

***

The dinner was quiet and awkward with the dynamics changed. We did our best to keep it on neutral topics. Noah smiled at me encouragingly as Angel and I spoke, coming to some kind of truce.

Now we're lying in his bed, my head propped on his chest as a show plays in the background. I'm so exhausted after this week that cuddles are the way to go. I snuggle into him tighter because I can. "Hey, have you talked to Tony yet?"

Tony's tried to call him a few times since he left the other night and Beth has sent him several messages. He hasn't responded because he wants time to process their argument. I don't want to push him, but I don't blame Tony for what he said about our relationship. I didn't know I was willing to come out. Even then, I loved Noah, but if Tom hadn't outed me, I don't know if I would have taken that leap.

Noah groans, not wanting to talk about it. "Yeah. He called me again today. We talked. He apologized."

"Did you tell him what happened?"

"I told him Angel knows, but I don't know if he deserves to hear the rest yet." I glance up at him, then run the pad of my thumb between his brows, smoothing out the line.

"So protective." I know he doesn't like what Tony said about me. If I can forgive Angel, he can do the same with his best friend.

He pulls me tight. "Damn right. Someone needs to protect you when you put everyone else first."

I pat his chest. "He's your best friend. He'll get over it. I hardly need protection anymore, anyway. Or did you forget that I'm possessed by the devil? Probably a demon now. I've heard those are pretty scary."

He scowls, clearly not amused. "That's not funny, Eli."

I run my hand down his cheek, cupping his jaw. I pull him close to my lips. We're less than an inch away when I whisper, "I know. But it's laugh or cry. And we're going to need friends now more than ever. I'm not upset about what he said, so it's time to forgive him. He was being reasonable."

Not giving him time to protest, I seal my lips firmly against his own. He hums with contentment before sliding me back to his side as the main character of the show gets into trouble. He strokes my back and I run my fingers through his hair, happier than I could have ever dreamed thanks to the man by my side. And who'd have thought going back to get my album and a few notes would have led to all of this?

"Hey, I just thought of something," I say.

"What?"

"You never told me how Dante's story ends."

The small lines around his eyes fan out with the glowing smile he gives me. "It ends happily. Very happily."

I can't help but feel like he's talking about us again and it makes me blush. "Yeah, but what happens? Give me all the details."

He kisses me on the nose. "You're going to have to wait and see like everyone else."

I whine. "I'm not everyone else. I'm your boyfriend."

A dark, lusty look has him sitting up. "Mmm. I like that word in your mouth."

"Is that the only thing you like in my mouth?"

"You know damn well it's not. I'm trying to be good. You're tired."

"Fuck being tired."

His eyes go to the ceiling like he's looking for strength. "Thank fuck. Come here."

Epilogue

Eli (Two Weeks Later)

The day of our ice cream trip arrives—a beautiful blue, sunny afternoon. Not wanting to discuss anything taxing, Carmen and I comment on the weather as we drive to the shop. I'm extremely nervous, though I can't quite pinpoint why. I know they'll be here because I spoke to Adriana and Dani late last night.

I try to think about anything else other than my nerves, so I look out the window, catching Carmen's car in the reflection of a store window. She drove because I don't have a car anymore, which is fucking inconvenient, and obviously a much better topic to think about… I'm loving my mind today.

We are working on getting me one, though I told her not to worry about it. I can take the city bus. Of course, when I voiced that option, she argued saying it would take me almost an hour and a half to make a half-hour trip. I would have to take three separate buses to get to campus. It's doable, though not ideal. We'll figure it out. Somehow.

Really, I should be excited to see my siblings. Most of them asked if Noah was going to be there too, but he insisted on staying home since it was the first time I'd see them again. He told me we would have plenty of time for them to get to know him later. As always, the thought of forever caused my heart to melt.

He wants forever with me. He wasn't explicit with his words. We weren't talking about moving in or anything more serious, but he told me we're forever in the little ways. The smiles, kisses, whispered reminders of how much he cares. The understanding that I have to figure this shit out on my own, for me. My life is crazy and I know he wants to come in and help, to offer more than his support, but he realizes it's not what I want and respects that. Respects me.

My sister pulls onto the street, finding a spot along the curb, and we step out into the fairly mild day. "Are you nervous?" I ask her.

"You have no idea."

I take her hand and give it a squeeze. "I am too. But they're gonna love you. They already do."

She looks at me skeptically, but doesn't disagree. I let her hand go to open the door and she steps through first, the air conditioning making me shiver as it hits us. It's already on the cooler side for the area, so it feels downright chilly. Maybe I can convince everyone to sit outside once we get everything.

I step forward to follow Carmen, but I am so distracted that I don't realize she's stopped until I run into her. I catch her around the waist, steadying both of us. "Sorry, got lost in thought. You okay?"

Taking in her posture, I follow her line of sight. She's rigid, eyes pinched with distaste, as she looks at where our siblings stand, our father right behind them. My body stiffens, preparing to be on the defensive. They all approach as a group when they realize Carmen and I aren't moving. Unlikely that we will anytime soon. Adriana arrives a moment before the rest, whispering an apology. "He followed us. I'm so sorry."

I tell her it's okay without taking my eyes off him. His expression is unreadable, but it doesn't look outright hostile. He looks at me and Carmen, his hands going up, as if to signal he means no harm. It's too late for that. "I only came to talk. I know you might not want to hear me, but I'm not here to fight."

Carmen snorts, breaking out of her frozen state. "Sure. That almost sounded sincere."

The others turn to my father, looking surprised, like they too were ready to hear him berate all of us. "Will you give me five minutes? After that, I'll leave and you all can spend time together. Alone."

Everything inside of me screams not to trust this. It's suspicious. He hates me as much as my mom does. Another, much smaller part of me, buried so deep I can barely admit to it, hopes he's here to tell me they were wrong and that he loves me. That we're his children and he never believed that other bullshit.

Carmen speaks first. "If you had anything of interest to say to me, you would have said it five years ago when you kicked me out of your life. There is nothing you could fucking say to me that I want to hear. I'm not going to… to sit here and listen to this shit." She turns to our siblings. "I'm sorry. I'll see you around another time."

She storms out the door before I have time to say anything, my siblings' eyes pooling with tears. Shit. I'm not sure if I want to hear anything he has to say, but I can't leave them, which means I should make sure Carmen's okay but come back to listen to him. "I'll be right back."

I run out, catching her arm. "Hey, stop."

She looks back at me, a fierce scowl pinching her face, doing little to mask her own tears. "I'm sorry, Eli. I can't sit there and listen to his bullshit. Did you want to come back with me, or should I hang around town until you're done here?"

Glancing back at the ice cream shop, I feel a deep longing to return, not only for my siblings. I shouldn't want to talk to him. I should tell him to fuck off, or stay silent like he did when I needed him. But I want to hear him out. "I don't want to upset you."

"You want to talk to him…"

"I'm sorry. I just need to hear him out. Are you mad?"

Taking a deep breath, she steadies herself and wipes at the moisture in her eyes. "Of course not. You don't need to apologize. If you want to hear him out, that's your deal. Call me when you're done."

I nod, choked up myself. Every day she's attempted to remind me that our relationship will be strong. She shows me she cares about me unconditionally. It's so different, and I treasure it. It makes me wonder why I'm stupidly walking back into the shop to hear what my dad has to say. "Yeah. I'll let you know."

Walking inside, I catch them as they take seats by the window, ice cream melting on Miguel's face. Each sister has ice cream in front of them, but is waiting for me to get back. I appreciate the solidarity, especially knowing how much it's killing Valeria not to inhale her ice cream before it melts. I approach the table and my father pushes a hot fudge sundae with extra whipped cream, extra fudge, and a splash of caramel in front of me. My favorite. "Thanks."

He nods, not quite meeting my eyes.

It's already started. If he wants to make me feel bad about myself, then he can leave. "Why are you here?"

That gets his attention. I see the internal struggle cross his face to reprimand me for being disrespectful, but he holds his tongue. "I don't understand why you would choose that lifestyle."

Feeling duped, I stand, ready to storm from the shop. "I knew this was a fucking mistake. I'm leaving."

He grabs my arm. "No. No. I'm sorry. I didn't mean to make it sound that way. Let me rephrase that. I don't want to lose you because of something I don't understand. That's on me, not you, to figure out. The other day, when you said this is how God made you, it made me stop and think. You're right. I don't have the answers, I don't know what He's thinking. Would God truly ask me to turn my back on my children who he blessed me with? I've spent five years asking myself that same question. Seeing you both when you walked out… I don't want to lose you."

I slide back into my chair. "What are you trying to say?"

He wrings his hands together, as if he's nervous. "I love you and I don't want to lose more of my children because I don't understand. I… I'm willing to learn."

"What about Mom?"

"She doesn't know I'm here."

"And she doesn't feel the same way?"

He shakes his head. Obviously she doesn't, otherwise she would be here too. Pain lances through me, but I push forward. "Did you two suspect I might like men? Is that why you pushed me toward Angel?" I didn't realize how much I cared to know the answer until it passed my lips, but I'm sitting on the edge of my seat, waiting to hear what he has to say.

"Your mother suspected." He looks sheepish.

"And you?"

He sighs, looking tired down to his soul. "I tried not to think about it. I only wanted to raise you to be a good man."

Up to this point, my siblings have been quiet, letting us hash everything out. At that comment, Adriana says, "He is. Eli is the best. Being a man looks different now, Dad. Being good, loving one another, that's what makes a good man. Understanding and listening to others even if you don't agree."

"Thanks, Adriana," I respond as she offers me a sweet smile.

My father clears his throat. "You're right. And I hope I can show all of you I can be that man if you give me the chance."

"I need time to think about it."

"Of course. That's understandable."

I don't know how to feel. The words swim through my mind, none sticking for long. It seems too good to be true. I'm still so angry. If he felt this way, why didn't he speak up? His silence condemned me as much as my mom's words, so I should hate him. Why don't I? Not wanting to think about it, I choose to focus on what little time I have with my siblings.

When I don't respond to his comment, my dad asks, "Will you drive the kids home when you're done here?"

"I don't have a car."

He pauses, reaching into a jacket pocket, producing car keys. My car keys. He tosses them in front of me and I look down at them dumbly. "What is this?" If he's trying to bribe me into forgiving him, he has another think coming. I'm not so easily won.

He doesn't respond, only pulls out a piece of paper, flipping it open and laying it in front of me. "The title. It's under your name now. It's your car. I know it's not much, but I want you safe. Traveling the bus system to get to school from Carmen's isn't ideal. You should have your car. No one can take it from you again."

"How do you know where she lives?" I look at my siblings, but they only shrug their shoulders.

He looks sheepish. "I—Uh, this whole time, I've kept tabs on her. I wanted to know she was okay."

I take the keys and pocket them. I can't manage anything else. All my words seem to abandon me. Sensing that, he nods and walks out the door, his head hung low.

I spend the rest of the afternoon with my siblings. I call Carmen to tell her he's left, and she ends up joining us a while later. We laugh and catch up and the kids hang on Carmen's every word, fascinated to learn as much about her life as possible. I leave my old home after dropping the kids off, smiling. I can't wait to tell Noah how my day went.

Epilogue

Noah (Four Years Later)

I finished my lecture for the one and only class I have this semester, so I head to my office to get a few other things done before heading home. I throw my bag down and set the coffee mug on the desk when my cell rings. Glancing at the caller ID, I smile as Eli's name pops up along with the very cute picture of him cuddled against our two cats, Dante and Callan.

For the record, I did not choose their names. I argued that they can't be named after my characters because it will make me look like an egotistical jackass. Eli argued that his fanboy nerdiness needed an outlet because a streaming service picked up my novels to turn them into a TV series. I conceded, naturally. Anything for that man.

It's been amazing, though… getting to see my world made into something visual and so breathtakingly beautiful. It's worth it even though we're constantly stalked by paparazzi now. They knew me before, but nothing like this, and Eli takes it in stride. I hate having my privacy invaded, but he's my rock, helping me get through all the craziness. In fact, he's the one who encouraged me to cut down to one class in the fall, so that I'm on set during filming each spring. That way, I control the content, ensuring I preserve the books on screen. With the popularity, the demand for more books has increased as well. Cutting down on classes has given me more time to write. I'm always busy, but I fall asleep every night the happiest I've ever been with the man I love.

The main reason for my happiness chirps through the phone as I answer. "Hi, love. Wanted to call and let you know I'm headed home to get ready for our date night." I promised to take him out because he spent the last month interviewing at a top five publishing firm for an editorial assistant role.

After graduation, he got a position with a small publishing house that specialized in helping indie authors, but a position opened up recently, and I encouraged him to go for it. At first he wasn't sure, thinking he'd never have a chance, but he went and landed an interview. Visiting the headquarters, only an hour away, he fell in love with the firm. He would have to travel on site every so often, but the position is remote and paid well enough.

"Hey, babe. I have a few things to get done here. But I'll be home soon. Did you hear from the publishing company yet?"

I can practically hear the smile through the phone. "You'll have to wait and see."

His teasing makes me laugh, his words echoing my own. Every time I start a new project, he asks what it's about, how it's going, and my response is always the same. You'll have to wait and see. Payback is fair, I suppose. "Oh, come on, babe. Please. I'll give you your present early if you tell me." I make my voice deeper, gravelly, knowing full well how much he loves the sound, both of us knowing what present I'm really offering.

He moans. "Fuck. I'm driving. Don't do that."

"Then tell me."

He hesitates, a soft sigh traveling through the phone, as I imagine Eli adjusting himself while fighting the urge to tell me. "Fine. Fine. I got the job. I start next month!"

"Fuck yeah. I knew you would. Congrats, babe. I can't wait to celebrate with you." What Eli doesn't know is that I'm also proposing tonight. I rented out the diner where we had our first unofficial date. Cara was so thrilled that she offered to do everything. She's been sending pictures of the decorators coming in and transforming the space so it has a romantic, fun atmosphere. She's also catering, though I told her she's wanted there as a guest.

"As long as I get my present first," he jokes.

Hmm, I like how that sounds. "It'll be the best, most mind-blowing present, babe."

"Hmm. See you soon."

***

I did, in fact, give him a present before we arrived at the diner. Unfortunately, that means we're running a little late. Everyone else thinks they're here to celebrate this huge next step in his career, except for Carmen, Vi, and Cara. They've been helping me arrange everything, so it's perfect.

I open the door for him, and he walks through, gasping at the sight. Getting my first proper look, I can't blame him. It looks nothing like the usual retro diner we've grown to love. Instead, the normally dingy walls have gauzy red and black fabrics draped over them, and fairy lights twinkle from the ceiling. It casts a soft glow, creating a magical ambiance. In a word, the place is perfect.

"It's beautiful. Did you do all of this just for me?"

"Of course, babe. This is getting you one step closer to your dream job." He spins toward me and plants a hard kiss on my lips. While he faces me, I signal to everyone.

They jump out, yelling, "Surprise," his body jerking in my hold. He turns around, eyes wide, face flushed.

"Uh, hi, everyone." He hits my chest lightly. "A party? This is too much."

I pull him to me, plastering him against my chest. "Nah. It's everything you deserve."

After that, everyone streams toward us, and we spend the next hour greeting and mingling with friends and family. With each congratulations, Eli blushes, and the sight is as beautiful as ever. I love that even four years later I can still fluster him. I smile, knowing he hasn't seen anything yet.

The crowd of well-wishers thins, and those who are closest to us, who we see regularly, come up to us. First to step up being Carmen, followed by Vi. They give Eli a big hug, but quickly pass as others stream forward. Angel finds her way up, whispering a few happy words along with her date. Then the rest of the Ruiz clan; his brothers, sisters, and father. Finally, Tony and Beth approach. Tony slaps me on the back, winking like he knows this is about more than a new job. I haven't told him, but I'm sure they've suspected for a while.

Soon enough, Cara comes out, informing us that dinner's ready. We take our seats and the meal is served— a simple pesto pasta dish with bread and salad on the side—the first meal we made together when he moved in after college. He looks at me knowingly, smiling fondly at the memory. We all dig in, but as the time comes closer and closer to the proposal, I get nervous. I know he's going to say yes, there's no doubt in my mind how much he loves me, but I want this to be perfect.

Okay, now or never. I can do this. I clink against a glass, pulling everyone's attention. "Hello, everyone." Eli gives me a funny look. "I wanted to thank you all for being here tonight to help celebrate Eli's wonderful accomplishment. He's worked hard and dedicated so much of his time to become the best damn editor this side of California has ever seen." Everyone cheers and it only makes Eli's cheeks flush harder, my mind supplying the rest; a blush creeping over his chest, turning his body the most beautiful pink over tanned, rippling skin.

Then I turn to Eli, addressing only him. "That's not the only thing that we're here for tonight. Eli, you are everything to me. From the start, you challenged everything I thought I knew. For instance… liking men. Or liking a man, I should say." A few people chuckle, but Eli's too enraptured to sass back. "You made me realize I was only living, functioning, but not truly happy. Not in the way I wanted to be. You showed me with word and action that I was deserving of love when I thought I should give up on it entirely. You have tenderly cared for my heart every day since, and continue to make me better. I have the best partner, and you already know you always have me. I'm here today, in front of our families and friends, to ask… will you be mine?" I drop to one knee and pull out a small box, a platinum band nestled in the fabric. "Eli, will you marry me?"

He's frozen to his chair, tears streaming down his face, and I wait for his response. The silence stretches, and I start to sweat. God, was this the wrong way to propose? Should I have done it at home, only the two of us? "Eli?"

"Oh, fuck! Sorry. Yes. Yes, of course I'll marry you! I'm yours. Always." I slide the ring onto his finger and he pulls me into his warm, hard chest.

"I love you."

He pulls me tighter. "I can't wait to have you home. All alone. All mine. Showing you exactly how much I love you, fiancé."

Fucking hell. He always knows how to rile me in the best sort of way. All I want to do is drag him home, have him show me just how much he wants me. For now, it's time to celebrate. After all, he will have me forever.

The End

———

Thank you for reading Have Me Forever
by Ally Blythe.

If you enjoyed this novel…

Please leave a review. This is the best way to help us authors. I greatly appreciate it!

Join my Newsletter for updates on new releases and bonus content. I promise I'll make it fun. I love speaking with my fans and staying connected. If you join my newsletter, you'll also get a free bonus chapter where you see Noah's reaction to catching Eli in the pool!

You can also join me on any of my social media platforms.

Keep an eye out for Carmen's story in…

Want Me Always

How does one find herself involved with her brother's best friend *and* said best friend's boyfriend? Well, turn to her for advice—then run into the couple, you know, *together*—crap. She really meant to look away.

Carmen Ruiz has always struggled to connect with others, either caring too much or too little, which is why she loses her best friend and gains a new roommate, her long-estranged younger brother, Eli, in one fell sweep. She's reeling with no one to turn to… except for her brother's best friend, Violet Hartford.

Vi is charming. Fun. Everything Carmen is not. Is that why she feels a pull like she's never quite felt before? That has trouble written all over it.

If that wasn't problematic enough, there's the other complication in Carmen's life. Cade Albrecht. A tech mogul's son, assigned to develop a grant for her school and Vi's not-quite boyfriend. He's an instant headache… until he's not.

As they grow closer, Carmen worries history will repeat itself, so she fights the draw. That is until she can't anymore.

The solution is easy. Make an agreement—casual and fun. A secret. One that protects their relationships and their feelings. But what will Carmen do when she realizes she wants them always?

Want Me Always is a bi/demi-awakening MFF brother's best friend, billionaire boyfriend romance with deep connections, scalding heat, no cheating, and a HEA.

Acknowledgements

First and foremost, I want to thank my two cats and dog. If not for them, I would have probably finished this sooner.

This book is the first manuscript I've ever finished, though I've been writing and re-writing different projects for years. Eli and Noah's story is near and dear to my heart. This is one hundred percent my book baby. I love these characters, the sass, the love, everything. I hope you did as well.

I want to thank my Critique Partner, W.H. Lockwood, for making this book what it is today. Without your amazing insight and support, this project would not be nearly as wonderful as it's become.

Thank you to my beta readers, Ana, Ida, Jean, Doni, and Patty who provided me with many laughs while reviewing feedback, and great input as you each added life to the story with your comments and corrections.

Lastly, I would like to thank those of you who gave my book a chance. I appreciate each and every one of you, and

HAVE ME FOREVER

I hope you'll continue to journey with me through future projects.

About the Author

Ally Blythe is an up and coming author who writes books about friendship, love, and acceptance in every form. She is an avid knitter, TV enthusiast, and reader. Basically, anything that has her sitting down and inactive. Occasionally she does things like hiking and kayaking.

Though she loves a good romance novel in most any genre, LGBTQIA+ is by far her favorite. The acceptance and love of the community has always impacted her life in a big way. What better way to return that love than through books?

Born and raised just outside of Chicago, she now travels the US with her husband, two cats, and dog. Our current stop, Mississippi, our next stop… who knows?

To learn more, or to connect with her, follow her socials.

Website: allyblytheauthor.com
Instagram and Facebook: @allyblytheauthor